THE CONVALESCENT

by

JESSICA ANTHONY

McSWEENEY'S BOOKS

SAN FRANCISCO

www.mcsweeneys.net

McSweeney's and colophon are registered trademarks
of McSweeney's, a privately held company with
wildly fluctuating resources.

ISBN: 978-1934781-10-4

for Bunky, with Love and Squalor

THE CONVALESCENT

For many years I had been lonely.
Then many people visited.
I'd have been happy if they'd stayed.
You are alone, was what they said.

—Attila József

CHRYSALIS

JUNE 15

On June 15, 1985, at 3:42 p.m., a six-point-seven magnitude earthquake hit Puebla, Mexico, destroying two hundred and ninety churches, three hundred schools, and four thousand houses, leaving fourteen people dead and over fifteen thousand homeless. Among the living was a young girl named Adelpha Salus Santino who, after digging through rubble at the old Vehiculos Automotores Mexicanos factory to find both of her parents suffocated, picked up a dusty knife, held it to her middle, and then stabbed herself quick in the stomach. She was rushed to the emergency room by paramedics who, when they could find no identification, asked the girl *¿Como te llamas?* to which Adelpha Salus Santino replied, "Mariposa," which means butterfly.

At the exact same moment, a team of astronomers at L'Observatoire de Paris witnessed the birth of a star ten times the size of our sun. The star was located in the center of a nebula formerly obscured by dust and gasses, but when winds produced by the newborn star cleared the debris, its unusual shape could be seen for the first time. At 3:42 p.m., one of the astronomers excitedly observed that the nebula possessed two round, adjoining clouds instead of the regular single cloud, and named it Papillon, which is French for butterfly.

Back on earth, a thousand miles north of Mexico, Ms. Mary Pierce, a single, middle-aged woman with an acute case of agoraphobia, was standing at the front door of her two-bedroom ranch home in a suburb of Youngstown, Ohio, wringing her hands to keep them from shaking. She was trying to summon the courage to open the door and go outside when the mail slot flew open, and through it the mailman shoved a promotional copy of *Explore Other Galaxies* magazine. At 3:42 p.m., trembling, Ms. Pierce opened the magazine. A brown butterfly spun out from underneath the pages. Specifically, the butterfly was an *Adelpha salus*, which is known only to remote regions of Mexico. Lepidopterists call it "Lost Sister."

Also on this day in history, on June 15, 1985, at 3:42 p.m., my parents, János and Janka Pfliegman, drove their car into a telephone pole on Back Lick Road in Front Lick, Virginia, dying on impact. They didn't own the car; the car they owned was a 1963 Rambler American station wagon, assembled at the Vehiculos Automotores Mexicanos factory in Puebla, Mexico. The Rambler had given them transmission trouble, and they'd left it, abandoned, by the side of Back Lick Road. The car they were driving was a shiny red Ford Mustang that belonged to a nearby rental agency called Galaxy Car Rentals, which had opened its doors on the cool morning of April 8, 1973, the day that I, Rovar Ákos Pfliegman, was born.

I have no life. I have no known relatives, no known friends. No church, no office. No warm and embracing community. No formal education.

Other people, who have lives, seem to live their lives pretty well. Achieving, aspiring. Whatnot. Other people are always busy doing big and important things like running for president or voting for president, or thinking about running or voting for president.

I sell meat out of a bus.

I consider myself to be a Hungarian. My grandfather, Ákos Pfliegman, was born in Szolnok, Hungary, in the county Szolnok, and the name Ákos is a Hungarian name. It's pronounced AH-kosh, and it means "white hawk." My last name, however, is German. It's pronounced FLEEG-man, and comes from the German derivation *fliegendenmann*.

That means "flying man."

As a Hungarian, there are times I would prefer a Hungarian last name, but my ancestors were given the name a very long time ago. The closest Hungarian translation of the Pfliegman name that I've found is "Csupas-zárnyrepülőgépemberi." That's pronounced TSOO-PASH-SAHR-ny-RE-POOL-IR-dee-EHP-EHM-BEH-ree. It means "flying wing human."

So Pfliegman works just fine for me.

Besides, for centuries historians have bickered about where the Pflieg-mans actually come from. If you want to be technical about it, technically I'm part Hungarian, part German, part Illyrian, part Celt, part Mongol, part Turk, and part Ugrian. As Grandfather Ákos once said, "To be a Pflieg-man is a collective neurosis."

All I can say is that I was born in a town called Front Lick, and my parents were also born in Front Lick, and I'm probably more Virginian than anything anyway, though that has yet to be officially decided: for if to be a Pfliegman is a collective neurosis, to be a Virginian is a quite singular neurosis, and neither leaves much hope for me. After all, I am a man who lives in a bus. A bus in a field. A field by a river—

There are wolves.

The bus used to be called PFLIEGMAN'S TRAVELING MEAT BUS. I'd drive to people's houses and offer them large-quantity discounts, until one day the engine coughed and sputtered. I veered off the road, into this field, and painted over the TRAVELING. So now people come to PFLIEGMAN'S   MEAT BUS to buy their meat. They come because my meat is very fresh. The fresh-est in the state. I've turned over the horsefields behind the farmhouse to the cows, pigs, and sheep, which I raise to slaughter. I am thirty-four years old. A self-made man.

I have an awning.

Sometimes the Virginians will stand beneath the awning and look at the bus. They'll pinch their faces. They'll turn to me and say, "You *live* here?"

Which is fine. The outside of the old school bus is not impressive. It's got four flat tires, busted directionals. The headlights stare off in one direction, like a person with a broken neck—

But the inside of the bus is pleasing: it's warm and dry, the color of hospital gowns; the ceiling is low, divided into several dome-shaped pan-els; a clean gray corrugated rubber flooring runs the length of it, all the way from the driver's seat to the Emergency Exit door; and the windows are all perfectly functioning, eleven on each side.

Underneath the windows I added some wooden paneling to give it a classic look, like I saw in the magazine *This Bus Is My Home.* The magazine said that today one in every three hundred people live in an RV. It also told me that many people live in refashioned school busses like mine. All in all, it's a "perfectly normal life-choice," said the magazine, and nobody who lives in a bus should be made to feel bad about it, like it was a socially awkward thing to do.

To prove that bus-living isn't socially awkward, the magazine had all these pictures of people in their homemade busses, standing in the center of their accoutrements, smiling amidst the here and there: the toaster ovens and microwave ovens, televisions and stereos, heating devices, cooling devices, and staying-the-same-temperature devices. "See?" the magazine said. "It's all portable. Just imagine being able to take your whole life with you, from place to place."

But my bus is not an experiment in an efficient, portable life; it's an experiment in stasis. There's a less sophisticated assortment of here and there: a sink attached to a rusty drainage pipe that keeps the water going where it's supposed to go, an electric stove with one working burner, and a tall white meat refrigerator for storing the meat.

I've looked for a magazine called *This Broken-Down Bus Which I Inhabit Like a Small Woodland Creature Is My Home.* I haven't had much luck.

But after seeing how the Bus People color-coordinated the interiors of their busses, I was inspired. I bought some bathing towels from an Indian when he was passing through. He was wearing a cowboy shirt and loafers, and a long black ponytail swung down his back. His grandmother, he said, was in textiles. He reached into his bag and handed me two blue towels with yellow pom-poms. "They're slightly stained," he said, and looked around. "What's with the bus?"

I didn't answer.

When I didn't answer, he just shook his head and said, "White people."

What else—I have a few pots and pans, a wool blanket half-shredded from the moths that come scouting at night, and a big pink sweatshirt that says Disneyland. The sweatshirt was given to me by a Virginian who was buying some meat. She was wearing the sweatshirt, and she was with her family, and they were also wearing sweatshirts. First she thought I was charming.

"Look at how little he is," she said.

"Hairy too," said her husband. "Get a load of that beard. What is he, a midget?"

The woman peered down at me, suspicious. "What *are* you?" she said. "Are you a midget or what?"

Which is fine. I am small and hairy. Fetid-looking. I'm so small, sometimes my meat customers will ask me if I am a midget, to which I respond in my brain, "I'm not a midget, but I'm probably about as close to a midget as a person possibly can be without actually being a midget."

"He's a *dwarf*," said the husband. "Dwarves are hairier than midgets."

"Whatever he is, I think he's just charming," the woman said.

I remain bewildered that someone like me could be considered charming by anyone, but she placed one hand on the side of the bus and whispered in my ear that she had just come back from Disneyland and I was more charming than Disneyland.

I brought out my writing tablet. *Am I more charming than your husband?* I wrote.

She pursed her lips. (Midget's got a fresh mouth.)

How about clouds? I wrote. *Am I more charming than clouds?*

A magnanimous look filled her eyes. "He must be a mute," she said, and clucked her tongue. "Poor thing. How sad. Isn't it sad, George?"

"God's got a funny sense of humor," said George.

The woman thought that it was very sad. She took off her sweatshirt and gave it to me. She patted my arm. She whispered, *"Here you go."*

Which is fine. The Virginians will often take one look at the hairy little man living out of a bus in a field, at the mountain of meat that surrounds him, and then there's no holding back the magnanimity. I've been given many items over the years: boots without laces, a stained coffee carafe. A brand-new silver towel rack, still in its original packaging. Virginians are big on magnanimity. They practically bathe in it.

I bathe in the river behind the meat bus. It's called the Queeconococheecook. My side of the Queeconococheecook is covered in long green grasses; the far side is covered in mud. I bathe in the river with the Indian's towels, and then hang them to dry on a clothesline that runs from the top of my bus to a nearby pine tree. The pine tree has wide, swooping arms, underneath which I keep a bucket for the containment and removal of bodily fluids and other unsavories.

These I deposit into a hole in the ground.

What am I, the Virginians all want to know? I live in a bus. I cut up animals. *Je chie dans un seau—*

I am the last remaining descendant of a line of the worst sort of losers on the planet.

II
EVOLUTION OF THE PFLIEGMANS:
THE ELEVENTH TRIBE

My story begins one thousand one hundred and eleven years ago, across another continent, in another age. It is an age not unlike the age we currently
inhabit. It is an age of very rich and very poor. Of men and non-men. Of
wars and entitlement.

Wolves *baroo* in the distance.

It is an age when Europe is defined and undefined by changing borders:
Charlemagne has drawn lines between the Frankish Kingdoms, but the
maps of the East remain lineless. The future countries of Eastern Europe
exist only as floats of pale color. Accidental fingersmudges. Places where
the ice turns to tundra, where glassy-eyed animals stumble hopefully
toward nourishment, where barbarians and nomads roam the landscape
in packs with names that sound fictitious: the Borussians, the Mazovians,
the Drehgovitians, the White Volhynians, the Avars, the Khazars, the
Pechenegs, the Magyars—and of course, the Pfliegmans.

By the year 896, we are living north of the Ural Mountains, hidden
amongst ten early Magyar tribes, in a field next to a river leading straight
into the heart of the great Black Sea. And this is where the story of the
Pfliegmans begins. In a field, next to a wide, tumultuous river.

Luxuriant green grasses coat one side of the riverbank; the other side is covered in slippery, rock-laden, gets-all-over-everything mud.

On the mud side live the Pechenegs, a cluster of barbarians who gather every morning to stand at the edge of their sloppy embankment in their bare feet, mud squishing fatly between their toes, and stare across the river. They stare with a lean, bright hatred. They stare until their bodies over-flow with the desire to touch just *one clean blade*, then they bare their sharp teeth and leap into the water, emerging on the other side to wipe their muddy paws all over their neighbors' fine grasses, kick down the posts of their tents, break all their clay pots, and ravage the weakest among them.

On the grassy side, the Magyars are not without flaw: historians have described them as "a people devoted to leisure, given over to vanities, and extremely libidinous." While in a matter of a few short years they will em-bark on a campaign of incursions so deadly, so horrific, that all of Western Europe will pee its pants at the mere whisper of their name—*De sagittis Hungarorum libera nos, Domine*—for now they are utterly without interest in incurring any incursions at all. They are perfectly content to do nothing but make love in their fields of long grasses. To admire each other's hair. These are the world's future Hungarians.

Thoroughly a peace-loving people.

Ultimately, they decide that anything is better than having one's god-damn clay pots broken for the millionth time, so one evening the heads of all ten tribes agree upon exodus. Already their people have many skills. They can ride horses, shape iron, make pots, and build huts. They fight with swords, with bows and arrows, and they all speak the same language—a unique Finno-Ugric language, closest to Vogul and Ostak—and they prac-tice animal husbandry, caring for their own horses and cows and pigs and sheep. The early Magyars are underdogs, but underdogs with a *purpose*: they will leave this grassy spot to seek another river. They will search for safe and fertile flanks of land to call their own. After all, having one's own land means a person is getting settled. Establishing himself. They all close their eyes that evening imagining whole fields of useful, prosperous dirt—

We Pfliegmans, however, are incapable of imagining anything.

From the get-go, Pfliegmans were outcasts in a country made of out-casts. We were then, and probably always have been, whole ages behind the progress of the company we kept. When men were bashing rocks together to make tools, Pfliegmans were slithering from the ocean, coated in a greenish muck; when men were grunting, sneezing, and lighting fire, hirsute Pfliegmans lay recluse in a dark musty corner of a cave, hissing; when men began wearing pelts and eating meat and painting walls, Pfliegmans were stealing pelts to make fun of the pelt-wearers and would return to a cold cave *hungry again, goddammit*; when men began forming languages and speaking in recognizable tongues, Pfliegmans snorted and threw their heads in the mud in protest; when men began eating with forks, Pfliegmans licked their dirty nails; when men were building factories to work in and homes for themselves to live in, Pfliegmans rolled in the grass, deliciously; when Edison illuminated the world, Pfliegmans squealed and covered their eyes; when Ford made the world go faster, Pfliegmans stood at the curb, fearing for their lives, gaping at the shiny wheels, which explains why my father, János Pfliegman, who, one Christmas morning in 1984, after receiving a VCR as a Christmas present from my mother, spent four minutes examining the buttons and one minute examining the manual before bashing it in the face with an elbow—

But I digress.

Despite the fact that most historians only acknowledge ten tribes who migrated over the Ural Mountains that year; that the very word "Hungarian" is not a derivative of "Hun," as so many people stubbornly and incorrectly assume, but actually stems from the Finno-Ugric word *onogur* meaning "ten arrows," one for each tribe—despite this, I'm here to say there was an eleventh tribe. A tribe known for tripping over their own feet. For growling menacingly at perfectly friendly strangers. For stealing other people's food. We are a tribe that suffers yearlong, incendiary illnesses, and our presence will be eclipsed by the history books. We participate in none of the world's major events, and we have no official leader, as we know nothing of leaders and followers. We blink with uncertainty at quick-moving objects. We clean ourselves with our own tongues.

We are the Pfliegmans.

As the Magyars throw saddlebags over horses, don their finest hats, and set off into the wilderness, we are huddled around a dirt pile, trying to scurry up a fire for the scrap of deer we've stolen from a nearby tent. My great-great-great-great-great-great-great-great-great-grandfather is blowing the ashes. His wife, the she-male, is humming softly. Look at them:

they're emaciated. Their muscles are butter on the bread of their bones, bones that point out from their skin painfully, like they're being pierced from the inside out.

The male Pfliegman removes the deer from the fire and takes a large bite. It's too hot; he spits it on the ground. The female smacks him on the head for being so foolish and wasting perfectly good meat.

"*Monga*," she admonishes, and grabs it.

The male Pfliegman punches her hard on the shoulder. "*Thpits!*" he replies, and grabs it back. He eats it and swallows, despite the burn. The roof of his mouth singes, dislodging from itself in one long peel—

This is the woman-Pfliegman's fault.

Later that night, holding his sore mouth, he watches her body lying underneath a pelt, the scrawny-boned back shifting, the hard-knobbed breasts rising and falling, and he feels hotly, overwhelmingly cheated. He leans forward and smacks his wife on the back of the head for not being greater than she is, and then he leaps on top of her.

Between them, this night, they conceive a boy. A Pfliegman boy who will one day save the lives not only of his own people, but those of the entire Hungarian nation. A Pfliegman whose own child will begin the line of Pfliegmans who defy the simple laws of evolution and survive for little more than a thousand years until, one by one, we each drop off, and only a single near-midget, living across an entire ocean, selling cheap meat out of some bus in some field of some weedy armpit of North America, remains.

III

WHITE PEOPLE

I may be the last remaining Pfliegman, I may live in a bus in a field, and out of this bus I may sell meat for a meager-yet-adequate living, but I'm not one of those introverted scoundrels. I don't sneer at the beautiful, I don't wax philosophic, and I'm not without a *glimmer* of urbanity: I have electricity, for example. I have a bed.

I wear a stylish woolen cap.

The cap was a given to me by a meat customer so impressed with the girth of his rump roast that he removed the hat from his own head and placed it, gently, on mine. My bed is a mattress flopped over two passenger seats at the back of the bus, made of arching springs that knuckle my back in a pleasing manner. Outside the bus an old battery-powered generator shudders, charging the stove, the meat refrigerator, and a lightbulb which hangs over my bed in a single dangling strand. The lightbulb illuminates a small bookshelf which holds a modest collection of literature: a shiny pamphlet titled *Your First Hamster*, by Peter H. Smith; *The Complete Book of Water Polo, With Pictures*, by Captain Jerry Aldini; *Madame Chafouin's French Dictionary (Concise Edition)*, by Madame Chafouin; *The Collapsing Universe*, by Isaac Asimov; and *The Rise and Fall and Rise of the Pagan Hungarians*, by a writer known just as "Anonymus."

I keep these books on the bus because although I have read and returned nearly every book in the Lick County Library, these books came to me instead of me to them. I obtained *Your First Hamster* one afternoon when a customer brought her six-year-old son out to the field to buy some meat. The boy stared at me while I wrapped his mother's rump roast. He tugged her arm. "Is that a *kid?*" he whispered. "A kid with a *beard?*"

"Shhh," his mother said.

"This place is weird," the boy said. "I want to go to a normal store. I want to go to the Big M."

"That's not polite, Michael," she said, and turned her back.

Michael looked at me and stuck out his tongue.

So I stuck out my tongue.

The boy's eyebrows raised, then he burst into tears. His mother spun around to see me standing with my tongue out. "I came here to be *charitable*," she said. "But now we're leaving, and I'm not going to buy a single thing. What do you think of that?"

I rolled my eyes. I wagged my tongue. I opened my mouth, and gagged a little.

"You are a *horrible* man," she whispered. "A horrible, horrible little man!" She grabbed the boy and ran back to the car. They sped off down Back Lick Road. I looked down and saw that the boy had left the pamphlet behind on the grass. On the cover was a picture of a clean, soft, apricot-colored hamster, perched on the branch of a tree. I picked it up.

"*Dwarf hamsters*," it said, "*are being seen more and more in the United States. Their petite size and charming ways point the way to an ever-increasing popularity.*"

I'd never thought about taking care of a hamster before, but ever since that moment, I've considered having one for company. There's something in the photo that makes me long to hold the tiny creature. To nuzzle him against my hairy cheek. To let him crawl down my arm and back up again.

But I don't really need company. Although it may seem as though I'm alone, I'm really not; I am surrounded by a whole community of living and nonliving things, and each plays a small but vital role in the sustenance of Rovar Ákos Pfliegman, and Pfliegman's Meat Bus as a whole.

* * *

About a year ago, I came across a cardboard box at the bottom of a dumpster of a Mrs. Kipner's Family Restaurant downtown. The box was packed with nonperishable canned goods. There was Mrs. Kipner's American Beans-n-Wienies, Mrs. Kipner's Bavarian Tomato Beef Stew, Mrs. Kipner's Hungarian Goulash. I carried the box back to the bus, and unpacked it. That's when I noticed that one of the cans felt light. Empty. I cranked open the lid.

Looking up at me was the biggest beetle I have ever seen.

He was enormous, with a waxy brown shell. He looked like a giant pecan. The beetle had apparently consumed the entire contents of a Mrs. Kipner's Hungarian Goulash and grown so wide that his thorax stuck sharply into both sides of the can. He was trapped. I moved over to the window to get a better look at him and he blinked at the light. He flapped the hard-shelled blades of his back aggressively. His right eye was bright and healthy, but his left eye hung low, clouded with a white mucous. One of his wings was coated in little white spots, and he kept throwing his head back, in a futile attempt to scratch them. When I tried to reach in and help, he twirled his leafy antennae in a threatening manner, so I went into the fridge, found a rotten tomato, and dropped it into the can. He quickly lowered his pucker into the tomato and made long, satisfying slurping sounds.

I call him Mrs. Kipner.

Once I tried to rescue Mrs. Kipner from the tin can by popping him out with a knife, but he wouldn't budge. I pressed down too hard, and the knife slipped a little, accidentally shucking off a small piece of shell. He squealed with unhappiness. Every time I came at him with the knife after that he twirled his antennae, so for the most part I keep my distance from Mrs. Kipner. I feed him slices of tomato and keep his tin can open, perched on a windowledge of the bus, so if he ever wants a peek at the big old world, he'll have a nice view.

But even without Mrs. Kipner, I'm not alone. Not by a long shot. Moles burrow underneath the bus, searching for the heat that travels underground from the generator; wolves bay in the distance, their breath spooling out in long clouds; and then there's the field itself. The presence of the bus, the human being, his beetle, and his collection of literature has somehow altered its natural state. Grass out here grows like it's pushed from the earth and fed by the sky. There's this one blade of grass that's taller than I am. She greets me every morning at a window of the bus with an endearing *tap-tap* sound.

I call her Marjorie.

In the summer sun, Marjorie hangs like a palm frond. In the fall, she waves in the wind in a friendly manner, and in the winter rains, she slaps the wide flat of the windows. In the spring, she grows. So you can see that I am not alone.

But there are those who do not understand my small and vibrant community.

"White people," said the Indian, shaking his head. "You live out here all by yourself?"

He was standing in the center of the bus, leaning one large hip against a passenger's seat. I couldn't remember how he even got here. He glanced at the books parked on my bookshelf. "Those belong to you?" he said.

I didn't answer.

He reached into his bag and produced a copy of Charles Darwin's *The Origin of Species*. He said he was reading it to understand how white people think. "Turn to page one," he said.

I turned to page one.

"The existing forms of life," the Indian recited, *"are the descendants by true generation of pre-existing forms."* He produced a toothpick and began cleaning his teeth. "My grandfather said white people have no history. As a consequence, they always have to change to fit their environment. It's how they have survived, and it's why they can't be trusted. Saying one thing and then doing another—"

The Indian went on for a while, but I was more excited about the book. New reading material is rather scarce when you live in a field in a bus. I went to the meat refrigerator, reached for my highest priced section, and handed him a blushing, swollen lambshank, the color of spring peaches. He looked pleased. "My grandfather said all white people are made of hate and Elmer's glue," he said. "But you don't seem like a glue sort of fellow to me."

I tried to laugh, but a cough bubbled up instead. I stumbled over to a passenger's seat and slumped into it, hacking away. Something wet flew from my mouth and landed smack on top of *The Origin of Species*.

"That doesn't sound good," the Indian said. "Would you like something hot to drink? I'll make some tea." He stood up and looked for the food cabinet, but I am a man who lives in a bus. I do not have a food cabinet. "Some hot water then," the Indian said, and wandered over to the stove. Outside the sky darkened, and thunder rolled above us. The air inside grew hot and thick. The Indian found a rusty pot hanging from a nail and went to the sink. He turned the knob, but the water never came. Slowly, he replaced the pot on the nail, just as it was. Then noticed a pile of envelopes lying next to the sink. "*Rovar Pfliegman*," he read. "Is that you?"

I coughed again.

The Indian picked up one of the envelopes and turned it in his hands. "It says that it's from Subdivisions LLC. It looks important. You're not going to open it?"

I held on to the Darwin tight, suddenly nervous for some reason that the Indian might want his book back, but he stayed focused on the envelope.

"It's marked Urgent," he said. "Would you like me to open it for you?"

It was clear that the Indian was looking for some conversation, it was clear that he wanted to open the envelope and chat, but herein lies the rub: I don't talk. At all. Certainly not since Ján and Janka died, but I'm not even sure I ever really talked before.

I'm no mute—let's just get this out of the way right now. I don't speak words, but there've always been noises, and as far as I know mutes don't make noises. I make all sorts of noises. The loud *blat*, the long *shhhhug*, the *murgle*. The heaving *wherge*.

And I've always been coughing. My coughs are full-bodied, lung-flattening coughs that give me headaches and nausea. The occasional, errant nosebleed. I once counted the number of times I cough in a day, and it was over two hundred before I fell asleep. That means I cough over a hundred thousand times a year. A million times since I've lived in the bus.

Two million times since the death of Ján and Janka Pfliegman.

When he realized that I don't talk, that I just sit in this bus, coughing, the Indian put the envelope back on the pile. He ran a finger around it one last time. "I'll leave it here for you, in case you want to read it," he said, and then a drop of water splashed onto his hand. He looked up. Rain hit the bus all at once. It sounded like beans being poured on a snare drum. "There's a crack in the ceiling," he said. Then there was nothing else to say. He climbed down and looked around the bus, nervously. He wiped his brow.

I sat back in the passenger's seat, watching him. Listening to the pleasant hum of the meat refrigerator. He could have been nervous about the bus, but I think he was more nervous about me.

Most people are.

I expected the Indian to leave at that point, but instead he sat down next to me, reached into his bag, and produced two cans of beer. He offered me one.

I shook my head.

He shrugged and snapped one open. "I don't get it," he said. "My grandfather said white people can't exist without speaking. He said they're all just imitations of each other, so it's like they have to speak to distinguish themselves." He took a long drink of the beer and roundly belched. "They're like mirrors or something. Illusions."

If I could speak, I would have told him about the time a Virginian drove up to my bus with a mirror in the back of his truck. The mirror was big and oval-shaped, framed in gold leafing. He said it was something his ex-wife bought and it'd been hanging in his living room for twenty years and he couldn't stand the thing. The man looked tired. "The dump won't take it," he said. "So I thought you might want it."

Of course I didn't protest, so he hauled the mirror out of the back of the truck and laid it down on the grass by my bus. "There," he said, and wiped his hands. "That looks super!"

After he left, I walked over to the mirror, took one look at what was staring back at me, promptly started gagging, and found no reason ever to look in it again. Weeds quickly engulfed the frame, and now the mirror looks exactly like a gentle frog pond.

Which is fine.

"Hell," said the Indian, "this bus could be an illusion." He polished off the beer and stood up, rubbing his stomach. "I don't suppose you have anything to eat that isn't raw?" he said. "A sandwich?"

I shook my head. He walked to the front of the bus and opened the door of the meat refrigerator to look for sandwiches. Then he craned his neck around the driver's seat, but there were no sandwiches there either, so he slung his bag of textiles over his shoulder. He stepped down from the bus and crossed the wet field, swatting at field ticks, and did not turn around to wave. Which was fine.

I rapped a knuckle on the side of the bus to see if the bus was an illusion.

It wasn't.

But I liked the Indian. I would have liked it if he'd stayed. If he'd stayed, we could have listened to music together. I could have brought out the tape-radio and played some music. Silence, I've noticed, makes people uncomfortable, and music always helps.

Most people are not content to listen to the hum of a meat refrigerator.

I suppose it's just as well, since I only have two cassettes for my tape-radio: Bach fugues and *The Best of Carly Simon*. They were given to me by a magnanimous Virginian who thought I'd get lonely living out here in a bus in a field by myself. I played the Carly Simon once all the way through and then suffered a twenty-four-hour panic attack. So I never listen to the Carly Simon. But I listen to the Bach. I enjoy the way the notes are simple at first, and then become complex. Mrs. Kipner likes the Bach as well; he likes it when the notes get faster, tripping over each other. When this happens, he lifts his head and makes a sound like a tiny drumroll.

There's also the radio part of the tape-radio, but the antenna broke a long time ago. I put a paperclip in the hole, so now I only get a station that plays German pop songs from the fifties, sixties, and seventies, with an announcer who cries, *"Deutsch Hits aus den Fünfziger, Sechziger, und Siebziger!"* I've tried placing other items into the antenna hole: a tack, a rolled-up piece of aluminum, but then I get no reception at all. So I don't listen to the radio too often. Which is fine. If I listened to music it might seem like I was an active part of the community, the general populace.

And this, I am most definitely not.

IV

EVOLUTION OF THE PFLIEGMANS:
THE SACRIFICE OF ENNI HÚS AND HIS FINE HAT

According to *The Rise and Fall and Rise of the Pagan Hungarians*, the old history book that is, at this precise moment, leaning slumped to one side of my small bookshelf, as the Magyars throw saddlebags over their horses, don their finest, pointiest hats, and set off into the wilderness, we Pfliegmans perk up from our holes and chatter disagreeably. We do not know much, but we know that we cannot endure the raids of the Pechenegs alone. Hatless, horse-less, and saddle-less, we hop on donkeys and, unbeknownst to the good and civilized Magyars, follow their horses in a long, slow fumble away from the Steppes of Asia, southwestward to the Carpathian Basin.

As they march confidently over the Ural Mountains, through the Verecke Narrows, easily passing the Impassable Forest, we miserably stumble our way up one precarious slope of the Urals, and begin slipping farther and farther behind them. Before now, life was divided into categories of Things That Will Hurt Us and Things That Won't, but now life's not so clear. As a consequence, we Pfliegmans fear the whole earth: the forests that sway and whistle in wind, the bad ice that sometimes cracks beneath our feet. Most of all, we fear the Man in the Sky. We fear His frigid winds, His omniscient darkness. We fear His rain.

Our fear is not wholly unfounded: we Pfliegmans fear the rain because we are more prone to sickness than other people. We are prone to all kinds of sickness. In fact, I think it's safe to say that, as a people, we are just plain *prone*. There was every chance in the world the little Pfliegman tribe would never make it. In *The Origin of Species*, Darwin writes, "*If any one species does not become modified and improved in a corresponding degree with its competitors, it will be exterminated.*"

It is the design of the Pfliegman, it seems, to live according to Nature's bitchy whim.

Still remaining among us on the journey, however, is the she-Pfliegman who suffered the cruel misfortune of becoming pregnant before we left. She stumbles along the slippery rocks, cutting her fingers on sharp branches as she reaches for support. Nine hundred years earlier, another pregnant woman named Mary followed a similar path, keeping an eye out for the inn or whatever, settling for a barn, but this little troll is not the Virgin Mary; she does not know the story of Mary, nor does she even know that she is Woman. She is a Pfliegman. Right now she's hoofing it up a mountain, gasping for air, hot with sweat and dirt and body oils. Right now she would *kill* for a frigging barn. The child growing inside of her presses down on the coils of her gut. Breathing is difficult. Fever boils in her throat. She wheezes painfully, looking for the male who made this happen to her, but he's ditched her for another she-Pfliegman, one who can walk faster than she can. One with swooning, pendulous breasts. If it were possible for her to say it, if she could possibly formulate the words, she might mumble "Mother-*fucker*"; instead, she reaches forward and grabs on to the pelt of one of the Pfliegman men in front of her. She gives him a desperate, pleading look.

Annoyed, he shoves her off.

So when she reaches the crest of the mountain, she stops walking. With relief, with sorrow, she realizes that she cannot continue. She steps out onto a large rock, balances herself and her large belly for a moment, and then, as though nudged by a gentle breeze, pitches herself forward down the mountainside.

Of the half a million early Hungarians on the march, only one, a man riding high up on horseback, happens to glance behind him. He is an extremely healthy and appealing early Magyar. Muscles pepper his body. He wears a thick warm cloak secured with a strap of leather, and a pointy hat made from fabrics the color of sunset, peaked with a shiny gold button. The world has been easy on this man. He overflows with inner resources. He is happy for his people and often surges with pride. He will throw his hands in the air and cry, "We are a new people!" or "This is an historic journey!" But as he turns his horse around to gaze at the shoulder-shaped peaks of the Carpathians, at the wide, sagacious eastern sky, he watches, in horror, as a pregnant woman tumbles down one side of the mountain.

"Hooy!" he cries, and digs into his stirrups.

He rides quickly back to the mountain, maneuvering his way up around the rocks and switchbacks until he finds her. She is alive, albeit uncomfortably embroiled, amidst a tangle of branches and sap and pine needles. He has never seen a woman like her. She is small, he observes. Inordinately hairy. Her belly is enormous, like a well-fed tick. He dismounts and squats down next to her, studying her face. He cringes. Her eyes do not look like regular eyes, he thinks. They are wide. *Black.* Exacerbated by the dark half-moons beneath them.

Politely, the Magyar removes his hat and holds it to his chest. "Are you all right, Madam?" he says.

She does not answer. She only stares, dumbly, at the gold button on his hat.

"What is your name?" he asks.

"*Pshaw*," she gags, and passes out.

So the Magyar reaches his arms beneath her body. He picks her up. "Even pregnant, she is *remarkably* small," he thinks, then ties a long sack from the horse's neck to his saddle. He places the woman in the sack to lie, hammock-like, until they reach the New Region. He talks to her, even though she does not talk back. He gives her a proper Hungarian name.

"I will call you Aranka," he says. "For 'gold.' For the way you looked at my button."

From that point on, the handsome Magyar stays close to watch over the Pfliegmans. He gives us water to drink. He gives the children pieces of sweet bark to chew. He smiles at Aranka, swinging in the sack. But despite his many kindnesses, we Pfliegmans distrust him. This man is too friendly, too *pink-cheeked*, and where we only drink water, the smiling man drinks warm animal milk. He also eats meat every day.

Come evening, he builds a campfire to cook his meat, and we Pfliegmans twitter around it, attracted to the light. "Careful," he says, but a few of us get too close. Our fingers singe, and we howl into the darkness.

"No!" he shouts. "Get back! Now look here…"

So he shows us how to make a proper hearth; he shows us what to do with fire and what not to do, and then brings out thick slices of salted meat. He sticks them into the fire.

Watching this man gobble his meat and not share it, watching his lips become slick and shiny, we begin quivering with want. We sniff the oils that hang in the air. Our dark eyes glow. We lick our lips.

We call him *Enni Hús*, for "eat meat."

As the weeks pass, we Pfliegmans scuttle along behind Enni Hús's horse, watching and waiting to see if perhaps one of those fine slabs of meat might fall from his pockets. We snigger behind his back, "Enni *Hoosh*, Enni *Hoosh*." We shake our fists, imitating him. We mock the sounds he makes on our sticky tongues:

Oo-wee-goo! Oo-wee-goo!

Alas, there is nothing more irritating to a handsome man than mockery. Enni Hús stops his exultations. He also stops giving us his food and water. He no longer allows us near his fires at night, and when Aranka groans inside the sack, it is not past Enni Hús to give her a swift kick in the side to shut her up. By the time we reach the Carpathian Basin, he decides that there is utterly no point in being of service to a people who are not interested in being serviced, so he dismounts from his horse, unties Aranka from the wrap around his saddle, and drops her body to the ground.

"*Oof*," she says, and rubs her butt.

The rest of us, cold and shivering, stare at him. We clutch our exposed skins.

"What more can I give you?" he says, bitterly, but we do not answer. We only stand there, blinking at his hat. Shivers sprinkle over his arms, his neck, like he's being covered by insects. He shakes them off. "May the Man in the Sky save you," he mumbles.

Then Enni Hús abandons us.

A brutal rain begins spitting out of the sky. We see the other Hungarians pitching their tents, so we quickly cobble together our own, which is not tall and erect, fortified with a strong bundle of sticks, or tightly secured with animal pelts; our tent is erected sloppily, made from the Leftover Pelt Scrap Heap. It leans east and west, with far too many people living in it.

As the proper Hungarians begin digging holes and planting seeds, milking cattle and roasting swine, as they conceive of other, more intellectual projects, like wine production, tax collecting, and beekeeping— beekeeping!—all we Pfliegmans can do is take care of the living, take care of our many dead, and stare wide-eyed at the enormously pregnant woman suffering in the corner of the tent. We click our fingernails against our teeth. We cough, miserably. We listen to the relentless, interminable rain.

Late one night, all of us packed into the bulging tent in the manner unique to our own perverse ochlocracy, we decide that we must pacify the Man in the Sky, to stop the rain and bring out the sun. Darwin writes, *"Many more individuals are born than can possibly survive,"* and although we don't know the word "expendable," at this point we somehow can sense it.

An elder Pfliegman pulls out one of his eyelids as far as it will go. It snaps back into place. "Sacrifice," he says.

We whistle and scoot around him.

The following morning, we Pfliegmans move quickly in a pack until we find what we're looking for: a young man on horseback, wearing a pointy hat made of lovely fabrics, silks the color of a broken sky. At the top, a gleaming circle of gold. Enni Hús has just finished digesting a plump and satisfying leg of deer and licks the sweetness from his lips, watching the progress of his people with his usual pride, even a bit of wistful awe. "My brothers," he says, and pulls a sentimental tear from his face with a long and healthy finger. Then, from an unknown corner of his keen peripheral vision, something flashes from behind one tent to another.

A shiver scampers up his back. He looks for any sign of danger and sees only a dog growling with a scrap of food. He settles back comfortably in his seat. The grass turns slowly in the wind.

"Enni Hús!" we shout.

He cries out for help, but we gather him too quickly; we smother him in our cloaks and drag him behind our tent, hurling rocks until the healthy and able Hungarian collapses at our feet. We form a circle. Everyone is given a small axe. This is the routine: each member of the Eleventh Tribe must take his own piece of Enni Hús, and then together we will sacrifice him to the punishing Man in the Sky to stop the rain and bring out the sun.

The elder Pfliegman raises his axe, and then solemnly lowers it.

And this is how the Pfliegmans make themselves known for the first time in history: sneaking up behind some perfectly good citizen, knocking him off his horse in broad, gray daylight, pummeling him with rocks until he is unconscious, and then dragging him behind a tent and chopping him into several chunky, loaf-sized pieces.

"*Man*," writes Darwin, "*selects only for his own good.*"

One Pfliegman receives a large piece of thigh. He tries to have a taste of Enni Hús, but another Pfliegman growls and slaps his hand. A female Pfliegman appears wearing Enni Hús's hat with the button. Everyone sees her and cheers. She smiles at the luck of her booty, but then another Pfliegman tries to take the hat from her. He scampers over to her and tugs it from her head. She screeches out in protest, but he pulls back, and then everyone wants Enni Hús's hat. We fly upon each other, Pfliegman upon Pfliegman, until tent collapses, the fire goes out, and everyone's pieces of Enni Hús get mixed up with everyone else's in a grisly mise-en-scène.

A hoary elder roars at us to stop, and so we stop, panting, and begin trying to sort out which pieces of Enni Hús belonged to whom. The elder demands the hat from the Pfliegman who found it.

She reluctantly hands it over.

We rekindle the fire in the exact manner Enni Hús taught us and then drop in our meats. Together, we mouth the words we heard him use, "My brothers, my brothers," as the fire roars up and the meat boils off the bone, and when every trace of Enni Hús has been transformed into a husky, awful-smelling spiral of smoke, the elder hobbles over to the licking flames and gamely tosses in the hat as well.

V

A PILL FOR EVERYTHING

This morning an extraordinarily fat Virginian jokes in a very funny manner that I should have some kind of outfit to wear while I sit out here in my green plastic lawnchair in front of the bus. He's wearing a baseball cap with an M on it, and suggests that I wear a hat that looks like a pig's head. Because I sell pork. Or, the man says, I could have different hats for different meat, like when I'm giving someone a steak I would wear a cow hat, and when I'm giving out lamb I could wear a lamb hat. "It might make you easier to look at," he says.

And then he laughs.

If I could speak, I might argue that he himself is not so exciting to look at. I might say that there's nothing particularly enthralling about the way his stomach swells over his pants, or the way his nose is so round it looks like a lightbulb. I might mention that his eyes are so close together it looks like his head has been caught in a vise—but I am not an angry man.

In fact, sitting here in my lawnchair, out in the open air, packages of meat passing from palm to palm, I think it's fair to say that ever since I left the farmhouse and moved into this bus, I've only had one single, throbbing emotion:

Her name is Dr. Monica.

Dr. Monica is a pediatrician. She wears a white hat. Underneath the hat is a tiny blond bun, but her hair isn't long enough to wear tied up like that, so the shorter pieces fall about her neck, giving me erections.

Rovar, you say, that is a rather disgusting notion, but you must understand that I'm a feeble man. They're only feeble erections. Perfectly benevolent.

It's like holding your finger for a second and then letting go.

Pfliegman men suffer Benevolent Erections very easily. I get them from cross-breezes, the smell of laundry detergent. The color orange. But Dr. Monica's neck is way up there. She hides the neck with sweaters, a gold cross gleaming above her breasts as if to say, "Back, Vampire." I get anywhere near that neck and St. Benevolus starts to tremble.

I go to Dr. Monica's office once a week, which is paid for by me, in cash. It always costs thirty-five dollars.

What's wrong with me? It's a fair question. Unfortunately, I don't have a fair answer. No doctor has yet been able to identify the reason for my panoply of disorders, therefore it suffices to say that I suffer because I am a Pfliegman, and Pfliegmans have been physically gypped in every way imaginable: my left knee is bent, and drags along the road as I walk; my head is lumpy and bulges outward, like it's made of potatoes; my stomach is uncouth and easily flummoxed, leaving me in a perpetual and contradictory state of nausea and starvation; and my skin is so dry it tends to peel on its own. Every day, flakes of skin parachute from my body. Occasionally a meat customer will look down and spot the tiny dry coils that have crashlanded on the reaches of my lawnchair, and they'll cough politely and take a step back from the line, or look at me funny and take a step back, or just take a step back.

Before I met Dr. Monica, I felt so lousy I could barely sell my meat. I would just lie in bed all day watching the rainwater leak from the crack in the ceiling. Fatigue boiled away at my anemic Pfliegman marrow. It got so bad that I couldn't even focus my eyes, not even enough to read, and for every different thing wrong with my body, I saw a different doctor. I saw a cardiologist, a gastroenterologist, neurologist, urologist, traumatologist, an orthopedist, eye-doctors, ear, nose, and throat doctors, endocrinologists, dermatologists, and an allergist. I carried all of my medicines in a backpack, and the doctors said there was a pill for everything. It was true. There *was* a pill for everything, and taking just one of the pills for one of my ailments might have done me just fine, but if you take Drug A, there may be inflammation, which means you have to take Drug A and B, which causes emotional disorder warranting Drug C, however Drug A and Drug C are catalysts for severe rashes and should only be taken at midnight, and if you forget to take them at midnight, you need Drug D to counteract the vomiting, which negates the positive effects of Drug B.

I was up to Drug R before I sat in front of a histopathologist, a pale, trembling wreck of a human being, and she recommended that I give up all of my independent treatments and go to the hospital for a very, very, very long time—all of this was before I met Dr. Monica.

It happened at the G&P.

Mister Bis's Grocery and Pharmaceuticals is a small grocery market on a corner of the Front Lick Village Square. The Virginians call it the G&P. The man in charge, Mister Bis, has a wide, protruding stomach, and black hair that falls over his head in five distinct fingers. He is an Indian, but not like the Indian who sold textiles. He's an Indian-from-India, and his real name is Tharavaad Bis Ghandi. He says that *tharavaad* means "ancestral home," and *ghandi* means "grocer," but *bis* doesn't mean anything, so as long as he lives in America, he'll go by Mister Bis.

The G&P used to have the largest meat display in Lick County, but ever since the Subdivisionists subdivided a large parcel of Virginia farmland and the BIG M supermarket opened, business has been slow for Mister Bis. He walks the aisles with a worried look, nervously tugging the collar of his shirt. When the first letter from Subdivisions LLC arrived at the bus, I brought it into town and showed it to Mister Bis. He read it and scowled. "How many letters have they sent you?"

I held up a finger.

"You let me know if you get more," he said. "They're trying to rezone the zoning laws. They can't kick you out without the proper zoning." He crumpled up the letter and threw it in the trash. "The Subdivisionists want to turn this whole goddamn country into a goddamn amusement park," he said.

But Mister Bis is a devoted, earnest meat-seller, and he buys all of his meat from me. We cut each other deals. My meat is arranged in neat rows with a white forked sign above it that says PFLIEGMAN MEAT. I buy my medicines, groceries, and wax paper wrapping from the G&P, but other times I like to go when I'm not going to buy anything at all. I like to go to my section and hover around and see who buys my meat.

I met Dr. Monica on one of the hovering days.

I was standing next to a pyramid of canned vegetables, keeping an eye on my display, when a short woman with blond hair turned the corner from dairy. She was shorter than most Virginians, almost as short as I am, but with large, appealing thighs. As she walked, her thighs shifted quickly back and forth underneath her doctor's coat in a professional, off-pace manner. She was headed straight for the Pfliegman meat. Her eyes were low, and she blinked more often than I'd ever seen another person blink before. (This is Dr. Monica's single imperfection. An eye condition that makes her blink a lot. If only *one* of my dozens of diseases was so endearing.) As she came closer, I smelled her: a scintillating combination of tuna fish and Kaopectate. She tossed her hair over her shoulders, leaned one thick hip against the display case, and inspected the meat. She pressed her fingers to it and it swelled from the pressure. It was pork. She lifted the pork and inspected it from all angles.

I began shivering. It was cool by the display, but I wasn't shivering from the temperature. It was the first beautiful thing I'd seen in years: Dr. Monica, next to my meat! Iridescent lights buzzed above us. A slight mist hovered about the display case, and when she reached in the mist wrapped itself around her. Mister Bis's radio yawked out an advertisement for a universal bathroom cleanser.

She put the pork loin back on the shelf and coolly inspected another.

I wanted to tell her everything about meat. I wanted to show her which shanks and loins were the freshest. I wanted to explain the subtle differences between April meat and October meat. I wanted to reach up and put my arms around her narrow shoulders and rub them and do what I had seen other men do to the women they adore: the rub. The kiss on the neck. "Darling," I wanted to say, "we need to fatten you up!" I wanted to stroke her back, tousle her hair. But I was not then, nor will I ever be, in a position to do those things. Instead, I coughed. A real loud one. A wracker. My lungs sounded like they were being gutted with a sharp-edged spoon. A kernel of phlegm flew from my mouth like a tiny bullet, landing smack on the sleeve of my Disneyland sweatshirt.

Dr. Monica turned to look at me. Me, the dark little creature looming by canned goods—

"Why, hello there," she said.

Her voice sounded so sweet, so lovely, it beckoned for me to say something civilized and gentlemanly, like "Ma'am," or "Fine morning, isn't it," but I am a Pfliegman. A primordial pre-being. Homunculus. I'm nowhere *near* that evolved. I grasped the front of my sweatshirt and held it. My face flushed, my eyes burned. I tried to hold back and contain it, but it was no use: a half-dozen sharp coughs exploded from my lungs like bats from a cave.

Dr. Monica wrinkled her nose. "That doesn't sound good," she said.

Miserably, I leaned away from her and, in five retching howls, finished the job.

She dug into her purse and pulled out a cough drop wrapped in a bright yellow wrapper. On it was a picture of a Dutch person dancing on a mountainside. I couldn't tell if it was a man or a woman dancing, but the person looked joyful. Three birds hovered above, and the birds also looked joyful. The brand was called "Evermore." She held it out to me.

I hesitated, uncertain what the woman might expect in return.

"Go on," she whispered. "*Take it.*"

I grabbed the sucker from her hand and shoved it in my mouth. Lemon and sugar coated my tongue. I bit into it greedily, and was rewarded with a mouthful of honey. I had never in my life tasted anything so wonderful. Dr. Monica removed a thermometer from a breast pocket of her white coat, and gestured to ask if she could take my temperature.

"I'm a pediatrician," she explained. The thermometer was yellow with a picture of a frog at the tip. It had been resting on her breast. "May I?" she asked.

I opened so wide, I gagged a little.

"Now close," she said. "Keep it under your tongue."

The thermometer was warm, and bitter with disinfectant. "*Muh,*" I said.

I hadn't meant to speak—it just slipped out. My throat vibrated and tickled, making me grin for the first time in weeks. None of my former doctors had ever gotten me to speak before, and it wasn't a beautiful sound, but even if I sounded like gravel being poured from a bucket, I didn't care. *Adorable Darling!* I wanted to cry. *Aphrodite! My perfectly stout Pediatrician!*

Then Mister Bis came over. Sometimes Mister Bis gets nervous about having me hanging out in his store. I can't say I blame him. He's a nice man with a nice family that lives in a nice house with a tight peaked roof. Mister Bis is very protective of all his nice things. Which is fine. I'd be nervous too if I had a real store, perishable items to worry about, and me as a customer.

"What's all this?" he said.

Dr. Monica removed the thermometer. "A hundred and one," she said, and placed her palm on my forehead. "What's your name?"

"That's Rovar," Mister Bis said. "Rovar Pfliegman. He's a butcher. Sells us our meat."

"Can you speak, Mr. Pfliegman?" Dr. Monica asked.

Hearing my name unfold on her tongue, I grinned. I stared at her rosy lips, and the bottom lip suddenly looked so sweet, I suffered a very real and pressing urge to nibble on it.

"Actually, Rovar is a—" Mister Bis said, but then he stopped himself. "Sick. He's always sick. He's just here to pick up his prescriptions."

The pharmacist at the G&P is Mister Bis's son, Anil. Anil Bis is a pale seventeen-year-old with all-season allergies. He prefers to be called Richie because "everyone always gets it wrong," he says. That day, Dr. Monica followed me to the pharmaceuticals counter, where Richie had arranged my medicines in a row. She leaned over the counter and began reading them off.

Richie appeared upset about someone reading his prescriptions. He sneezed, and then looked over Dr. Monica's cherubic head to mine. "That will be ninety-seven dollars," he said.

"Wait," said Dr. Monica. "You don't need all this." She selected two of the little brown bottles and nipped a packet of Tylenol from the shelf. "You've just got a small fever. You should go home and rest."

Richie blew his nose. "He doesn't *have* a home," he said.

Dr. Monica looked up. "No?"

"He lives in a bus."

"A bus?"

"That old school bus," said Richie. "The one by the river."

That's when Dr. Monica looked at me—really looked at me—for the first time. My brow went hot and my chest burned. I wanted to hold her and absorb the tuna fish scent in her hair. I wanted to lie on a long verdant stretch of grass and listen to her read Darwin and eat Evermores, but instead she reached into her jacket and gave me her business card: DR. MONICA, PEDIATRICIAN. Next to her name was a picture of a small blue butterfly.

I brought out my writing tablet. *I think you can help me*, I wrote.

She read it and smiled. "A body," she said, "cannot fight itself and expect to win."

VI

WRITE HOW YOU FEEL

The following Tuesday, I take my seat in Dr. Monica's Waiting Area and flip through women's magazines (none of which give me even the most benevolent of Benevolent Erections) and wait to see her. It is your typical doctor's Waiting Area. The walls are square and white. A border of wild-flowers is pasted around the center of the walls in a garish floral belt. Above the border hang a few unframed pastel paintings of bucolic farmyards, and beneath it, wooden chairs line the walls. The chairs have rounded edges and bulbous legs so the Sick or Diseased children who crawl about the Berber carpeting all day cannot injure themselves. The Sick or Diseased children and their mothers are always looking at me funny: why would a tiny bearded man who always wears an oversize pink Disneyland sweatshirt be coming to see a pediatrician?

No doubt it is a relevant, probing question.

I'm not allowed to schedule an appointment with Dr. Monica because I am over the age of eighteen. Dr. Monica says it's illegal in Virginia for me to schedule appointments to see her. But she also says there are exceptions to every rule. I'm allowed to see her only when there's a cancellation, so every Tuesday I come to her office and wait.

Right now the receptionist, Mrs. Himmel, is glaring at me. It's perfectly understandable. Dr. Monica's office is small, and I take up a valuable seat.

I'm not exactly sure what Mrs. Himmel's responsibilities are other than to answer the telephone and shift folders. Sometimes she looks at her computer monitor. She lives in a subdivision behind the park called Whispering Acres. I don't understand how an acre, a unit of area, can whisper anything, but Mrs. Himmel says that Whispering Acres is the best place to live in the entire state of Virginia. Everyone's subdivision, she says, is cared for by a management company, so there aren't any worries. "Your drain clogged?" she says. "Call management. Want your lawn mowed? Your hedges trimmed? Call management." Mrs. Himmel thinks that everyone should want to live in Whispering Acres, and gets angry when people do not.

"Maybe it's about originality," says Dr. Monica.

"Originality?" she balks. "They won't think it's so original when the plumbing fails!"

Then she goes back to shifting folders.

Mrs. Himmel doesn't think a full-grown person needs a checkup once a week, however small he might be, however weak or sick, and definitely not by a pediatrician. She frequently lowers her horn-rimmed glasses and cautions Dr. Monica about certain *safety issues* regarding certain *little bearded men who live out of a bus* and the Sick or Diseased children.

"It's criminal," she whispers, shooting me glances. "Someone will *sue* you if you keep him around."

I may be unappealing-looking. I may not speak. I may suffer from a hundred debilitating and unidentifiable illnesses, but I can hear just fine, so whenever Mrs. Himmel says something hurtful I remember that Mrs. Himmel has an ass the size of two sleepy, domesticated pigs. I'm not being judgmental of Mrs. Himmel by saying this—to be honest, I'm quite admiring of it: I wake up in the morning sometimes, picking at the skin that clings to my bones, and wonder how convenient it must be to have an ass like that. It's a perpetual cushion. A portable sofa.

Think of the space an ass like that would save on a bus.

"Adrian!" Mrs. Himmel shouts. "I need folders!"

Adrian, Dr. Monica's intern, walks into the Waiting Area carrying a tower of heavy medical folders on one arm. Adrian only works here part-time, and is tall and fit in the exact same way that Mrs. Himmel isn't. She wears shoes made entirely of brightly colored rubber, and clothes made of things with names like Gore-Tex and Windstopper and Polarguard. Adrian has climbed the fourth-highest mountain in the Lower 48 and is training for the third highest, called Mount Massive.

I can't imagine what it must be like to climb mountains. I can barely make the walk from the bus to Dr. Monica's and back.

To get here, I have to cross Back Lick Road and walk through the forest. Then I follow a highway for a mile or so, and this takes awhile. My bad leg gives me trouble. Most people don't notice the hairy little man limping along the highway, but sometimes they'll pull over. They'll ask if I want a ride. Usually the drivers are large men in business suits with kind faces, but I always decline. It's not that I don't want them to feel good; I just prefer to walk.

This is hard for them to understand. After all, they're Virginians. They're part of the community, the general populace. That's when they become angry. "Suit yourself," they say. Or occasionally, "Whatever you say, *midget.*"

The first time I walked to Dr. Monica's office, a Ford Escort stopped in front of me and a Virginian climbed out. He looked sharp and neat, like he'd just stepped out of a catalogue. The man's face was evenly tanned, and the sleeves of his shirt hugged his considerable biceps. "Need a lift?" he said.

I shook my head, but he walked over anyway. He linked an arm around my neck. "C'mon," he said. "You look like you need a lift." He ushered me into the car, and smiled at me with two rectangles of clean white teeth. He asked where I was going.

Of course I didn't say.

"I'm Ted," he said. "What's your name?"

I brought out my writing tablet.

He read it and his eyes lifted. "Ro-Var," he said. "What are you, a Muppet?"

I stared at my feet. On the floor of the passenger's side was a book called *The Complete Book of Water Polo, With Pictures.* Ted saw me looking. "That's my team," he said, and plopped the book on my lap. On the cover was a glossy photograph of fifteen evenly tanned white men who all looked exactly like Ted. They all had the same round muscles. Skin so greasy it shone off the page. They were standing in a semicircle with their arms crossed over their glistening pectorals, and they all wore the same black swimming trunks—except for one. One was holding a yellow water-polo ball under one arm and had a funny mustache. It looked like a caterpillar had crawled across his face and stopped.

"That's our captain," said Ted. He revved the engine and the little car took off down the highway. He reached beneath his seat and offered me a white triangle wrapped in plastic. "You hungry? It's bologna. You look like you could use it."

I shook my head.

"Suit yourself," he said, and wolfed the sandwich down in two bites. He looked impatiently around the car, like he didn't know what to say next. His fingers galloped over the steering wheel. "How about sports? You do any sports?"

As soon as he said it, he realized the absurdity of the question. He pointed at the book. "All those guys there? Those wetnecks? You might not think it to look at them, but they're real jerks." Ted fussed with the knob to the radio station again. "I'm the worst, though," he said. "I'm the worst jerk." He looked at me and grinned. "I've got two wives."

I didn't know what Ted wanted me to do after he said that. So I just grinned back. I showed him my own teeth, which are not white and impressive, but yellowed, sharp, and crooked. Barnacles of the mouth.

"Aren't you going to say anything?" he said. "I just told you, I've got *two* wives." He took his hands off the wheel and rolled down the window, threw an arm in the air, and shouted, "I have two wives!"

His voice disappeared into the wind.

"You can't *imagine* how good it feels to say that," he said. "To be honest, that's kind of why I picked you up today. To get it off my chest. If I didn't tell someone, I'd lose it, I swear."

Then Ted shifted gears, and the car stopped, right in the middle of the highway.

"So that's it," he said. "You can get out."

I looked at him. He wasn't smiling anymore.

"Get the fuck out of the car."

I scrambled out and shut the door. Ted roared off. I didn't realize until he was gone, dust spiraling behind the Escort in two long cones, that I was still holding his book. So now I am the owner of *The Complete Book of Water Polo, With Pictures.* I keep the book on my bookshelf with the others because despite Ted's marital failings, these men on the cover are the best physical specimens of men that I've ever seen. Men with two beefy legs.

The most enviable biceps.

Sitting here in Dr. Monica's office, my eyes tripping along the pattern of the floral wallpaper border, the television murmuring hypnotically, I think to myself, "If I weren't sick, I'd have a shot at looking like one of those men." I'd stand up straight and shave my beard and stick out my chin. The dark holes in my face would illuminate, the lumps on my head would disappear, and my hair would fill out thick and smooth. My eyes would clear up, and I would impress people by how far away I could read roadsigns. My shoulders would right themselves, my ankles would turn from in to out, and my bad leg would heal. I'd be able to walk in a straight line with my head up, not conspicuously studying the ground for any crack or split in the pavement, holes where my foot might catch and send me catapulting to the ground— No! I'd smile with a frown and shake my head good-naturedly and talk about sporting events and the rising price of gasoline. I'd have friends with man-names like Joe or Jack or even the Captain.

Here we are, the Captain and the Creature, standing waist-deep in the waters of the Queeconocacheecook! Our shirts are off. I've shed my pink sweatshirt and my stylish woolen cap on the embankment. We're both in Speedos. My body is somehow bigger today: swollen, bronzed. Rippling with meat. My face is shaved clean and my eyes are functioning so well I don't need eyeglasses. I'm almost *good*-looking. The rapids are strong and the wind blows our hair back and we're cold. A shimmering white net appears out of nowhere. The Captain looks at me and silently puts on his helmet. A yellow ball floats down river. He grabs it and tosses it high in the air and punches it. It hurtles toward me. I jump high, as though lifted by the water itself.

"Spike it!" the Captain cries.

I raise my arm and the ball crashes into the river. The Captain claps and laughs. "Well done, Pfliegman!" he shouts. "Woo hoo!"

I'd do all of these things if given the chance to be anything other than what I am now: this withered cretin, this gimp, this half-finished mold. This golem.

He who has never been woo-hooed by anyone.

I summon some Manliness to feel less feeble than I really am. "*Rrrr*," I say.

Mrs. Himmel looks up from her computer monitor. She stares at me. Then she picks up the phone and begins urgently whispering: "I'm sorry, but I don't like the way he just sits here all day, looking at me. It's unnerving."

Moments later, Dr. Monica appears in the doorway of the Waiting Area. She's holding an enormous baby in her arms. It's one of the biggest I have ever seen. Its head is nearly as large as her own. Even the limbs look adult. She struggles to move it from one hip to the other as she walks to Mrs. Himmel's desk. She grabs a long yellow writing tablet and then comes over to me. She hands me the tablet. A pen. "It's just something to keep you occupied while you wait," she says, and shifts her weight.

I pick up the pen. *What should I write about?* I write.

She shrugs. "Just write how you feel."

But my Darling, I want to say, it's difficult for Pfliegmans to write how we feel because we are not now, and never have been, a sentimental people. After all, it's difficult to romanticize anything when one is so hungry one licks one's own arms for the salt. When one can fit one's fingers underneath each wing of one's own ribcage. When one's own limbs feel as though they don't fit the rigid frame of one's own body. To understand this bus-dwelling creature, this Rovar Ákos Pfliegman, you need not know how he *feels*, you need only understand the history of his people—

Dr. Monica turns to the babe's mother. "Give him two drops of Tylenol before bed," she says. And then, considering his size, adds, "Perhaps three."

The babe hears Dr. Monica's voice and lifts his large head, his face contorted in hot agony. He finds her pear-shaped breast above him and reaches for it, smooching and bobbing his mouth, and then arrogantly kisses it. He turns his head and looks at me.

He smirks.

I imagine throwing myself down on my stomach. I imagine crawling slowly toward him, reaching for his giant infant ankles. I Can Bring Him Down—

VII

EVOLUTION OF THE PFLIEGMANS:
THE BIRTH OF SZERETLEK

My Darling, My Pediatrician. Although it is difficult for me to write how I feel, I can tell you how Aranka felt as she lay on her side in front of a fire amidst the pungent, simmering remains of Enni Hús. She felt thirst, but there was no water. She felt the weight of isolation, of inevitability: this child would take her, or she would take the child. She gazed up at the uneven flaps of the tent, listening to the purring sounds of a hundred dozing Pfliegmans—she felt savagely alone. Most Pfliegman fetuses, she knew, did not survive birth. As though they could sense it, as though they could see their whole lousy future before they even had a chance to live it, they hoped for better luck in the next conception and gave up in the womb. If they managed to be born, the babies were often so small they looked like little blue fish. Babies born off-color, with elongated heads, mealy skin. Feet that hung inward in hackneyed flippers. An aura of general malaise.

We called them *hal*.

If a baby had been born *hal* north of the Ural Mountains, we would have picked it up and scuttled it over to the river and dropped it in, sending the little fish back where it came from. But now we were no longer living next to a river.

We were nowhere near water at all.

"*After the sacrifice of Enni Hús,*" writes Anonymus, "*a curious dry spell descended upon the Carpathian Basin.*" As the rest of the Hungarians worried about their crops, we Pfliegmans were extremely pleased with ourselves. We sauntered confidently around camp, soaking up the sunlight, muttering "Enni Hús, Enni Hús" so often that it didn't take long for the Hungarians to hear our strange chants, miss their good cousin, see us licking our lips, and totally misunderstand what happened. They logically concluded that because we had no meat of our own, we had kidnapped Enni Hús and cooked and eaten him.

In whispers, they began calling us the *Fekete-Szem Hentes*, the Black-Eyed Butchers from the Black Sea—

But Aranka needn't have worried. Her baby would not be born *hal*—far from it. One morning, late in the year 897, she was lying on the ground of the Pfliegman tent when her body finally seized, torquing the infant. She grabbed her belly with both hands. Her water broke and she began kneading, dough-like, into her unapologetic Pfliegman cervix. The water came fast, like a faucet, and did not stop. Aranka looked down, saw it rushing from her body, and unleashed a low and awful moan.

We Pfliegmans heard the moan and stirred from our various angles of repose. We clicked our fingernails and scampered over. We prodded Aranka to turn her body, looking for the baby as if it would be born from her back. She tried pushing us away, but we swirled around, tugging her hair, smelling her moist skin. She lifted her head for air, taking in short, horrible breaths as the baby shifted inside of her—*That's it*, she thought, *it will take me*—when the flaps flew open and six women from the Hungarian tribes entered, marching straight into the center of the tent.

"Out, Cretins!" one of them shouted.

The Hungarian woman was small, with ill-fitting limbs that had never seemed to broach adolescence, and yet no one questioned her authority. She clapped her hands, and in a flurry, dozens of little Pfliegmans scurried outside.

She knelt down next to Aranka and ran her hands over the massive arc of the great white belly, noting immediately the problem with the water. A strange look passed her face. She whispered something to the other women: "Get back," she said. "Make more room." Then she leaned into Aranka's ear. "Do not speak," she said. "Not a word. If the child hears you, he will want to stay close to you, so you must not make a sound. If you keep it all in and hold your breath, he will pop out like a cork. Yes? Good. Now, what is your name?"

"*Aranka*," the mother whispered.

"That's a good name," said the woman. "It means 'gold.' My name is Kunigunda, but you may call me Kinga. Now let's get a look at this sonofabitch *kisbaba*. We need to move you up higher. Up onto the hearth. Careful of the water," she said, and looked curiously at the water that continued to flow from between Aranka's legs.

Together the six women moved the stones of the hearth to create a flat surface, over which they tossed assorted pelts, burlap. All the loose accoutrements of the miserable Pfliegman mundane. They hoisted Aranka up on top of the pile and watched as the water came faster now. They grabbed a few bowls and moved them beneath her to catch it. The bowls quickly filled. The women moved Aranka's legs back to inspect the source and a long lace of green slipped from her body. It fell into one of the bowls with a quick, wet slap. One of the women grabbed a poker from the hearth and lifted the green thing. It hung long off the poker, dripping like a soaked feather.

"It's algae!" she cried.

The women all gasped. Kinga put her finger to her lips and shushed them, and then she took Aranka's hand. She leaned in close, offering up soothing whispers: "How wonderful you're doing, Mother. Keep going, there's been some real progress now." But as the labor wore on, the baby, perhaps resenting the fact that his mother wanted him to leave a happy warm place for the Carpathian Basin late in the ninth century, only burrowed himself deeper inside her. The water was now running even faster, spilling out from between Aranka's hairy legs in a fat and even spout. The floor of the tent turned to mud. Spongy. Viscous. The women groaned and lifted their feet, and when the ground had absorbed all it could possibly absorb, the water began to rise. Quickly it became ankle-deep.

The women looked at each other. "The water is still coming," they whispered. "Perhaps there is no child. Perhaps there is only water."

Then one of the nurses gasped. "Look!" she cried. "A fish!"

Aranka, in a daze, heard the women talking. She lifted her head, breathing in sharp, uneven breaths, and looked down just in time to watch herself giving birth to a silvery, spoon-shaped fish. Certain that her child had been born *hal* and there was nothing to be done, she closed her eyes and allowed her mind to carry her to a place far more sane and comfortable. She found herself standing on the wide grassy embankment of the river where she once lived. She dunked her toes into the water, and it cooled them. Her body felt light, almost weightless, as though she might rise, as though the sun itself were pulling her up with two warm hands. From far off, a tinny voice rang in her left ear, but she deliberately ignored it. Why go anywhere? Her eyes rolled into the back of her head as she looked at the sky and admired cloudshapes.

The women, meanwhile, covered their mouths and watched carefully as a small, narrow fish, a fish the color of metal, slithered out of her body and fell into the rising water. The fish wiggled for a second, then, in a quick line, deliberately darted outside the tent. The women waded over to the flaps of the tent and peeked out at the Pfliegmans scurrying up the embankment. "It's everywhere," they said. "It's a deluge. The water is filling the land."

"Wait," Kinga said, and watched as another fish came, slipping from the mother's body, and then came another. "There's more now! Help, all of you!"

The women tugged their skirts through the water back to the body. They pulled out whole pieces of furry, arm-length algae, but it was difficult to manage and slipped easily from their hands. One of the nurses grabbed her dress and held it up as the top of the water licked her knees, as fish slapped her ankles. She looked at Kinga. "This creature is giving birth to a *river*."

"We don't know that," said Kinga. "Not yet. Now get to work! All of you!" Kinga pressed her hands against Aranka's face and then noticed Aranka's rolling eyes. She grabbed her head. "Mother!" she cried. "Do not leave this baby behind!" She snapped her fingers in front of Aranka's face. She pinched her cheeks. The little she-Pfliegman did not respond. And yet the water still came. It rose higher now, and nearly reached their waists. The women all tried to jump up onto the hearth. "Do something!" they cried. "We'll all be dead and drowned!"

"No one is drowning," Kinga said. "Grab the poker." With one hand, she held the mother's chin so she could not breathe, then leaned down and firmly bit her on the nose. The nose was oily and soft, but Kinga held tight. She motioned for the poker.

The woman tossed it across the water.

Kinga caught it, and immediately stabbed Aranka, deep in the shoulder.

Flung from her grassy embankment back to the tent where she could only see the strange, wide orb that was her vastly pregnant belly, heaving like it was its own, separate animal, Aranka forgot her earlier promise to Kinga not to make a sound, opened her mouth, and cried out:

It was a sound that seemed to come from somewhere outside of herself. Louder than any Hun entering battle. Hungarian farmers two tribes west heard it. It startled Kinga, it startled the women, and it startled Aranka. She pushed the baby, who, at that precise moment, happened to be rocking comfortably back and forth on the cushy inner lining of his mother's fat, extraordinary uterus. The push caught him off guard, and out he went. Two women tried, but he was so big they could not hold him; he slipped between their hands and splashed into the water. The impact caused a considerable wave.

"*Szörny!*" the nurses cried. "He's a monster!"

Aranka lifted her head and saw her child. She reached for him: "*Szeretlek*," she whispered, and then collapsed back onto the hearth.

The women threw their arms into the water, holding on to the enormous baby with four hands. They managed to slice off the umbilical cord, thick as an eel, but the water was by now so deep that it had developed a current. They struggled and splashed in the water to hold him, but the grip was lost.

"Get him!" Kinga shouted, as the baby began floating outside.

Someone managed to grab an ankle and pull the child out of the water. Together the women lifted him, dripping, from the river. They held him high above their heads. "Out!" they cried. "Everyone, out!" But Kinga would not yet leave Aranka. She turned back to the mother's body, floating like some grotesque and useless bauble in the waters. Her legs had fallen back, and her shoulders slid away from her neck. Kinga placed a cold, wet hand over her chest. There was no movement, no lifepulse. "Welp," she mumbled, "that's that," and pulled herself to the edge of the tent. She yanked back the flaps, but at that moment the pegs affixed to the ground finally gave way. The entire Pfliegman tent lifted up from the mud, twisting into itself in the current—

Kinga barely made it out alive. She swam across the water to the dry part of the embankment, surrounded by a gaggle of chattering Pfliegmans. We were laughing idiotically, inching ourselves away from the rising waters, and Kinga's nurses were kicking us back with their heels:

"Hiss!" they cried. "Shoo!"

We Pfliegmans danced and howled, watching our home collapse in the water. Kinga ignored us. She walked up the embankment and reached for the gigantic baby. The women had bundled the boy in a dry wrap, and in it he lay oafish and uncomfortable. The size of the cloth was too small. His large face pinched, and he wailed with unhappiness. Fat arms and legs stuck out all over. There was no disagreement that the baby was unattractive: he had a wide, moonish forehead. A mouth that hung agape, like his nose didn't work. His eyes looked as though they had been tossed on his face.

"That's the ugliest baby I have ever seen," one of the nurses said.

"He'll be of use," said Kinga.

The women quickly got down to the business of naming the child and recording him in the Log of Births. As we Pfliegmans were not official members of the Magyar tribes, we had no name or traditions of our own to speak of. We certainly didn't follow any of the common conduct practiced in the Magyar camps, and everyone argued over what to name him.

"We will name him Szeretlek," Kinga said.

"But that's not a name," the women protested. "Call him a proper name, like Odon or Zoltán."

"Szeretlek," said Kinga. "It was what his mother called him."

"I love you?" the women said. "You can't name a baby 'I love you.'"

"Watch me."

As it happened, Kinga knew a little more about this particular baby than the other women. She knew that the baby's father and Aranka's father were cousins. She knew this because she and Aranka were sisters. Kinga was a Pfliegman as well, and was frankly a little surprised that no one noticed her hairy, flaking skin, her fingers like little claws, her lips as thin as wire. But had she said anything, the women might have been even more frightened of her and the child than they already were. They would not have even bothered to name him.

They might, in fact, have even killed him.

Kinga held on to her nephew tight. "Szeretlek," she said again, and from the top of the embankment, Pfliegmans teeming about her legs like needy, monstrous vermin, she watched as Aranka's river filled the dry landscape. The Pfliegman tent turned along the surface of the water, rolling itself around Aranka's body, and floated down the bend.

Miles away, the Hungarians stopped their farming and ran for cover as the water roared past them, a river carving out the path for the cities of the long and distant future: Győr, Komárom, Esztergom, Visegrád, Vác, Szentendre, Budapest. They lifted their pointy hats and cheered as Aranka's body floated past, pulling with it the waters of the wide Black Sea.

VIII

MARCH 18

"And don't you forget it!" Mrs. Himmel shouts. She slams down the phone. Mrs. Himmel always slams down the phone after speaking to her daughter, Elise. Elise is graduating in June, and Mrs. Himmel wants her to be a model, but Elise hasn't got the looks. She has thick bones, her hair frizzes weirdly in the back, and she has a stiffly bent neck. Her head looks like it was placed crooked on a mantel. Elise is also the name of the lead actress in one of Mrs. Himmel's favorite television sitcoms. Dr. Monica has a television set going all day that hangs from the ceiling in the Waiting Area. Whenever Mrs. Himmel's program comes on, she shushes everyone, all of the Sick or Diseased children, so we can watch.

Today is no exception.

"Everyone quiet!" she demands, and picks up the remote control.

The Sick or Diseased children all stop what they're doing. They stare mournfully at the screen.

Television Elise is a mother who looks after her children all day and is misunderstood by her husband. She does her best to appear strong before her family, but always ends up losing her marbles over some small thing, like not being able to buy 1 percent milk at the grocery store. At the end of every episode, Television Elise cries to her family and makes them feel guilty for ruining her life. Then the husband gets a Bright Idea, and hustles the children to the flower shop so they can buy Television Elise roses, and all is forgiven. One episode they surprised her with a trip to Cancún.

Mrs. Himmel watches every episode with her hands on her chin, a wistful look about her face, and then, when the program ends, she sighs in one explosive breath, replaces her eyeglasses on the tip of her nose, pulls her fingers through her short, tightly permed hair, and, quick as a lightswitch, returns to her regular, acerbic self. Today when the program ends, Mrs. Himmel picks the phone up again and makes a phone call to Daughter Elise's modeling agent.

Perhaps I was tough on Daughter Elise. She has big brown eyes and nice skin, and she's great with the Sick or Diseased children. In fact, if she weren't under so much pressure to be a model, I'd say she was quite beautiful. Suddenly I feel compelled to tell this information to Mrs. Himmel. I tear off a piece of paper from my writing tablet, and quickly write:

Your daughter is quite beautiful.

I hold the paper in my hand and imagine getting up out of my chair and walking up to reception and giving it to her. The look that would cloak her face! But upsetting Mrs. Himmel could make me lose privileges with Dr. Monica, and that's just one risk I'm not willing to take.

I fold the piece of paper and stick it in the pocket of my trousers as Adrian pops her head into the Waiting Area.

"Mr. Pfliegman," she says. "You're up."

I follow Adrian down the hallway that runs behind the reception desk, passing more pictures of bucolic farmyards, and into Dr. Monica's office. Adrian flips a few pages of her clipboard. "Dr. Monica wants you to change into the examining gown today," she says, and closes the door.

Mrs. Himmel had to order the special paper gown for me because I'm obviously not like the other patients. The Sick or Diseased children's gown has trains on it if you're a boy and daisies if you're a girl, but Mrs. Himmel insisted on ordering me an adult-sized gown. It's big and blue. Sterile-looking. It's much too big for me, and hangs poufed over my limbs as though inflated. I put on the gown and then take a seat on the child-sized examining table. Stuffed animals are scattered all over the place. They're everywhere: on the windowledge, the examining table, the counter below the cabinets where Dr. Monica keeps stacks of paper cups and glass containers filled with tongue depressors and throat swabs. Color-coded anatomical illustrations of children's bodies hang on one wall, and on another is a poster of a white kitten hanging by its claws off the branch of a tree, its eyes squeezed tight in terror. Beneath the kitten, the poster says HANG IN THERE! The first time I came to Dr. Monica's and saw the kitten, I brought out a scrap of paper and wrote *Life is not worth living.*

Dr. Monica said that everyone has to believe in something in order to make life worth living.

Like what? I wrote.

Dr. Monica shrugged. "Most people believe in God," she said.

She wanted me to write down for her what I believed in, but I just sat there. I couldn't write. I couldn't put into words a single thing that I believed in, because to believe in something is to have hope, and that is something that the Pfliegmans, in our stinking, wayward lives, have never had.

Dr. Monica believes in water. As soon as she saw my peeling skin, she took away all of my prescriptions and made me start drinking eight glasses of water a day. It's helping, although now every forty minutes or so I have to leave my post at the meat bus to take a piss. I also sweat more, which is extremely unpleasant for my customers. So she gave me a tube of fiercely pine deodorant. It covers my natural odor, a ruddy mixture of grass and meat and oil, and hovers about the small space around my lawnchair. It's called Spice of Life. It keeps away the mosquitoes, which is a big relief, but the field ticks are still present, popping around my ankles. They are not afraid of Spice of Life. They are not afraid of anything.

As it says on the tube, Spice of Life is *For Men on the Go!*® and there's a picture of a tall, handsome man in a leisure suit, smiling like someone just complimented his pectorals.

Maybe that's my problem. I have no pectorals.

But Dr. Monica believes there's nothing better for the body than water, and she prescribes large quantities of it for the very sickest of her patients. I'll often see the mothers of the Sick or Diseased children lugging around a plastic gallon, and there are two water fountains on either side of the Waiting Area alone. Sometimes Dr. Monica herself will appear for a drink at one of the fountains. She'll bend over the fountain and wrap one delicious ankle around the other. A foot will delicately scratch her calf, all the way up one leg and then back down again—

It's enough to make one throw one's hands in the air and denounce civility altogether.

I look at my own hands. I should have washed them. I have darkly stained fingernails that will probably never be the proper color from all the animal cutting, the blood handling— Footsteps approach! I quickly pinch my cheeks to give them color; to give the illusion of vim, of vigor.

Dr. Monica knocks, and then opens the door. "Hello, Mr. Pfliegman," she says.

Her blond hair is loose today, not bunned, and falls flat against her back in a yard of silk. Her white coat is open, and underneath is a soft blue turtleneck sweater. Tan slacks one size too small cinch her large thighs, pulling at the seams, and around her shoulders a Kermit the Frog stethoscope hangs like a piece of reliable rope.

"GODDESS!" I want to shout.

She smiles, turning the stethoscope in her fingers.

"You've got some color in your cheeks," she says. "How are you feeling today?"

Dr. Monica always says "you" instead of "we." All of my other doctors always referred to me the other way, as in: "How are *we* today, Mr. Pfliegman?" To which I would respond in my brain, "What *we*? We are not both Pfliegmans. We do not both live in a broken-down bus in a field. We do not both hold our cramping stomachs over the bucket, or cough until we bleed. We do not both dream worms are nibbling at our fingertips."

Dr. Monica is better than that.

"Your vitals are up," she says. "You're drinking your water, I can tell. That's excellent." She produces a clean sheet of paper to write on. "You're still not eating right, though, and you're not doing your stretching exercises."

Stretching exercises?

"Like I showed you last time, remember? Bend down, rise up, breathe?"

Dr. Monica puts down her clipboard and bends at the waist. Her long hair spills in front of me in a waterfall of blond, exposing a creamy slice of neck—

St. Benevolus shivers like an orphan in the cold.

Her fingers quickly smooch the tips of her white pediatrician's shoes, and then she stands up again. Blood rises to her face, coloring her cheeks. "Remember?" she says.

Ah yes, now I remember, I write. *I am a complete and total idiot.*

"You've got to work on rehabilitating that leg," she says. "There's absolutely no reason why it should be dragging like that." She points to my bad leg with her pen. "The kneecap's a little off, but that really shouldn't affect anything," she says, and she frowns at the kneecap. "Does it hurt to stretch?"

I shake my head.

"Okay then." She sits back down and returns to my folder. "Have there been any more nosebleeds?" she says.

A few.

"And your leg? Is there any stiffness?"

There is some stiffness. You could say that there is some of that.

"What about headaches? Are you still getting those?"

Actually, those have eased up a bit, I write.

"Good!" she says, scribbling. "And how's the coughing? Is there any expectorating?"

I nod.

"And when that happens, what color is it? Is it white?" She wrinkles her nose. "Or is it yellowish or greenish?"

Most of the time?

"Yes."

Red. Or yellow. But most of the time, red.

"Red, huh," she says and looks at me sideways. She blinks, officiously, sucking in one part of her upper lip as though to hide it. Around the room the stuffed animals stare at me, unblinking. The white kitten looks panicked: *Hang in there!*

"You know you have to be honest with me, Mr. Pfliegman. If you're not honest about how you're feeling and what's happening to you, I won't be able to help you. You won't be able to see me anymore. Do you understand?"

I nod vigorously.

"Okay then," she says, and then stops writing. "Tell me, if your pain were on a scale from one to nine today, one being the least pain you've ever felt, and nine the most, how would say you feel?"

I look at her. Is she serious? She is.

Four?

She closes the folder. "All right, Mr. Pfliegman, let's have a look at you."

In one swift, breathtaking movement, Dr. Monica pulls all of her hair into a ponytail. The elastic hairband snaps like a hasty prophylactic.

I shudder a little.

"Take it easy," she says. "I'm just going to see what your muscles are doing." With cold hands, my pediatrician begins professionally squeezing my shoulders, my arms and legs, stopping along the way at every hinge of my small, oddly shaped appendages. She squeezes elbows, wrists, ankles. The wide part of my little plate-shaped feet. All the way down every phalanx of my awkward, reaching toes—

"Joints seem fine," she says. "Sit up now." She kneads my head, pressing her fingers lightly against the lumps. "Does this hurt?" she says. "Does this?" She reaches around and presses the base of my skull with two cold fingers, then slips the other hand behind my beard and politely prods my throat, balancing my head on her hands as though it's a fragile egg. She's searching for something, I know not what, but it feels nice.

"It's important to try and speak every day," Dr. Monica says. "Even if you can only make noises. Sometimes rubbing the throat helps loosen things up. Can you try and say something now? As I do this?"

I am terrified of what would happen if I actually spoke. If I spoke, I would tell her that when I look at her, every circular cell in my body aches. I would tell her that if she wouldn't mind, I should very much like her to lean over the examining table and let me unbutton her blouse and gently unwrap the Kermit the Frog stethoscope and nuzzle my beard into her neck. I lean forward slightly to see if my head might accidentally bump against her head, to see if she might accidentally brush her lips against mine and accidentally slip her tongue into my—"*Algh*," I say.

Dr. Monica looks up and blinks, hopefully. I try again.

There's nothing left.

She makes her final notes, checks her watch, and then hands me the folder. "Return this to Mrs. Himmel," she says. "And I think it would be useful to see your parents' health records. Can you get them for me?"

I nod.

"Okay then," she says, and smiles again. "I'll see you next week."

I watch her leave, thinking that I don't have a clue about Ján and Janka's health records. They never went to a doctor. As far as I know, there aren't any records of anything about my parents beyond what sparse pieces of furniture lie moldering in the farmhouse that leans both east and west, and what was written in the *Lick County Gazette* on the day following the accident, June 16, 1985:

János and Janka Pfliegman of Front Lick were killed yesterday afternoon when their car crashed into a telephone pole on Back Lick Road off Rural Route 9. The car, rented from Galaxy Car Rentals, was in showroom condition, and it has been determined that the accident is not the fault of Galaxy Car Rentals, which always provides Safe Cars and Safe Service®, but rather the fault of Mr. János Pfliegman, who was driving under the influence. The couple is survived by their son, Rovar.

The article is divided into two columns. Directly underneath the second column, underneath my name, is a picture of a snail-shaped galaxy. In his extreme haste to meet the five o'clock deadline, the junior editor hadn't read the column. He only knew that Galaxy Car Rentals was paying a hefty sum to have their advertisement advertised in this issue, and he was trying to find room for their logo. At the time, however, this wasn't what bothered me about the article, nor was I bothered by the car rental's disclaimer pinched into the text, nor was I even bothered by my name, detached, hovering. I was only bothered by the word "couple."

Nothing could be further from the truth.

Imagine. In the busy hey-ho of life, tooling around in your automobile, you drive past a scrawny little man shuffling down the side of the road. He's wearing a silk shirt with an anachronous paisley print. The long collar hangs from his neck in a limp frown. His hair is oiled and licked to one side with a comb he keeps in the back pocket of his creamy slacks. They're not in fashion—wide, aggressive pockets buck out from either side—but his shoes are black Italian leather, finely polished. Every few steps or so the man stops walking, reaches down and rubs dust from the road off the tips, and then stands up again. His face is small and pointed, with eyes that dart like flies. His given name is János. It is a Hungarian name. It's pronounced YAH-nosh. It means "God is good." You drive past this man, you pass him, but something about him warrants a second glance; you grab a look from your rearview mirror, and it's then you notice that the man is not alone: a small boy is walking next to him with skin so pale it's almost transparent. You swear you can see his blood vessels and arteries churning. You can see the holes that hold his eyes. He stares at you, mournfully, and the look on his face makes your heart feel wet. You feel, suddenly, as though the arms of a thousand miserable children are reaching out to you, begging you to stop the car, but the skinny man catches you in the pause. He catches your eye, and smiles. The smile is handsome, but not genuine. It leaks to the edge of his face. At once, all the blood in your body makes for your feet, so you do not stop. You press the pedal. It's just a boy and his father, you tell yourself.

Walking home.

Home is a farmhouse is east of the Queeconococheecook River with large barn in the back, out of which János Pfliegman works as a butcher. Today, on March 18, 1983, two years and three months before he will die in a terrible car accident, Ján and the boy are walking along the side of Back Lick Road. They have been wandering the horsefields behind the barn for hours, looking for a violin that they did not find. They climb the stairs to the front porch. "I'm going back out," Ján says, without looking at the boy. "Get in there and help your mother."

The boy watches his father walk back down the road to the horse-fields, hopping around the weeds, and then slips inside the farmhouse. He ducks past the kitchen, where his mother, Janka, is stirring tomato soup at the stove.

Janka is short, and sloppily fat. She is only slightly taller than the stove itself, and has to stand on a footstool to cook anything. All day she waddles around the kitchen wearing an oversize men's golfing shirt that says VIRGINIA IS FOR LOVERS GOLFERS. Janka stops stirring and reaches down to scratch her legs. Her legs are hairy, pocked from plucking. She spends hours in the bathroom trying to manage them. When a tickle appears at the back of the boy's throat, he moves quietly away from the kitchen doorway. He covers his mouth to keep from coughing, and moves up the stairs to his room unseen. He lies on his bed, picking at his sweaty clothes. Janka buys all of his clothes two sizes too big at the secondhand store, where she also buys his toys. Toys broken, with parts missing, discarded by the sticky hands of Other Children. One day the boy climbs off his bed and plays with an Indian doll, holding a small sack. The sack is filled with miniature towels and clothing. Assorted textiles. He plays with the toy, and the next day he comes down with a prickling fever. He lies in bed gulping air for four days, as images of the fever-carrying Indian appear in and out of his brain. He vows never to touch any of the toys again. But Janka scolds him for not playing with them. She comes into his room and sees him lying motionless on the bed and scowls, "I don't know why I buy you a damn thing, Rovar."

They named the boy Rovar. It is a Hungarian name. It's pronounced RO-vahr. It means "insect."

Today, as he lies in bed watching a fly hurtling around the edges of the windowscreen, the boy wishes he were an insect. If he were an insect, he thinks, he would be invisible. *O, to be a fly, a flea*, he thinks, observing the small things about his room. The things that insects observe. The curl of paint on the windowledge. The jagged fray of the blanket. The sound of bees throwing themselves at the windowscreen. He pinches his arms and watches the hairs rise up. He presses his fingers on his eyeballs until globes of light appear behind the eyelids, each taking the triangular shape of the wings of a butterfly—

"Shit!"

The boy props himself up on his elbows and looks out the window. His father stomps onto the front porch, thumbing mud from his shoes. It's gotten dark.

The violin will not be found today.

It belonged to Grandfather Ákos. The old man came to visit the farmhouse only once, three years ago, when the boy was nine years old. Ján had told him that Grandfather Ákos was very rich, but the old man didn't look rich. He was a bus driver, and pulled up to the farmhouse in a yellow school bus. He wore a big wool coat that made him look, the boy thought, like a vagrant. His grandfather was thin, with knees that jutted out from the top of his shins like small lightbulbs. His face was shaped like Ján's, small and pointed, but flaked with age. On his chin he sported a white goatee that looked like he'd just kissed a sticky cloud. He carried no bags or luggage, just a violin case, shaped like a small side of beef.

When Grandfather Ákos stepped down from the bus and saw the boy for the first time, he dropped the case on the grass. He looked at Ján and Janka.

They said nothing.

He beckoned the boy forward. He took his chin between his fingers, holding it as though examining an egg: "*Mi ennek a neve?*" he asked. "What is the name of this?"

Janka scratched her legs. "We call him Rovar," she said.

Grandfather Ákos smiled at the boy. His mouth was full of rotted, ill-spaced teeth. "That's not a good name," he said. "I will call him *Kis Ákos*. Little Ákos."

"Now look here," Ján said.

But Grandfather Ákos ignored him. He spent his visit sitting outside on the front porch in his wool coat, eating lemons, his favorite food. He peeled them with his rotten teeth, and unfolded the *Lick County Gazette* over his lap like a blanket. He liked to read a section in the newspaper called "Today in History, by Eldridge Cooner." It was merely a list of events that have all happened on the same day over time, but the old man loved them. He would read them out loud, and the boy never left his side. He would sit next to him on the front porch for hours, waiting for the lemon peels to drop. Waiting to be called Little Ákos. Once Grandfather Ákos spit a lemon seed into the palm of his hand and showed the boy. "Notice, Little Ákos," he said.

In his palm, the seed was white and shiny. It looked like a diamond. The old man grinned at the boy, and the grin looked wicked. "Eldridge Cooner never writes about the small things," he said.

After the newspaper had been read, he would reach into the violin case, then stand up and play underneath the porch light. His arms swooped as he grabbed and pulled at the strings. In his small hands, the instrument made high-pitched crying noises that ached over the horsefields, setting off the wolves. He was a terrible violinist. One evening, as he played, Janka couldn't take it anymore. She ran out from the kitchen, grabbed the instrument from his fingers, and threw it off the porch. The violin whistled through the air and landed, invisibly, in the long weeds of the horsefields. Crickets exploded into a chattering mayhem.

Grandfather Ákos said nothing. He stared, motionless, into the dark fields. Mosquitoes *zizz*ed above his head, drunk on the porch light.

"I'm sorry," said Janka.

For a long moment, Grandfather Ákos did not move or speak. When he finally set his eyes upon her, they were round. Black. Janka stepped back into the hallway of the farmhouse. "I'm *sorry*," she said, but the old man leaned in. Something shifted beneath the shoulders of the wool coat—

"Ján!" she cried.

Ján came running out from the barn, and together they searched the horsefields. They searched all night, and into the next morning. When they returned to the house empty-handed, Grandfather Ákos led them to the couch in the living room. He sat them down.

"I said I was sorry," said Janka.

Ján kicked her.

The old man looked at them both carefully. He breathed out through his nose. He cleared his throat. "*Nincs kegyelem*," he said.

Ján jumped up. "What?"

"You're cut off."

Ján opened his mouth to protest, but Grandfather Ákos held up one finger. "Until," he said, "you find it." He stood up and began buttoning his coat, and it was then that the boy, watching from behind the kitchen door, noticed the buttons. They gleamed as he maneuvered them between his fingers. Ten perfect circles of gold. Grandfather Ákos finished buttoning and walked towards him into the kitchen. He rolled up the newspaper, and then took the boy's head in his hands once more. He bent down and looked so closely, the goatee tickled the boy's chin. He clucked his tongue, the clean smell of lemons on his breath—

"They say it's in the eyes," he said, and then turned and left the farmhouse.

Now, years later, Ján Pfliegman still has not found the violin. He pours himself a glass of whiskey and plunks down at the dinner table. "Screw it," he says, rubbing the mud from his shoes. "We don't need the money."

"That's right," says Janka. "We don't. We have everything we need without him."

She brings over a large glass jar full of pickled eggs and places it on the table. A piece of masking tape is taped to the front of the jar that says *Tojás*: eggs. Janka keeps big glass jars above the cabinets in the kitchen, and writes everything on the masking tape in Hungarian: *Bors.* (Peppers.) *Káposzta.* (Cabbage.) *Krumpli.* (Potatoes.) *Kompót.* (Stewed fruit.) She brings over a bowl of tomato soup, and Ján starts shoving in spoonfuls. He reaches a hand into the jar of eggs and removes two. He eats them whole, like cookies. He takes another drink of the whiskey and then he looks over the table at the boy sitting across from him. He seems startled, like he'd forgotten the boy was there, and is suddenly struck by a moment of unpredictable hilarity. He takes another egg and pops it in, chuckling that he has a hairy little son who won't speak to anyone. He giggles like a child.

Janka thinks he's laughing at her cooking. "You better cut it out," she says, but the man cannot help himself. The weird little frame. The lumpy head! He bursts out laughing. In a fury, Janka turns and hurls the stirring spoon from the stove.

It slaps him, hard and wet, right on the neck.

He jumps up from the table and reaches for Janka, punching her clean on the head. She kicks him with her wooden clogs and gets him swiftly across the shins. Ján cries out and grabs his legs. Then he stands up and throws a fist into her back. She bends over and grabs one of his hands. She takes his thumb in her mouth and bites it.

This is how they fight. Like children.

Where is the child in these pretty environs? He goes to the same place he always goes when they start fighting. He leaves the farmhouse and runs to the mailbox at the end of the driveway. He takes out the newspaper and reads "Today in History, by Eldridge Cooner." And today in history, on March 18, many big and important events took place: In 1766, Britain repealed the Stamp Act. In 1850, the American Express company was created, and in 1932, John Updike was created. On March 18, 1965, Russian cosmonaut Aleksei Leonov left his Voskhod 2 capsule and hovered in space for twenty minutes. Four years later, on March 18, 1969, President Nixon's "Operation Breakfast" began, as the payload from B-52 bombers lightly fell from the sky onto supposed communist base camps in Cambodia. These events have all been forever recorded down in history by Eldridge Cooner. But it's true, the boy observes; Grandfather Ákos was right. Eldridge Cooner does not keep record of the small events; he does not record what happens in the rubble of Mexican earthquakes. He makes no record of the discoveries of faraway nebulas, the fear of the agoraphobe. He most certainly does not record the Pfliegmans. He does not write that on March 18, 1983, a ten-year-old boy living in a farmhouse that leans both east and west wished his parents would die. He does not keep record of us, but these, Dr. Monica, these are our records.

IX

PROPERTY OF SUBDIVISIONS LLC

This morning I wake up, pull on my sweatshirt, slice off a fat piece of to-mato for Mrs. Kipner, go out to the tree, spend a few unpleasant moments trying to contribute something to the green bucket that does not want to be contributed, and then unroll the awning, lean the chalkboard against the side of the bus, plunk down in my lawnchair, and sell my meat.

The chalkboard is for writing down everyone's orders, so people know how much meat is left, et cetera. For the most part it's a reliable system, but occasionally someone will come around who hasn't been to the bus before, who doesn't know that I don't talk, and who gets in a huff because I'm not answering their important business-related question, because I'm just sit-ting there in my pink sweatshirt, staring at them from behind my beard as though I'm merely an extension of the bus itself. But before things get out of hand someone usually clues the new person in, and then they get an altogether different look on their face.

"He doesn't *speak?*"

Then it's like I'm deaf and I can't hear what they're saying.

"Why doesn't he speak?"

"He's a mute."

"But everybody speaks."

"He's a midget *and* a mute."

Today we have a wrangler.

"Look here, boy, how come you don't speak?"

A tall, square man with a buzzcut orders four sirloin strips, and when I don't respond, just make a few quick marks on my chalkboard, the man decides that he's insulted. He marches over to me, grabs a fistful of sweatshirt, and hoists me five inches above ground with one arm. "Listen here," he barks. "I'm a retired general. Now speak!"

I don't say anything. I just hang there, like a coat.

"Speak!" he shouts. He shakes me a little.

Then a fat man comes running up from the back of the line of meat customers. "Hey!" he shouts. "Hey you! Knock it off!"

He's wearing a baseball cap with an M on it, and I recognize him immediately. He's the one who said I should wear hats when I sell my meat. He's the one with the swollen stomach, the head like a vise. He's got a walkie-talkie clipped to one side of his belt. From the other side, a long black billy club hangs like a second, misplaced penis.

"Just drop him," he says. "Leave him be."

The general scowls. "I'm not doing anything. I just don't believe the boy can't speak, that's all."

The fat man places a threatening hand over the billy club. "*Drop him,*" he says.

"Who are you?" says the general.

"I'm a security guard," he says, and taps his baseball cap.

The general laughs out loud. He lifts me a little higher. "The Big M supermarket? You're a security guard for a supermarket?"

The fat man moves his arms away from his considerable stomach. He places a threatening hand over the billy club. "So what?"

I look back and forth between them. They don't move. So I open my mouth and gargle, "*Bawr.*"

This is good enough for the retired general.

"See?" he says happily. "The boy's no mute." He drops me back into my chair.

The security guard watches him leave, and then turns to me. "You okay?" he says.

I nod.

"You ever need anything, just come by the Big M and ask for Herman. I mean that," he says.

I give the billy club a nervous look.

He holds it up. "This? Don't worry about this," he says. "It's a fake. Made of polymer or something." He snaps a finger against the club. It makes a stubborn, plastic sound. "I'm not supposed to tell anyone," he says. "But only the police get the real ones. Not too many people know that. Security Guards don't get the real ones." Then his mood abruptly changes. A troubled look consumes him. "Baseball caps and plastic," he says. "I was in Desert Storm, for Chrissakes."

A soft breeze passes through us. Next to his leg, the billy club lifts like a feather.

"You got any hamburger?"

I point to the chalkboard.

"A dollar a pound?" he says. "Is that right?" He fidgets with the rim of the baseball cap as if he can't believe it. "This place is cheap," he says. "Cheaper than the Big M supermarket, even with my employee discount." Herman removes a wallet from the nether regions of his gigantic pants. "Gimme two pounds," he says, and flakes out the dollars.

Dr. Monica would be proud. She wants me meet people. "It's important to try to interact, Mr. Pfliegman," she tells me. "Look for opportunities to have social encounters. After all, look how much you've improved just meeting with me. You don't cough as much, and your lungs are clearer. If you can communicate with me, then I'm sure you can communicate with other people."

"But Darling," I want to say, "you are not 'people.'" And I've had encounters. Just the other day, a meat customer was so pleased with the weight and texture of his top round that he held out his hand, intimating that he wanted me shake it. He beamed at me in a friendly manner, so I reached out to him, but as soon as he saw my tiny hand, bony, quivering, skin flaking off like grated cheese, he quickly withdrew the offer. The truth is, most Virginians aren't looking for encounters with hairy little men who do not speak, who wear bristling, cakey beards and Disneyland sweatshirts. Men who cough greedily at the slightest cross-wind.

Most Virginians buy their meat from me and then return to their cars and drive back to wherever they came from. They don't talk to me or about me. They pretend I don't exist. Which is fine.

I just read the books that I keep in the bus.

Take *Madame Chafouin's French Dictionary*.

A few weeks ago, on my way out of town from Dr. Monica's office, I happened upon a carton of eggs at the bottom of a garbage can in the Village Square. I cracked one of the eggs and it didn't smell terrible, so I was planning on bringing the carton home for Mrs. Kipner, and that's when I noticed the dictionary. It was heavy, bound in fake brown leather. It looked like a present no one wanted. So I took the book along with the eggs, but when I brought it back to the bus, I realized that it was not an ordinary dictionary at all, that the word *chafouin* in French means "weasel-faced," and every word in the dictionary is something unpleasant. So now I'm learning Unpleasant French. I'm up to the D's. Today's word was *la diarrhée*.

That means "the diarrhea."

Come evening, after the meat customers have left and the gray spring sky has gone grayer, I'm rolling up the awning when a large black sport utility vehicle drives past. It moves slowly at first, and then speeds up, disappearing around the bend. Sometimes cars will drive by the meat bus like this. The drivers want to see what a human being is doing out here with a broken-down bus and a fridge full of meat. They always want me to be doing something interesting, but when they see that all the hairy little Hungarian does is sit in his green plastic lawnchair, leisurely enjoying the scents that float across the field, stroking an exceptionally long blade of grass with one finger, just waiting for meat customers, they become impatient. Sometimes they shout, "Do something!" or "Do a trick, midget!"

So now when Virginians drive by the field, I stay seated in my lawnchair. I remain so still that I've started practicing not moving at all. Not even blinking. Sometimes I get so absorbed in not-blinking that I don't even notice when a customer comes up to the bus. Not even when they stand right in front of me, waving a hand in my face, which is what a female Virginian of a tall, gangly variety happens to be doing right now.

"Hey, are you still open?" she asks.

She pokes me with the tip of her shoe.

I go inside to wrap up the woman's steaks, but it turns out that I do not move fast enough for her.

"Come on, come on," she says.

I hand her the meat from a window.

"You've got terrible service," she sneers, and sprints across the field. She jumps in her car and roars off. As she goes, she passes the same black sport utility vehicle returning to the field. But this time it doesn't just drive by the meat bus; it expertly backs up around the bend and comes to a shuddering stop at the side of the road. The doors swing open and three men hop out. They're all wearing clean-pressed black suits, and they all possess these strong, remarkable chins. They remind me immediately of FBI agents I'd seen on a television program at Dr. Monica's office, but these are not FBI agents. One holds a fresh white letter in his hands, while the others remove a wide sign attached to a stake from the backseat:

PROPERTY OF SUBDIVISIONS LLC

The Subdivisionists look both ways, walk to the edge of my field, and then, with a rubberized mallet, wordlessly pound the stake into the ground.

X

EVOLUTION OF THE PFLIEGMANS:
THE PECHENEGS ADVANCE

It is not always easy for people to move from one region of the world to another and make a fresh go of it. It is not always sufficient to live in an unpopulated field, or even an entire unpopulated freshwater basin, and call it your own. Sometimes a person must possess certain things that declare ownership. Pieces of paper, et cetera.

Possessing pieces of paper, it seems, is extremely important to people.

Five years after Aranka's river redefined the quixotic geography of the Carpathian Basin, the Western Europeans were not at all pleased that these nomads from the East had acquired so much land so quickly. And so close to an actual *place*. They began spreading rumors, horrific rumors, as though the Hungarians were as bad as the Turks, the Huns, the Saracens, or even the Pechenegs, calling them, incredulously, "Child-Devouring Cannibals," or the "Bloodthirsty, Man-Eating Monsters from Scythia." To these people devoted to leisure, to vanity.

To public displays of affection!

Word traveled back to the Ural Mountains that the grass-lolling Magyars had discovered a river next to the nicest and grassiest of all nice and grassy spots to live, and so, without even finishing their breakfast cereal,

the Pechenegs migrated southwestward to once again wipe their filthy
paws all over our brand-spanking-new grasses, to kick down the posts of
our tents and bust all our clay pots, to thrust the wooden stakes of their
flags into our precious fields and claim our land as their own. To once
again ravage the weakest among us. And this is the reason why the early
Hungarians, who up to that point had been perfectly content to farm and
make wine, beekeep and fuck, were interrupted from the progress of their
own evolution.

They had to go to war again.

We Pfliegmans may have been the lousiest of the barbarian tribes, but
the Pechenegs were rivals in their own right: they possessed convex bodies
with hulking backs, they only wore black, they did not braid their hair,
and they all suffered from a peculiar out-jutting chin, a chin that weighed
twice as much as a normal chin should weigh, and which swung below the
mouth like a defiant fist.

They called us Magyar Assholes; we called them Big Chins.

"Natural Selection," writes Darwin, *"acts with extreme slowness."*

But the threat of the Pechenegs was not to be taken lightly. They painted
other people's blood on their faces; they used the dry skulls of their victims
for drinking cups; they sharpened both sides of wooden spears and thrust a
human head onto one end and plunged the other end into the earth; they
kicked bunny rabbits in the face. (Not in the *side*—in the face!)

Upon hearing that the Pechenegs had made their way over the Carpathians and through the Verecke Narrows, that they had easily passed the
Impassable Forest, that they were mere farts on the wind from the sprawl of
Hungarian camps beyond the Tisza River and would soon encroach Aranka's
river, the leader of the early Hungarians, the Grand Prince Árpád, mumbled,
"Well that's just fucking *fabulous*," and gathered the tribal heads together to
negotiate the situation.

Árpád was a tight little ball of pre-medieval energy, with a voice as
high and shrill as a child's. Some said he even looked like a child. The
Grand Prince was terrifically short, and tripped over his own cloaks as
he walked. A long sword hung awkwardly from his belt. He also wore a
large, shiny metal helmet in the shape of a hawk, which his father, Almos,
had given him before he died. The helmet wobbled over Árpád's small
head and hung so low over his eyes that often all anyone could see was his

wishful, roping mustache, shaped like a handlebar to a bicycle. But the Grand Prince walked quickly, raised his small fists passionately, and loved three things in life: fresh, warm bread; easy women with large, fleshy thighs; and killing his adversaries right through the heart.

As the members of the early Hungarian counsel sat quietly in his tent, waiting for the meeting to begin, Árpád was sitting quietly in a corner at a table. He would not look at any of them. "There are only eight of you," he said. "Where is the ninth?"

One of the men cleared his throat. "You mean Lehel," he said.

Árpád swallowed. "Right. I always forget. Lehel."

He frowned, thinking of Lehel's disappearance five years ago, and of the Fekete-Szem, the creepy little people who had followed them from the East. Rumor had it that they had snuck into the Hungarian camps in broad daylight, pulled Lehel from his horse, neatly slaughtered him, bone by bone, and then disappeared into their tent with his body parts. The Fekete-Szem had not yet been brought to justice for their crime because no one could say with certainty that they actually bore culpability; after all, there were no official eyewitnesses. And while Christian historiographers would like to believe that the pagan Hungarian tribes were barbarian savages, that they held no order in their communities, this wasn't true; Anonymus reminds us that behind every tent, around every sweaty pagan corner, a person was innocent unless he was judged to be proven guilty by his own ignoble behavior: "*Anyone caught defying the counsel of the early Hungarian community*," he writes, "*without offering a pretty darn good explanation, would be cut in half or, at the very least, exposed to hopeless situations.*"

But Árpád knew the real reason he had not gone after the Fekete-Szem. These were the very same creatures who had somehow created the Danube River out of the great blue nothing. It was along the Danube that the Hungarians had flourished over the past five years, and it was along this very same river that they would campaign against all possible invaders. The river had by now swollen majestically, stretching from Black Sea through Bavaria and well up into the Germanic north, and it was Árpád's plan to use the river and other untouched marshes and wastelands for protection against the Pechenegs. They would build a *Gyepü*, a "natural blockade." They would fell trees, assemble rock piles. They would leave breadcrumb trails, and the trails would lead straight into dark and vacuous holes. And the Gyepü, Árpád explained, would serve other purposes as well: keeping the Pechenegs at bay would allow the brand-spanking-new Hungarians to invade the West. They would imitate the fighting methods of all of the worst barbarian hordes. They would pillage, they would plunder, and when word reached the Pechenegs that the Hungarians were the most vicious of all vicious barbarians, with whom no one, Christian or pagan, should want to reckon, only then, Árpád believed, would his people be able to live a life of leisure, given over to vanities and as goddamned libidinous as they wanted it to be. "It is *vital*," he argued, pressing a bulb of cold, stale bread into his mouth, "that we invade the West to secure our position in the Carpathian Basin."

The tribal leaders all nodded soberly.

The Grand Prince was true to his word. The Hungarians really did behave most abominably. Stories quickly spread both east and west, until every nobleman, civilian, and peasant knew and feared the vicious crew. Ape-men, with teeth like tiny daggers and no other interest in their lives other than overrunning small villages and slaughtering the *vivre* out of innocent, happy townfolk.

"Cut off one head, and thirty will grow in its place!" they cried. Or, "They slip through one's fingers like eels!" Or the somewhat less thrilling: "They emerge from the swamp like frogs!" Human heads were set upon spears and poked into the ground in their wake. (My Darling, I'm sad to say that they even did the ugly business with the bunny rabbits.)

But there were notable differences between the Hungarians and the barbarians: where the Pechenegs fought in a great black mass, bodies tripping over bodies, the Hungarians were organized, and rode on horseback. Their light cavalries attacked from all sides, disseminating across the countryside before anyone could mobilize against them. They would *pretend* to flee battle, and then, when the other side falsely believed that they had won, the Hungarians would regroup and charge again. They would agree to meet with the leaders of the Western nations and *say* that they accepted Jesus Christ as their Savior, gaining a higher rank and further access to their lands, then they would turn, stick out their tongues, and gleefully plunder.

Rather than err on the side of correctness, of civility, Árpád encouraged the rumor that they were indeed the sons of Attila, truly the new Scourge of Europe, a bunch of foul prevaricators, with no allegiances to anyone.

Civilized Europe shook its big, indignant head. It was not enough that the Hungarians were known as the Bloodthirsty Man-Eating Monsters from Scythia; they were two-faced as well. A fresh rumor spread that these men were a new, evil race of people with faces on *both* sides of their heads—

It was all in the interest of survival. In order for the Hungarians to survive, they had to become something they were not: bloodless, heart-less, ruthless, murderer-killers. They were so successful that when they were not off invading already well-established and civilized countries, the Hungarians would invade them in their dreams. Many a Christian feudal lord awoke at midnight with a sweat-soaked dressing gown, screaming about the invading hordes, and his mistress would have to calmly soothe him with talk of conquer, self-righteousness, and sexual favors. A single prayer could be heard in churches echoing across the quaint medieval pastoralia: *De sagittis Hungarorum libera nos, Domine*: "O Lord, save us from the arrows of the Hungarians!" Or the prayer heard somewhat more often: "Goddammit, we have got to *get* those sons of bitches"—

The phone rings. Mrs. Himmel, busy filing her fingernails into ten perfect points, grabs it after a single note. She's waiting for Daughter Elise's mod-eling agent to call about an interview with a famous modeling agency, but it's not the agent. It's a mother calling to get information about intention-ally exposing her child to chicken pox.

Annoyed that a mother is taking up the phone line, Mrs. Himmel grabs a handful of fun-size candy bars from the shelf behind her and unwraps all of them at once. She lines them up on her desk in a parade of chocolate turds. "Oh, just bring him in," she says. "If he spends ten minutes in the Waiting Area, I guarantee he'll catch it." Then she hangs up the phone, and shoots me a glance—

I catch it.

We are like two dogs, waiting for the other to flinch.

Mrs. Himmel quickly picks up the phone again, pushes the extension to Dr. Monica's office, and begins whispering, fiercely: "I can *smell* him from all the way over here." She slams down the phone.

Seconds later, Adrian fills the doorjamb. She strides over to Mrs.

Himmel's window with her mountain-climbing legs and quietly speaks to her about being respectful to Dr. Monica and to the people in the Waiting Area. That means *everyone*.

Mrs. Himmel looks at her like she's made of seaweed.

"He's harmless, Mrs. Himmel," Adrian whispers. "Dr. Monica would never let him in here otherwise. But if it makes you feel better, I can watch the desk until three o'clock."

"It's not right," Himmel says. "A thirty-four-year-old person seeing a pediatrician is just not right." She shakes her head. "A normal person would have better things to do that spend an entire day in the waiting area of a pediatrician's office. He's useless. A member of society should do something. Contribute. What does a person like that possibly contribute?"

Adrian glances at me. "He has a job," she says. "Dr. Monica said he's a butcher. He sells meat out of his bus."

Mrs. Himmel perks up. "*Meat* out of a *bus*? What does he butcher?"

"I don't know. He probably butchers what other people butcher. Pigs, chickens. Cows, I guess. Livestock."

Mrs. Himmel's lips curl into a sneer. The tight perm on her head somehow looks even tighter.

"My uncle was a butcher," she says evenly, "and I'll have you know that butchering takes a huge amount of time and money and manpower. Just *look* at him, Adrian. I want you to tell me how *that little thing over there* can hang up and drain a whole cow. How does he even cut off the heads?"

First you slit open the hide, I think, *cutting from the horn to the nostril. Skin out the front of the face, flip over one side and then the opposite side. Grasp the jaw in your hand, bend back the head, and remove it by severing the neck and atlas joint.*

Mrs. Himmel grabs a stack of folders and begins shuffling. "I don't believe it," she whispers. "Not for *one second* do I believe that." She assembles all of the folders into one firm, thick square. "There are *children* in here, for heaven's sake."

Adrian rolls an unsavory thought around her brain for a moment. But then she shakes her head. "He's only here once a week," she says. "Dr. Monica says to not worry about it, so I'm not going to worry. And neither should you."

Mrs. Himmel waves her off. "I'm not worried. Yet. But heaven help him if I *get* worried. If I *get* worried, I'll chuck him out of the Waiting Area so fast he won't know what hit him," she says, and then she looks right at me. She shoots me a real mean one and mouths, *"Don't you think I won't."*

—*Anyway*, as Árpád was busy conjuring military strategies, the rest of the Hungarians were trying to figure out how to deal with the fetid little people who had followed them from the Black Sea like lost children; the one who had lost their own tent in the flooding and built a new one right next to Bona Fide Civilization; the ones who stole their livestock from them, left and right, with no sense of place or courtesy; the ones who spent all day lying around the outskirts of camp, bitching and moaning about every small thing, hollering insults at passersby. The ones who just couldn't seem to get it together.

"They're totally *useless!*" one of the Hungarians cried.

It had gotten to the point where many actually feared the Fekete-Szem. You always had to keep one eye open walking by *that* tent, they said. You'd walk by and would get hissed at. Pieces of bone would be hucked at you. And then there was what had happened to poor Lehel.

"Get rid of them now!" cried another. "Before we *all* get eaten!"

Árpád was summoned to deal with the situation. He weaved in and around the Hungarian camps while riding his magnificent, tall white horse which he called, only, M.

When he arrived at our tent along the outskirts of camp, we Pfliegmans weren't up yet; we were lazing about on our backs, smelling our skins, chewing our toenails for breakfast. Peeling fleas from our long strands of hair.

"Come forth, cretins!" one of the Hungarians bellowed.

We Pfliegmans squealed and scurried about like veritable insects set loose from our veritable tin cans.

Árpád dismounted M, took one look at us, exposed and shivering, all eyes and elbows, and sighed impatiently. "They're not going to *eat* anyone," he said. "They're bored. What they need is something to do. Something to make them feel like they're part of the community."

"We don't *want* them to be part of the community!" shouted an angry woman with an exceedingly wide hind end.

Árpád gave her an impatient look.

"But what *can* they do?" a man protested. "They can't do anything."

"Sure they can," said Árpád.

"Like what?"

Árpád stroked his gorgeous mustache for a minute, rolling the ends into points between his fingertips. Then he thought of Lehel, and his eyes brightened. "They can cut meat," he said.

One of the Hungarians had an old cow, and complained of the cow's inability to give milk. A suspicious green color had blotched the udder, so it was universally decided that the cow would serve perfectly as the Practice Cow for the Fekete-Szem, to see whether we had any useful knowledge of meat and bone. We were given the cutting instruments. Wide-eyed, we curled our fingers around them like prized fighting swords, then one of the Hungarians stepped forward with a blunter.

"Who is the most able among you?" he asked.

Kinga pushed Aranka's child, Szeretlek, forward. The boy was only five years old, but was already the size of your average medieval Hungarian adult. He was neither handsome nor bright, not even by lowly Pfliegman standards. His face was dull and lifeless. A face like a loaf of bread. The large child was deeply distrustful of his own brain, and clung to Kinga for direction. She put him to good use. At five years old, he could dig pits and haul logs for the Gyepü. Trees fell with one swing of his axe. So when the time came to choose among us Pfliegmans, there was no doubt that Szeretlek was strongest and most able. The blunter was quickly passed to him.

The boy stared at the long piece of heavy wood.

"Make yourself *useful*," Kinga whispered. "A useful man is never lonely."

Szeretlek looked at everyone for permission. "If I can be of use," he said. He lifted his massive arm and clocked the cow over the head.

"*Wunh*," the cow said, and then fell over.

We Pfliegmans threw ourselves upon it. Like vampires, like piranhas, in a few flimsy seconds we held up heavy, dripping cuts of meat. Round, Loin, Flank, Rib, Plate, Chuck, Shank. All of it. The heart of the cow still pulsed in one of our hands.

"You can see the white bone," the Hungarians breathed.

It appeared there was a use for us after all.

Szeretlek, however, had not participated in the cutting. His big fingers were too thick, too clumsy. But as he watched his family carve and eviscerate the animal to the approval of the good and decent Hungarians, the boy felt, from a deep place in his large body, that things were about to change for the Fekete-Szem.

XI

KABÁT TOLVAJOK

An unpleasant odor is filling the air of the Waiting Area. It smells infested. Gluttonous. There's a dead rodent somewhere, I think. Oily hair, rotting flesh. A pungent, omnivorous mold—I look up.

Mrs. Himmel is eating a cheeseburger.

The Sick or Diseased children hold their stomachs in agony. I admit, even my own stomach is turning unhappily. For someone who knows everything there is to know about the meat business, for someone who sells meat of a bus in a field for a meager but adequate living—for all of this, I don't go near the stuff. Not long after Ján and Janka Pfliegman died, I took a bite of a ham sandwich and the meat tasted wrong. Heavy. For a while I only ate tomatoes and crackers, but then the crackers also started getting heavy. I couldn't work them down my throat.

In fact, for the last month, all I've been able to swallow with any modicum of appeal are Evermores. Mister Bis sells them by the box at the G&P, but Dr. Monica wants me to be working more with the rest of the food groups. "Listen to your body," she says, and so I listen, but I swear that Evermores are the only thing my body wants.

I reach into the pocket of my trousers and remove one. The Sick or Diseased child sitting next to me watches as I unwrap it. He thinks it's candy.

He looks at me. "Is that a lemon?" he asks.

I nod.

The boy slides off his chair. He walks over to the pile of coloring books on the sidetable, books colored over so many times the pages have torn, and picks up a blue crayon. With one eye, he watches as I bite into the Evermore and swallow the honey. He's wearing a T-shirt that says BANG THE DRUM! on it, and there's a picture of a snare drum with two drumsticks hovering in the air above. It looks like the drum's being played by an invisible man. He pretends to be importantly occupied coloring over a dumptruck that's already been colored.

I pick up my writing tablet. I draw him a quick sketch of a bumblebee and hold it up.

He ignores me.

His mother turns the pages of her women's magazine. She's reading a recipe for a banana-nut loaf with Tips for Decorative Icing:

1. Squeeze the tube from behind.

2. Use different nozzles for a varied effect.

3. Have fun.

She takes out a notepad from her purse and pointedly jots it all down. She is a Good Mother. I can tell the difference between the Good Mothers and the Bad Mothers. The Good Mothers make their children wash their hands in the bathroom before they see Dr. Monica. They wear clean slacks or skirts with pleats in the front, and raincoats on rainy days. They carry tissues and mints in their pockets. They are the ones with the water jugs. The Bad Mothers come into the office wearing T-shirts, with the straps of their brassieres showing. They smell like onions and cigarettes and tell their children to *shut up and go play with the toys*. They slouch in the chairs and don't even bother with magazines. They disconsolately watch the television in the corner.

I like the Bad Mothers. I'm not sure why. Maybe it's because of the snooty way the Good Mothers are always clearing their throats and shooting them glances, or maybe it's because the Bad Mothers sometimes talk to each other and try to make each other feel better about their Sick or Diseased child, and the Good Mothers never talk to anyone. Or maybe it's because of the familiar way the Bad Mothers troll around the Waiting Area like it's their own living room. When prompted, they laugh a startling, bellicose laughter.

Or maybe it's just because I have a slightly different perspective on the issue of Good and Bad. I imagine Janka sitting here in Dr. Monica's office. She'd sit next to the Good Mothers. She'd scratch her hairy legs and then reach into her bag and bring out a pack of cigarettes and, ignoring the sign hanging right above her head, light one. When a Good Mother would politely ask her to extinguish it, she would sneer and call her a *tight bitch*. Then she'd borrow one of the Good Mothers' tissues and blow her nose and then clean the bottom of her clogs with it. She would complain about the hard chairs on her *goddamn coccyx*. She would start ribbing one of the Good Mothers for showing off such a *fancy fucken purse*, and she would get a few snickers from the Bad Mothers. She would feel fed by them. Most of all, she would completely ignore her own Sick or Diseased child, passed out on the floor underneath the withering ficus.

Adrian reappears in the doorway with her clipboard. She motions for the BANG THE DRUM! boy to follow her. His mother gets up quickly, dropping her women's magazine on the side table. They linger, for a moment, in the Waiting Area, as Adrian explains what's going on.

"Dr. Monica would like to do an X-ray," she says, quietly.

The boy hears the word X-ray and bursts into tears. Whimpering, he takes his mother's hand. As he walks by me, I hold up my writing tablet and show the boy what I've drawn. Instead of a crappy bumblebee, it's a cowboy whirling a lasso above his head surrounded by a dying sunset and prickly cacti. From the cowboy's mouth is a speaking bubble that says *"Giddyup!"*

He smiles as his mother pulls him out of the Waiting Area. I'm pleased that I've made the boy smile. I even laugh a little. My laugh is dry and quiet, but unfortunately it's enough to command Mrs. Himmel's attention. She puts down the cheeseburger and glares at the man in the filthy pink sweatshirt cackling in the corner of her Waiting Area. Her eyes go narrow, thin as dimes—

Slowly, I stick out my tongue.

"That's it!" she shouts. She bounds from her chair and moves right in front of me. She leans down, so close I can smell her wet, acrimonious pores:

"I want *you* outside *now*."

I look around quickly, but Adrian and Dr. Monica are nowhere in sight.

I look to the mothers, but their faces are buried in women's magazines. The Sick or Diseased children are the only ones who notice. They watch me gather my writing tablet. They lift their pale faces.

"Get your coat," Himmel says.

I remove my coat from the rack and follow Mrs. Himmel's finger outside Dr. Monica's office. She points me to a circular picnic table parked on the front lawn.

"Wait here," she says. "Adrian will come and get you if there's a cancellation. If no one comes to get you by five o'clock, you can assume you can just go home."

The door closes behind her with a deliberate *click*.

I climb up on top of the picnic table and stare across the street. Directly across the street from Dr. Monica's office is the Big M supermarket. The place used to be a mini-mall, but now the supermarket takes up the entire complex. Inside, there's the Big M hair salon, the Big M coffeeshop, the Big M car mechanic. At the entrance to the parking lot, a three-dimensional box laconically spins: ENTER, EXIT, ENTER, EXIT, ENTER—

Above it all is a glowing red M.

Sitting here, evicted to a picnic table outside a pediatrician's office on this wet and frigid April afternoon, clouds splayed across the sky like spilt milk, I imagine climbing off the picnic table and crossing the intersection and walking into the coffeeshop and sitting down to have a cup of coffee like any normal, civilized person. But civilized people have something to offer each other, and all I have to offer is my unsightly visage. My swinging cheeks. My dirt, my peeling skin, my sickness. My beard hanging from my chin like a squirrel. And the civilized people would sit tightly, politely, away from me. Because they are Virginians. They're doing everything right in the world, and I'm mucking it up royally.

There's no question about it.

Wind blows mercilessly through the Disneyland sweatshirt, making my flesh pimple. I pull my coat over my arms. The coat is one of Grandfather Ákos's coats. There are ten in all, each made from heavy gray Hungarian wool. Each cinched with a row of gold buttons. Inside, the coats are layered with thinner, more refined wools, but behind what appears to be the final layer, behind a zipper, are a dozen or so wide pockets. Pockets made from soft, but extraordinarily durable, Hungarian cloth; pockets evenly distributed throughout the hidden lining, designed so that once filled, a person on the outside could never guess the nature of the ballast; pockets just large enough to fit assorted, prewrapped, loaf-sized cuts of meat.

A small light-blue silk label is sewn into each collar of the coats: KABÁT TOLVAJOK.

Coat of Thieves.

Grandfather Ákos never told me about the original function for the pockets, but once mumbled something about how being a Hungarian meant wanting nothing and being prepared for anything. "Or was it the other way around," he said.

Three Security Guards appear briefly in front of the glass doors. Herman lumbers fatly around the other two, moving in a winding figure-eight, observing the Virginians who walk past him with wariness and suspicion. He rests one hand on the walkie-talkie attached to his belt like a pistol; with the other, he fiddles with his baseball cap. The guards take one look through the glass doors and then spread out, abandoning their posts.

I stand up and stretch, then pull on the wooly sleeves. There has always been something about the Big M supermarket that makes me feel hidden. Invisible. It's something in the high ceilings, the gleaming white walls, the glass refrigerator units filled with colorful, prepackaged foods. It's in the sweet smells unfurling from the bakery ovens. It's in the rows of shiny green peppers, shipped all the way from Taiwan. Here, there are so many more interesting, more charming things to look at other than a hairy little man lingering in front of the meat display in a large wool coat, slipping cold, prewrapped packages into the pockets of the lining.

I lower my stylish woolen cap to cover my face, and then climb off the picnic table and cross the intersection. I hustle quickly through the parking lot, all the way up to the entrance of the supermarket, to where those shiny glass doors swing open.

METAMORPHOSIS

XII

THE CAPTAIN AND THE QUEECONOCOCHEECOOK

It's Saturday. People buy roasts on Saturdays. By late afternoon, the line of meat customers nearly reaches the road. Marjorie likes busy days. Her blade sways happily in the April wind by the bus, listening to the gurgle of the Queeconococheecook, feeling good about today. About life in general. The sky is clear for once, and inside, the tape-radio's playing some upbeat German pop tunes:

Hier ist ein übermäßiger Klassiker von den sechziger Jahren!

Even Mrs. Kipner's in a good mood. I perch the tin can on an arm of my lawnchair and drop in a fat slice of tomato, all brown and glistening with sugars. It lands on the shiny part of his back. Tomato juice runs luxuriously over his face, like water from a warm bath. He whirrs contentedly.

The Virginians all chat comfortably while waiting to buy their meat. Mister Bis is here today, in line with the others. A woman tells a funny story about losing her keys and a baked ham and everyone laughs. A man is buying meat for a church barbecue. He invites everyone in line to the barbecue, and walks along the line of people and gives them his flyer. He does not give me a flyer. Which is fine. I have no interest in flyers.

Dr. Monica says I need to put myself in social situations, but is selling meat out of a bus not social? This moment, my customers all in a row, is my main social engagement with the outside world. My convivial soirée. The whole world is busy and alive and I, if just for this fleeting moment, am alive in it—

I hand a lamb roast to a Virginian in a pressed suit.

"Well!" he says, laughing, marveling at the girth. He pays for the meat, then reaches into a bag and produces a loaf of dark, thick bread. "You look *hungry*," the man says.

Even if I could possibly consume it, the bread is old, and has already hardened.

"How magnanimous of you," I want to say.

Then the sport utility vehicle turns the corner onto Back Lick Road. It's the same one as before. Black. Shiny. It moves toward the field like a tank. An arrow of sunlight hits the window, illuminating the three of them inside: the dark suits. The curve of their massive chins. Another large square sign fills the backseat:

PROPERTY OF SUBDIVISIONS LLC

COME TO PARADISE

The car lingers for a moment, purring at the edge of my field, but when they see that I've got company, the Subdivisionists don't stop to hammer the new sign; instead, they drive past us, speeding quickly around the bend. Mister Bis comes up behind me and watches them leave. He clucks his tongue.

"Chickenshits," he says.

We sell out by noon. Everything goes. All the chops, shanks, loins. Mister Bis buys his half of it. "People need their carnitine," he says, helping me dole out three steaks to a woman holding a baby.

"What's that?" the woman says.

"It is the protein in meat," says Mister Bis. "If you eat your carnitine, you're good as gold. That's why those vegetarians have terrible posture and go shuffling around in their goddamn clogs all day. Not enough carnitine. They can barely keep themselves upright."

"Carnitine," says the woman, and nods her head.

"Carnitine," says Mister Bis.

At the end of the day, Richie arrives in Mister Bis's truck to pick him up. He honks the horn. Mister Bis ignores him, and gathers a bundle of wax papers that have been blown across the grass. Richie, impatient, honks again. This time he leans on it. An assembly of birds scatters from the trees.

"Get over here!" shouts Mister Bis.

In a sulk, Richie slides out the door of the truck and walks over to the meat bus, kicking at the grass as he comes. "*What*," he says.

"Help clean up."

Richie sneezes a dry, exaggerated sneeze. "I can't," he says and sniffles. "I have allergies. The stupid grass gives me allergies."

"I'll give you allergies, Anil," says Mister Bis, and throws him a handful of tongues.

Richie jumps aside.

Mister Bis and I fill up his boxes with chops, roasts, steaks. Assorted cutlets. It takes a while, but eventually we get it all loaded up in the back of his truck. The grocer slams the door and wipes his hands. "I honestly do not know how you do it, Mister Pfliegman," he says. "I do not know how you manage to do it all on your own. But I would be out of business without you." He gives me a warm look. Then he opens the door of the truck to leave. "Where's Richie?"

We turn around.

Richie has braced himself by the side of the bus, and is furiously tugging at Marjorie with all of his strength.

I make a run for it. I haul my bad leg across the field and throw myself upon the boy pharmacist.

"Hey!" he cries. "It's a *weed!* It's just a weed!"

I focus on his left hand, trying to pry Marjorie out from his insubordinate adolescent fingers, but Richie is considerably bigger than I am. He easily bends his legs around my legs until he gets a good grip on the bad one. He turns it.

"*Algh!*" I yell.

Then a man walks out from around the back of the bus. Stunned, I stop wrestling and stare at him. He's wearing nothing but a tight Speedo. He has glistening pectorals, a trim, two-inch mustache. Around his neck hangs a shiny whistle, and he's got a funny round helmet on his head that looks like he's about to battle kindergarteners. He looks exactly like the Captain from *The Complete Book of Water Polo, With Pictures.* As if cued, the Captain brings forth a yellow water polo ball from around his back. He begins expertly tossing it back and forth between his palms. His leg muscles twitch excitedly. "Take him away from the two-meter area!" he cries.

I give him an incredulous look.

"Go for the goal!"

Sensing that I've let up, Richie seizes the clear advantage. "Take that!" he cries, and elbows me deep in the gut.

"Push him out to four to six meters!" the Captain shouts, and tweets his whistle. "Get and hold one side!"

Half-bent, I climb up one side of Richie's body to his shoulder, and then, with my barnacle teeth, chomp down. Richie howls and grabs his shoulder. He begins whacking me on the head with his knuckles, then grabs my stylish woolen cap in his hands. He flings it across the field—

"Foul!" cries the Captain, jumping up and down. He blows the whistle, hard. "Use the legs!" he shouts. "Focus on the legs! Eggbeater, Eggbeater!"

I concentrate on my legs. I hook my good leg around Richie's knee, and am fairly surprised as it turns, sending him sideways to the ground.

The Captain is so excited he takes off his helmet. "Attaboy, Pfliegman!" he shouts, and gives me a thumbs-up. Richie wiggles under my grip, but I don't let go until Mister Bis throws an arm in and divides us. I look for the Captain, but he's gone. Back into the slice of air he came from.

Mister Bis gives me a light shake. "Are you all right, Mister Pfliegman?"

Richie spits on the ground. "No, he's not all right," he says, and spits again. He pulls the collar away from his neck to show his father his fresh wound. "He bit me on the shoulder! I probably need a goddamned tetanus shot!"

I hobble over to the front of the bus, looking around all sides.

"Go back to the truck," says Mister Bis.

Richie sniffles and wipes his nose on his shirt. "But I was bit!" he insists.

"I said go back to the truck!"

Richie rubs his shoulder and shouts at me: "Who goes around *biting* people? What are you, anyway? Some kind of *vampire?*"

"Get back in the truck, Teenager!" says Mister Bis. "Right now!"

"Fine!" Richie yells. He runs all the way back to the truck and jumps into the driver's seat. He turns on the radio.

Rock music blasts across the field.

Mister Bis picks up my cap and approaches the bus. "Are you all right,

Mister Pfliegman? Do you feel all right? What are you looking for?"

I beckon Mister Bis into the bus and point out the windows to the wide hanging arms of the pine tree, the muddy path leading down to the embankment of the Queeconococheecook. The Captain is meandering down the grassy side of the river, tossing the yellow ball between his palms—he slides into the water, disappearing into the froth and foam.

"What?" says Mister Bis. "What am I looking at?"

I go to my bookshelf and pick up *The Complete Book of Water Polo, With Pictures* to show him what I'm talking about—I point at the Captain on the cover—but Mister Bis doesn't look at the book. Although he has visited the field many times before, he's never actually been inside. He looks at the rusted pots, the barely used sink. The diamond-shaped crack in the ceiling. He spots a tin can perched on the windowledge and picks it up—a large brown beetle spins his antennae—he quickly puts it down again. He folds his arms over his chest. "Rovar," he says. "I think you should come and stay with me and Missus Bis for a while. I would have to clear it by her of course, and it would not be a permanent situation, but there is a cot and a few other things, and you'd certainly be comfortable. It's freezing in here. You shouldn't be living outside like this, next to a river. It's not safe."

I smile warmly at Mister Bis's generosity. This is no everyday gesture, and I am truly appreciative. I pick up my writing tablet.

Thank you, I write. *But no.*

He sniffs, and presses his hands together. "No? Why not?"

Please don't be offended. I have no choice in the matter.

"But it's the least we can do for you, for everything you do for us—"

I shake my head.

"All right," he says, and puts one hand on my shoulder. He fingers my filthy pink sweatshirt, the woolen cap. My everyday trousers, worn thin.

"Do you at least have a good coat?" he says. "I can get you a good coat if you need one."

Oh, I have one, I write.

Then Mister Bis notices the pile of unopened letters from the Subdivisionists. He picks one up and opens it: "*Due to re-zoning the zoning laws,*" he reads, "*this acreage is to be subdivided into eight elite, residential properties.*"

Outside, I watch the Captain climb out of the water and trod happily up the embankment in his bare feet, shaking the water from his body.

When he reaches the bus, he grabs one of the Indian's blue towels with the yellow pom poms, drying on the clothesline. He rubs himself with it.

"This is *bad*," Mister Bis says, shaking his head at the letter. "Have you not seen this? They've got lawyers involved now."

I slowly place the water polo book back on my bookshelf. There is no need for me to read the letters from the Subdivisionists. They always say the same thing. The pages are filled with all sorts of important-sounding words like *fiduciary*, *accrue*, and *facilitate*. I may not practice or appreciate language like *cost-effective* or *fiscal advantage*; I may not understand words like *accretion* or *adverse possession*; and yes, these may well indeed be modern words for modern times, but it seems that not all that much has changed from early medieval times, when people were most concerned with eating fresh meat, laying claim on land, and killing people right through the heart.

XIII
EVOLUTION OF THE PFLIEGMANS:
THE GREAT LEG-WRESTLING CHAMPION
OF TENTH-CENTURY HUNGARY

I once read that every person should live next to a body of water. That all forms of water represent change. Or the possibility for change. That landlocked people go bonkers. Living next to a river was an imperative for the early Hungarians, though purely for pragmatic reasons: these people of leisure, of vanity, fished and hunted along the many rivers which decorate the Carpathian Basin, and it's probably for this reason above all others that their civilization evolved so quickly there. By 926 AD, the Magyars had spread out over many thousands of square kilometers, a total combined area considerably larger than the area of present-day Hungary, which is thirty-five thousand square miles and roughly the same size as the state of Virginia. The original ten tribes had disseminated into hundreds of villages of smaller tribes, across various rivers, but mostly along the Tisza and the Danube, which divide the country into long and narrow thirds. But what is little known about the early Hungarians, even amongst the most fêted historians, is that among the Magyars who inhabited these rivers lived the best leg wrestler the world has ever seen.

Her name was Lili László.

Lili László, as the Virginians would call her, or László Lili, as the Hungarians called her, had long blond hair which coiled around her neck like a furry snake, and the largest thighs of any woman in camp. Lili would often challenge men to leg-wrestling matches, and everyone always came to watch. For an emerging, war-torn country, early in the tenth century? Entertainment-wise? It was the best bang for your buck.

This is the way it worked, as passed down from Ural Mountains to here, where we are now, in 926 AD, this flat, wet, and thankless place called the Carpathian Basin: *"Two opponents lay on their backs, facing opposite directions, their arms intertwined,"* writes Anonymus. *"Their legs lifted and locked into each other. A struggle, for as long as the wrestlers could hold, ensued. The winner turned the knees of his opponent, hauling him over his head."*

Lili László never leg wrestled for fun; it was always for grain alcohol or for extra portions of food, as Árpád had imposed strict rations in camp. Lili would pass through the food line with her tiny woman's plate and sigh, looking hungrily at the men's plates, piled with cold salted deermeat. She would bribe men out of their breakfasts by challenging them to a match and promising to allow them to *gurulni* her body if she lost.

She never lost.

One morning, she awoke to find a semicircle of men in their man-loins standing outside of her tent.

"You owe us," one said.

The men behind the speaker all nodded.

"We've all wrestled you, and you won't gurulni any of us."

"Yeah!"

Lili reached into her tent and brought out her breakfast, a flank of beef from last night's roast which she'd won by wrestling a one-legged deaf man. (And this was really the last straw, the men all thought, being that the man was deaf and one-legged and all.)

"So what?" she said.

"So we want a rematch."

Lili listened to the men, and began gnawing at her bone, thoughtfully. It was rather odd, she was thinking, that they all wanted a rematch. It was all very cute. "What do I get if I win?" she said.

"You get to gurulni any man in camp," one said.

Lili snorted.

The men looked at each other. "And you can eat with us every day."

"Every day? For how long?"

"As long as you like! Eat as much as you want."

Lili thought about it. She didn't really feel like gurulni-ing with any of them. Your average medieval Hungarian male was no hot ticket, and the last thing she could afford to do for her health in all this rain was open up and let somebody jostle around everything that she would just have to set right again—but in the end, the promise of all that food was too much to pass up. She wiped her hands across her chest and grinned. "All right," she said. "Who among you wants to fight me?"

The men smiled, and then, like a curtain parting, stepped aside as Szeretlek the Giant made his way through the crowd.

"If I can be of *use*," he said.

Lili took one look at Szeretlek and wavered in front of the flap of her tent. She held the lip of meat in her mouth. This was not what she had agreed to.

"This is not what I agreed to," she said.

Szeretlek grinned at Lili and sat down on the rounded earth in front of her tent. He landed with a thud. His legs unfolded beneath him, stretching out like fallen trunks—

The men practically danced around him.

Lili retreated into the solitude of her tent. How could she beat the Giant? She lingered for a moment and evaluated her resources. Although on the short side, with a trunked neck and an unimaginative bosom, Lili was not a completely unattractive she-pagan. She had blond hair, smooth shoulders. A playful soupçon of feminine beard. She could flirt with him, she decided. The idea wasn't completely outrageous. She hocked a burr of phlegm into her hand and smoothed her hair. She pinched her cheeks for color, wrapped her braids around her head, and unbuttoned the top of her cloak like it was accidental. She practiced standing at various angles that called attention to her fattest, most flattering body parts, and when she emerged from the tent a few moments later, she looked softer, in a way, than she had before, and the look on her face was clear and desirable.

She smiled a thin, disingenuous smile, and then Lili László lay down on her back.

The Hungarians erupted in cheers. What a match! Szeretlek the Giant versus the unflagging leg-wrestling champion of tenth-century Hungary! The people liked Lili; she teased the men and roughhoused with the children, and there was nothing particularly great about Szeretlek apart from his physical greatness. He was big, yes—but Lili's strength seemed to come from somewhere else. You could feel it if you stood too close to her. You could smell it on her breath. It was in her voice. Her screams were spectacular, louder than any soldier entering battle. Huns were known for yelling the loudest as they fought, Germans shouted "Kyrie Eleison," and the Hungarians cried out in wolf-like howls, "Hooy Hooy!" Lili screamed louder than all of them.

She locked legs with the Giant.

"Go!" shouted one of the slighted men.

Szeretlek, meanwhile, had not been expecting much of a struggle. He casually looked up from the position where they now lay, legs interlocked, and wondered what all of the fuss was about. Although feeble-minded, he was aware of the basic biological differences between them, and felt certain there were better uses for him at the moment. Kinga had trained Szeretlek to feel uneasy when he was not being useful in some way to the greater Hungarian society, and as he lay on the grass that afternoon, he had some difficulty keeping his mind away from the other, more important tasks at hand that day. The Gyepü always needed some kind of maintenance. There was the Vacuous Hole that needed filling again. He had been spending the morning watching the Moving Rock Pile when the Hungarians approached him about the match.

He looked back at Lili, between their nest of legs. Most women were afraid of Szeretlek. After all, his arms were like logs, his head was potato-shaped. His hair grew out in scattered, queasy sprouts. If the Giant looked at any woman and smiled, if he offered any sweet expression, she always gathered her things in her basket and hurried off in the other direction. Szeretlek noticed that Lili was not frightened of him; on the contrary, it was like she didn't even see his swinging limbs, his lumpy head. She coiled her hair around one finger and lowered her eyes. She puckered her lips and blinked at him coquettishly. Szeretlek stared back at her, and then it was like something stepped forward on a platform in his chest and plummeted deep into his gut—

I Love You was in love.

As the Giant tried to understand this fresh emotion, he absentmindedly released his grip. His knees loosened, and he felt Lili's legs go tight. Solid. All of a sudden it felt like he was trying leg wrestle a block of wood. He tried to focus, to find another strategy; he tried altering his torso right and left, lumbering his weight little, trying to take advantage of his considerable gravitas, but still the smiling girl *did not move*, and after only a few minutes, his forehead blushed, and the blush moved southerly. His face grew hot, his lips quivered. A thin trickle of spit slid from his mouth onto his chin. He couldn't be losing, but he was.

Szeretlek *was* losing.

It wasn't entirely his fault. Two things were at work against the Giant that day: first, although it may not look like a contest of the mind, there is a definite strategy involved in leg wrestling, and by locking in early, Lili had suggested to her thick-witted competitor that all she knew how to do was hold tight in one position, and eventually she would falter.

This was simply not true.

Szeretlek's other handicap was simply the place he had chosen to sit. On his side, the grass was long and plush and beckoning. As a giant boy, the giant man had enjoyed lying leisurely in grassy fields just like this one, feeling the soft tickle of long blades over his large palms, but in the end, Szeretlek's clean green grass that he adored, that all Hungarians adored, gave him absolutely no leverage.

Lili, meanwhile, was lying in a patch of unruly tenth-century crabgrass.

Clouds hung low above them, and the birds shut up. Rain was approaching from the east. Tents flapped open and the dogs whimpered and ran for cover, but nothing else moved. The whole camp grew quiet and watched as Lili and Szeretlek held together, tight. Lili's thighs quivered. She held on tight to the handles of crabgrass, and then a sound moved from her belly to her throat, up and out, orbiting around the crowd and nearly blowing the Giant's hair back:

Not since Aranka's scream while giving birth to Szeretlek had there been such a noise in camp, and that had been nearly thirty years ago. Chilled by the familiarity of the sound, the Giant lifted his head to try and see what she was doing, and then:

Lili had been taking a breath.

Szeretlek grabbed desperately at the grass that fell into withering clumps. He tossed the handfuls to his side and grabbed again until there was no grass left. He began grabbing at dirt. The dirt flew. It looked like he was digging a hole.

"He's digging his way to the Black Sea," an old woman sniggered.

Lili László's legs flashed left and jerked right, making the Giant's torso look like an enormous fish caught in a line. She reared his massive rump skyward and then just as quickly sent it crashing to the earth. She did this twice, and then the third time, she flipped her feet under his body and the thighs went to work.

In *The Complete Book of Water Polo, With Pictures*, the Captain examines every muscle in the body: *"The gluteus maximus,"* he writes, *"is the strongest muscle in the body and covers a wide part of the buttock. It allows the thigh to extend, causing the leg to straighten at the hip when a person walks, runs, or climbs. It is used to raise the body from a sitting position."*

It is also used to toss enormous Hungarians over your head.

The sky opened and it began to rain, but the crowd remained, cheering as Lili thrust her ass forward and—for a split second—flipped Szeretlek over onto his stomach. She held him up with her feet, the way that children pretend to fly. Szeretlek's eyes held, staring into hers, and he thought he saw something inside of them that he already knew of the world, something long and low and pulling, but triggered only for the quickest second, like a slippery memory of a smell. Then Lili found the position she'd been looking for.

She winked.

Szeretlek saw the wink, and believed that the woman he loved loved him back. His body went limp as her knees sprang up. The Giant elevated only a few inches, landing directly behind her in a patch of spider-shaped crabgrass.

The crowd thundered appreciatively, then quickly scattered in the rain. Lili wiped her face and stood up. She picked a thorn from the side of her back and then grinned at the men.

They were forced to acknowledge the victory.

"Fine," they mumbled. "Go ahead and pick someone."

Lili finished brushing herself off, and then asked for the impossible: "I choose Árpád."

The men looked at each other. "Shit," they said, and one of them ran off to tell him.

Lili turned to Szeretlek and stuck out one hand, helping him up from the wet grass. "You okay?" she asked.

Standing up, Szeretlek was almost a full human taller than she was. He rubbed his lower back, fighting the hot hold of tears in his throat. He nodded.

Then Lili turned with the men and went to find Árpád.

The Giant watched them go. He wondered how or when he had misjudged the situation. He felt deeply wronged, but could not articulate the wrongness, and as he walked back to work, his sadness swelled to anger. His feet left heavy imprints in the mud, footprints deep as bowls, until he reached the Moving Rock Pile.

All of the rocks in the Moving Rock Pile were identical, and it was terribly difficult to pull them apart. Occasionally one rock would become separated from the others, and then the entire pile would go in search of its lost member. Without warning, the rocks would move, and if the Magyars weren't careful, if the Moving Rocks were not closely watched, a person could easily be trampled in the middle of the night. The Moving Rocks needed constant supervision, and since Szeretlek was the only one strong enough to carry the rock that fell away, he was usually the one to watch it.

This time, however, he did not take his place; instead, he reached down and grabbed one of the rocks. He yanked and tugged it, forcing it away from its brothers. Once separated, the rock turned in his hands, squirming in the unhappy manner in which only the Moving Rocks could squirm.

Szeretlek walked over to the embankment. He held the rock above his head and then he threw it into the river. He watched it sink beneath the surface. Then he sat down on the grass and waited for the ripples to begin. He knew that the rock would eventually move up out of the water because just as the pile would search for any lost rock, the rock would also search for its pile. The Moving Rocks moved slower than freshwater snails, but they could always be counted on to move, and in that hard moment, Szeretlek the Giant needed something he could count on.

XIV

A PROBLEM WITH INVENTORY

The following morning, I awake on the bus to a tickle aggravating the lower part of my thigh, reach down to scratch it, and am fairly surprised when a patch of skin the size of my palm peels off. I hold it up to window, examining the crisscross pattern that reflects back to me, and then reach for *Madame Chafouin*.

"*Déloyauté*," she says. "*Disloyalty. Treachery.*"

Outside, frigid April wind woos over the stiff grass, blowing the milkweed. A crow barks. The crickets have all dozed off. Marjorie taps the window with her splintered blade languidly, making the whole field look emptier somehow. Vacant.

I pick up *The Complete Book of Water Polo, With Pictures* and study the Captain's face. It could easily not have been him, I think. There are occasionally swimmers who go swimming in the Queeconococheecook. But the swimmers usually come in the summer months, and this has probably been the coldest spring on record. I open the book and read the first sentence: "*The body is a tight and efficient unit,*" the Captain writes, "*and it works together, not each part separately.*"

I do not feel like a tight and efficient unit. I am a messy conglomerate. Flotsam and jetsam. Bad art.

I close the book and look out to the gray, inimitable sky, to the trees that line the field like patient grownups, and feel an acute pang of loneliness. Which is fine. Anonymus writes, *"The peculiar intensity of the Hungarians' existence can perhaps be explained by their exceptional loneliness,"* and as the last remaining member of a species, I would imagine that it is Normal, now and again, to feel a sense of longing for one's lost brethren. I pick up Dr. Monica's business card from the windowsill, the one she gave me when we first met, and finger the sharp corners. I breathe it in, deeply. It used to smell faintly of Dr. Monica.

Now it just smells like everything else.

Mrs. Kipner peeps from inside the tin can. He hates the rain, and it was pouring all night. Whenever it rains, his antennae droop, and he is overcome with malaise. Sometimes he won't even lower his pucker for breakfast. I get up to slice off a piece of tomato, but when I pass the tin can I realize that he's not moving; both wings are hanging weirdly off the sides of his back, and the little white spots have spread to the middle. He's not even trying to fidget around to itch them anymore.

I reach in to touch him as if to say, "You all right, Bub?"

He snaps his good wing against his thorax. His antennae twirl.

I pick up the can to make sure he's just in a bad mood and not something else, but it slips from my hand, hitting the floor with a shiny pop and sending the beetle tumbling out onto the corrugated rubber flooring of the meat bus.

Confused, rolling on his back, his numerous legs pedaling the air, Mrs. Kipner rocks his shell until he manages to flip himself over. The legs spread out evenly beneath him and he immediately practices moving them one at a time, and then all at once. When he's determined that all of the legs are functioning in the manner which they should be functioning, he jumps up, alert, and darts to the far end of the bus, following one straight ridge of the corrugated rubber flooring, dodging crumpled Big M labels as he goes. He scuttles all the way down to the empty driver's seat, and for a second I worry that he might flee underneath the door of the bus and disappear into the weeds—but he doesn't. When he reaches the driver's seat, he turns around and races back, stopping at my feet, breathless and a bit bewildered. He looks east. He looks west.

Then he begins to hop.

I never imagined how Mrs. Kipner might move if given the opportunity, but I never expected this. He hops all around my feet, the bad wing hanging off him like a broken backpack. Dr. Monica once said that in order to fully recover, to recover in body *and* spirit, one must believe in something.

I looked at the gold cross, dangling out from her turtleneck sweater. *Like God?* I wrote.

She paused. "Something like God."

I watch Mrs. Kipner go hurtling down the corrugated rubber flooring and wonder if an insect can believe in God.

Mrs. Himmel is in a good mood today because she was given a warm loaf of zucchini-nut bread from a grateful mother and is slicing off thick pieces for everyone in the office. Everyone but me. Which is fine. I couldn't stomach it anyway. But there are other pleasant things going on: the rain has given way to a warm breeze, the Sick or Diseased children are tumbling in a corner, Adrian's manning the phones with her big, I-Climb-Mountains way, and Mrs. Himmel is working her gob on the bread. Things, you could say, are as good as they get.

And then they get better.

Dr. Monica unexpectedly walks into the Waiting Area. She walks over to Mrs. Himmel's desk and leans over. *Far* over. She's looking for a goddamn paperclip and in the meantime pointing her refined and shapely ass in my undeniable direction.

Sitting here, in these cheap and uncomfortable chairs, helplessly staring as though I can see right through the flimsy white polyester material of her pediatrician's jacket, as though I can see the run of her sturdy thighs wrapped snugly in their tan slacks from the curved anchor of her lower back all the way down to her thick, alluring kneecaps, there are moments I fear that I really *am* more Animal than Man; moments when I don't trust myself *not* to stand up and walk over and lift the tidy hem of her jacket to expose those devastating thighs. Creamy. Limber. Delectable Darling. *Ma Plus Grand Amour!* Do you not feel the pulse of my probing gaze? Do you not yet see me blowing you imaginary kisses? Do you not feel my hot breath traveling toward your milk-colored neck? Do you *really* want to know how to heal me? I can tell you that right now. There's only *one thing* I need to recover, and that is for you to dim the lights, walk over to the crusty little bearded man who at this very moment is sitting so patiently next to a wheezing Sick or Diseased child, lean down, place your tender, pudgy hands on the arms of his wooden chair, and kiss him wetly on the mouth. It would be just like in the movies. Kiss him, and his lungs would clear, his bad leg would fill with muscle. His eyes would blink and brighten. He would tear his stylish woolen cap from his head, toss his thick spectacles onto the Berber carpeting, throw one arm around your waist and bend you over and—

Dr. Monica finds her paperclip and stands up, professionally cinching the child's report.

"Make sure he gets plenty of water," she says to the mother. "You also might want to watch the way he walks. If he seems to be crossing his legs a lot, or tripping over his own feet, then schedule another appointment to bring him back in— Otherwise, he should be fine by morning."

The mother effuses her gratitude to Dr. Monica and then leaves, passing a tall, fat man wearing a baseball cap on his way inside. It's Herman. I lower my writing tablet and watch him make his way into the Waiting Area. He's holding a bulky paper bag with a grease stain on the bottom in one hand, and a stack of books in the other. The Sick or Diseased children stop what they're doing and stare up at him from the floor. He tries to wave at them, but it's a lot to manage. The books are slippery, and fall from his arms onto the Berber carpeting.

"Hello Herman," Dr. Monica says, and disappears around the corner to her office.

The security guard gathers the books, approaches Mrs. Himmel's desk, and dumps everything over it. He sighs like a deflating balloon. "Elise forgot her schoolbooks again," he says.

This, I am amazed to learn, is her husband.

Mrs. Himmel reaches into her mini-fridge, pops a can of Coke, and hands it to him. "I'm busy," she says. "You'll have to take them yourself."

Herman grabs the soda and drinks it. He belches, softly, licking the sugar from his wet lips. "What do you want me to do? Be late again? If I'm late for work again, they could let me go. They could let me go just like that." He snaps his fingers, but the sound is soft. Ineffective. Like he's trying to snap éclairs.

"Fine," Mrs. Himmel says. "I do everything anyway."

"Fine," says Herman. But he doesn't leave. He points to the greasy bag. "By the way, that's your lunch. You left it this morning."

Mrs. Himmel picks it up, lightly. "What is it?" she sniffs.

"Cheeseburgers."

"*Again?*"

Adrian approaches the reception desk and picks up her clipboard. She sees the fat man sloped to one side. "Hi Herman," she says, but she does not make eye contact.

Herman shifts his belt and clears his throat. "Why, hello Adrian," he says. He speaks to her with exaggerated politeness, as though good manners could somehow diminish his corpulence.

But Adrian is not impressed. She doesn't say anything else. She studies her clipboard, then walks into the center of the Waiting Area. The mothers all look up from their magazines.

"Mary Ellen," she announces.

One of the Sick or Diseased children stirs. She has a sour face and ears that stick out a bit too far from her head. She's wearing jeans with yellowed knees, sneakers tied with pink bows, and a pink halter top that says, in glittering rainbow letters, HOT FOR RECESS. The girl hears her name and runs behind a barrel of building logs. Her mother stands up and grabs her by the wrist. The girl instantly falls limp and heavy to the floor, rendering her body immobile.

"It's your *turn*, Mary Ellen," her mother says, pulling her up.

Mary Ellen reaches for one of the bulbous legs of the nearest chair, and misses it. She screams.

Adrian points at me. "You're up after this one," she says, and whisks Mary Ellen down the hallway.

I quickly look at Herman to see if he's noticed me, but he's still standing at the reception window.

Mrs. Himmel glares at him. "What's wrong with you?"

"Nothing," he says, but the baseball cap is pinching his head. He removes it, shovels the sweat from his forehead with one flat palm, and wipes it on the front of his shirt. It leaves a dying smear.

"Bull," says Mrs. Himmel. "What's going on?"

Herman shrugs. "There's just some trouble at work is all," he says.

His wife tightens in her chair. "What kind of trouble?"

"The numbers don't match up again."

"So?"

"So it's one of *my* sections."

"But that's not your fault," she says. "Somebody probably counted wrong. That's Inventory's problem, not yours. You're Security."

"That's what *I* said," he says. "I told them that. Besides, everyone knows that Inventory's never exactly right. Everyone's always saying that since the place is so big, it's hard to keep track of what goes in and out."

Mrs. Himmel throws a finger at him like a dart. "Just see you don't get fired again, Herman Himmel. Elise has a lot of modeling appointments lined up, and every week we have to get new clothes and new makeup. It's extremely expensive. We can barely afford it on what you make now, and I've already taken on extra hours here," she says. "I'm doing my part."

Herman's face softens. He rolls each of his large lips around the other. "I know that," he says. "I know you are, dear."

Mrs. Himmel visibly bristles at the term. "Just stay on top of it. Make *sure* that someone counted wrong. Go through the paperwork yourself if you have to."

"All right," he says.

Mrs. Himmel shakes her head and selects another piece of zucchini bread. Herman stares at the dessert with a long face. Intuitively, he slowly lifts a large paw over the counter, but he isn't fast enough—Mrs. Himmel slaps it.

"Herman!" she scolds. "Your diet!"

The security guard stands up. His lips quiver. "I shouldn't be the *only* one on a diet," he mumbles, then he marches out the front door of the Waiting Area. Mrs. Himmel picks up her purse and removes a small vanity mirror with a tortoiseshell clasp. She stares at her reflection as though it has somehow deceived her.

"Mr. Pfliegman," Adrian announces. "You're up. Let's go."

I slide out of my chair.

Adrian offers to take my coat. "Here," she says. "Let me."

I wrap my arms firmly around my body. I shake my head no, but she just looks puzzled. "It's really hot in here," she says. "C'mon, let me just—"

I try to protest, and hold on to the coat.

"Don't be ridiculous, Mr. Pfliegman," she says, and reaches around the back of my neck. She tries to yank it from my shoulders. "If you want to keep coming to see Dr. Monica, you have to hang up your coat like every-one else. You know that."

I grab on to the lapels and fiercely pull back, creating an unanticipated heavy movement from inside one of the pockets. In a panic, I try to hold on to it with an elbow, but it's no use:

A perfect, two-inch, dinner-sized sirloin, still wrapped in plastic, slides out from one of the pockets and falls expressionlessly to the floor. The label shines in the Waiting Area:

BIG M

I glance at Mrs. Himmel, but she's got her face in the mirror, and Adrian has been fortunately diverted by one of the Sick or Diseased children deject-edly plucking a near-dead leaf off the ficus plant.

"Leave the plant alone, Muriel!" she shouts.

The meat is safely returned to its pocket.

Adrian shuffles me down the hallway and opens the door to Dr. Monica's office. She points to the closet. "You have to hang up your coat in here, Mr. Pfliegman," she says. "Dr. Monica can't examine you otherwise."

She watches, curious, as I go to the closet and remove my coat. She watches me pull out of the sleeves and hang it up. I close the closet door, plunk myself down on the examining table, and then I look at her, expec-tantly.

Adrian stares at my sweatshirt. She's had a tough day; first Mary Ellen, and now Dr. Monica has instructed her to take Mr. Pfliegman's blood pressure. Taking my blood pressure means she must go near the greasy sweatshirt. Even worse, a fetid little forearm. She lightly touches the sweatshirt, and moves her hand to her nose. Her eyes water. She quickly spins around and goes over to the cabinet above the sink. She takes out a paper mask and wraps it around her face, then she pulls on two plastic gloves, like what she's about to touch is toxic. She picks up the coil to the blood pressure unit. "I don't know why *I* have to be the one to do this, anyway," she says.

Then Dr. Monica walks up behind her. "How's everything going in here?" she says.

Adrian wipes her eyes with one wrist. "I haven't had a chance to take the blood pressure yet. The sweatshirt—" she says.

Dr. Monica looks at her watch. "That's okay," she says. "I'll take care of it."

Adrian leans in and whispers into Dr. Monica's ear, something so inaudible I can barely make it out:

(He *stinks*.)

Dr. Monica waves her off. "Finish up your paperwork, then go. You've done enough today."

The intern looks relieved. She snaps off the plastic gloves and mask and ducks out of the office before Dr. Monica can change her mind.

Dr. Monica looks at me perched on her examining table. "Mr. Pfliegman," she says. "I think it would be a good idea to use the examining gown today, all right?" She hands me the blue gown, folded in a tight clean square. "Put this on. I'll be right back."

She leaves the room for a moment to give me time to change. When she returns, she's carrying a pile of fresh towels and a can of Lysol. "No offense," she says.

None taken, I write.

Dr. Monica wanders around the room, huffing Lysol into the air. She lingers at the coat closet, holding her finger on the nozzle, then without hesitation, without even any plastic gloves, my pediatrician walks back over to me, plunks down in the swivel chair, grabs my arm, and straps on the Velcro to the blood pressure apparatus. She smiles, pumping air into the strap, holding my scrawny arm until the strap tightens. Air hisses out. She watches the gauges, carefully, and then rips off the strap. "Terrific," she says, and grins.

I reach for my writing tablet.

You're in a good mood, I write.

Dr. Monica laughs. "I guess I am," she says.

She brings out my folder and scribbles in it. She takes a minute and reads, allowing me to observe the delicate way she picks hair from her eyes and tucks it behind her ears. She sighs. She lifts one of her pudgy, flour-colored hands and rubs the back of her neck with it—

St. Benevolus shivers, like a child in a church pew.

"I'd like to start with a throat massage today," she says. "Massaging the throat can help maximize the opportunity for speech. Watch me."

Dr. Monica moves her hands along the rigid run of her trachea.

"Hold your throat with both hands," she says. "Like you're holding a drinking glass," she says. "Practice moving it up and down. Then I want you to try and make a sound. Not just any sound, you're going to make the sound *Ooo*. Are you ready?"

My hands are at my throat. I nod.

"*Ooo*," she says. "Now you."

I hold my throat and open my mouth, but nothing happens. I reach down to the bottom of my gut and grasp for the sound, but it's like trying to find the lightswitch in a big dark room.

"*Ooo*," she says. "Do you understand? *Ooo*."

I understand that I want her to stop speaking and take off her white coat and peel off her flesh-colored slacks. I want her to sit next to me on the child-sized examining table and uncross her legs and blow on my eyes. But she just keeps *Oooing*.

"*Ahhh*," I say, dryly.

Dr. Monica smiles and marks the folder. "A good start," she says. "Now, let's do an S.R.E. This is a Sensory Response Examination."

What's that? I write.

"All of our bodies are like two halves sewn together at the middle. I'm going to touch both sides at once, and you need to let me know if anything feels imbalanced on either side, all right?"

I nod. Dr. Monica gets up and begins moving efficiently around the examining table, placing her hands on parallel parts of my body.

"Does this feel the same?" she asks, swiping two fingers down my neck. Behind the ears, over the eyes. "Does this feel the same? Does this? Does this?" She's making sure the symmetry is working properly, that my body is not entering into a civil war; that one side is not acting more aggressively that the other side.

She swipes her fingers twice lightly against my ankles, as sharp as little rocks. "That's good," she says. "I think you're recovering well, Mr. Pflieg-man. You're off all of those horrible meds, you're drinking enough water, your vitals are improving, and you're not coughing as much." She taps me on the knee with a finger. "You should be happy. You're looking good."

Looking good? I want to say. I'm barely human. I'm a hairy little Hun-garian pulp. An incongruous mass of skin and blood and hair. I am a sorry gathering of organs. That is all.

Dr. Monica keeps smiling at me, but then her eye catches something, and she starts blinking very quickly. "What the," she says, and swivels the chair close to me.

I look down. A piece of skin has lifted away from my elbow and is calmly peeling down one side of my forearm. It's not like the usual flaky business; this peel is long and white. It looks like a grocery list. She turns my arm left and right.

"That's odd," she says. "Have you been spending a lot of time in the sun or something?" she asks.

It's a stupid question. She doesn't wait for a stupid answer. Instead, she wheels over to the counter and fusses with some gauze pads and tweezers and bottles of ointment. She produces a small bucket underneath a sink. The lid says HUMAN WASTE. Dr. Monica places a blue cloth on a tray that is also on wheels, and then sets up a small buffet of treatments. She picks up the tweezers. "Open your mouth if this hurts, and I'll stop," she says. "Okay?"

I nod.

Dr. Monica pinches the top of the skin with the tweezers and begins slowly peeling, glancing up at my mouth the whole time for movement. Which is fine. It doesn't hurt. When she's finished, her eyebrows raise as she holds it up and examines it. She deposits it into the bucket. The lid closes all on its own.

"So what's this all about?" she says.

I don't know.

She studies my face.

I honestly don't.

"Tell me," she says. "When was the last time you had a bath?"

A few days ago?

"A few days, huh," says Dr. Monica. She clearly does not believe me. "Look, I don't mean to sound harsh, but this is serious, Mr. Pfliegman. You could have some kind of rash or skin disorder. This could be some kind of advanced eczema, pityriasis rosea. It could be a serious fungal or bacterial infection, and I have to say I find it difficult to believe that you've taken a bath or a shower in the last few days. You need to be honest with me if you expect me to be able to help you. I can't help you unless I know your health history, what your genetics are. Your parents. I need to know—"

I am being honest, I write.

Dr. Monica inspects the raw pink patch on my arm and then points to my thigh. She moves a piece of my gown, and her face softens. "Oh Mr. Pfliegman, look," she says. "Here's another one."

She picks up the tweezers and starts pulling off another long white strand, but this time the tweezers get too close, tugging the raw skin. I jerk my leg to one side.

"Does that hurt?" she asks.

I nod.

She puts down the tweezers and goes over to the sink. She runs a sponge under warm water, then slowly prods my skin with it. She moves with care and focus. She uses these sweet little stabbing motions as she cleans both places, then applies Bacitracin. "I'm going to prescribe you an antibiotic," she says. "In the meantime, is there any change in your regular routine that you can tell me about? Your eating habits?"

I shake my head.

"What are you eating these days?"

I point across the room, to my clothes. She walks over and picks up the trousers. She reaches into the pocket.

A dozen yellow Evermore wrappers scatter to the floor.

"Is this *all* you've been eating?"

I nod, and then my head goes swimmy. My limbs feel heavy, like I've been consciously holding them in their sockets all day. I slump back against the examining table. I lean on one elbow, and the air that travels in and out of my body suddenly sounds deep. Hollow. My lungs try to open their valves, but the valves are paralyzed. Everything goes purple—

"Mr. Pfliegman," says Dr. Monica. "Are you all right?"

I grab the edge of the examining table and try to bring the air in, gulping like a dying fish. The potato-shaped lumps on my head begin throbbing. It feels like they're growing—

"Water!" she shouts. "Get some water!"

I leap off the examining table and make for the sink, but the swivel chair is in the way. My toes crunch into the wood. I grab the tower of paper cups and send them spilling all over the counter, then reach for the faucet but my hand slips off the handle—my head hits the edge of the counter and I slide to the floor and begin shaking.

"Rovar!" cries Dr. Monica. She rushes out of the room.

Lying here, shuddering on the floor of a pediatrician's office, staring up at the ceiling, a rivulet of spit rolling over my beard, I think about certain dark moments when I consider ending the entire Pfliegman line sooner rather than later. Rather than hanging out in a broken bus for the next four or five dozen years, coughing one's guts out, waiting like an injured bird to sputter the final sputter, gasp the last gasp, and in one shallow, anticlimactic breath, die off, why not just take care of the whole thing right now? But there is one thing that I have in the world that keeps me from carrying it out. It's not the meat bus. It's not Mrs. Kipner or Marjorie, and it's not even Dr. Monica—

It's Isaac Asimov.

In *The Collapsing Universe*, the last book on my bookshelf, Asimov writes: "*It is the gravitation force, and only the gravitational force, that holds the universe together and dictates the motion of all its bodies. All the other forces are localized. Only the gravitational force, by far the weakest force of all, guides the destinies of the universe.*"

One morning, as I was sitting in my lawnchair outside the bus, the book fell out of the sky and landed squarely on the grass in front of me, inches from my feet. Startled, I leapt from my chair, but the meat customer in front of me did not jump or flinch. She picked up the book and read the cover. She looked at me and said, "God knows you done something terrible."

XV

NOVEMBER 22

When Dr. Monica returned to the office yesterday, she brought Adrian and Mrs. Himmel. Mrs. Himmel was holding an oxygen tank. The women all peered down at me. Dr. Monica had never witnessed a seizure before—I can't imagine that that sort of thing happens very often at her office. I can't imagine too many of the Sick or Diseased children turn purple and knock over furniture and spill themselves all over her nice clean floor.

I tried to stand up. "Really," I gestured. "I'm fine," but Dr. Monica pushed me back. She took the oxygen container from Mrs. Himmel and began strapping on the mask. I smiled up at her, grateful, and then looked at the receptionist, leaning on the doorjamb, her arms folded over her swollen, domesticated bosom—

"*Faker*," she mouthed.

It's pouring out. Only one customer has come to the meat bus. I'm about to roll up the awning and pack it in when someone pulls up in a rusty sedan and parks at the edge of the field. It's a housewife. She's been to the meat bus before, but she only comes when no one else is around. She crosses the wet grasses in the rain, dragging two pallid-looking boys behind her. They're soaked, and cling to her arms and legs as though someone is about to take them away from her. When she reaches my lawnchair, she unfolds a wet five-dollar bill from her purse and gives me a tired look. "What'll this get me?" she says.

Up close, her cheeks are heavy, laced with white pimples. Her hair is wrapped in a kerchief in the exact manner that Janka used to wear her own kerchief, cinched tight at the neck. I motion for the boys to stand under the awning, out of the rain, and then hustle inside the bus. I reach underneath a seat for the cardboard box holding the Carly Simon cassette tape, load it up with hamburger, four steaks, and two pork chops, and then lower it down from the window.

The housewife takes the box. "That's too much," she says. "The Big M would charge me sixty dollars for all that."

For second I think she might refuse it, but the boys grip her tight— She lifts up the bill, limp as a leaf. I take it, and she does not thank me.

Which is fine.

When things do not belong to you, it is so easy to give them away.

But then the woman looks into the box again. "Boys, go back to the car," she says. They shuffle off across the wet field obediently. The woman reaches in and holds up the Carly Simon. "Cain't eat this," she says, and hands me the tape. Then she holds up one of the domes of hamburger. Squeezed into the far right corner is a bright red label: BIG M.

I accidentally left it on.

The housewife steps out from under the awning, into the rain. She gives me an angry, bracing look. "Why don't a butcher cut his own meat," she says.

There happens to be a very specific reason why.

A few hundred years ago, on the island of Mauritius in the Indian Ocean, the Dodo bird had lost its ability to fly. It had lived undisturbed on the island for so long, eating the fruit that fell from the fruit trees, that there was simply no need. So when a Dutch penal colony invaded the island, bringing rats, pigs, and monkeys along with the convicts, the flightless Dodo was the first to go. On November 22, 1681, at 12:29 p.m., the last of the Dodo, sick and alone, lowered its curved beak, coughed pitifully, and then expired.

Go east to the United States, all the way to the eastern seaboard, and over to Martha's Vineyard. On November 22, 1932, the last remaining heath hen, a sickly looking, wood-colored bird that resembled the prairie chicken, stood on the beach at Aquinnas, the wind ruffling his feathers. He was looking for his friends, but there were no friends left. At 12:29 p.m., he stared out at the great blue expanse of ocean.

"*Gaw*," he said, morosely, and then fell over.

Also on November 22, at 12:29 p.m., a motorcade turned the corner of Dealey Plaza in Dallas, Texas, making an easy left-hand turn past a schoolbook depository. Seconds later, some other bloodsuckers winked at each other, cocked their rifles, and took aim at the motorcade. It was 1963.

That was another kind of extinction.

And then there's the boy. The skinny, obeisant boy. The apodictic age of ten. The morning of November 22, 1985, Ján enters his room and pulls him up from the cot with one arm. "Go get that thing you write on," he says, and hiccups.

János Pfliegman has decided that it's time to begin educating his son in the ways of meat. He brings the boy out to the barn, where he's lined up pictures on the outside wall, one for each of the animals: Cow, Sheep, Pig. Each picture is covered in lines that map the bodies into trapezoids of standard cuts of meat. The boy is supposed to be homeschooled. There was once even rumor of a social worker, but the social worker never came. At her own desultory, apathetic whim, Janka shows him letters and numbers, and every year she fills out a form for the school. She licks the envelope and mails it. "You'd get killed over there," she tells him, as though school is a distant, foreign war.

This morning Ján points to the butchering pictures and explains each of the trapezoids in long and slow syllables, occasionally tripping over the Hungarian like a crack in the sidewalk. He starts with the cow, gesturing to all of its parts, stern to bow: "This is the Round," he says, "and this is the Hind, Shank, Rump, Loin, Short Loin, Flank, Rib, Plate, and Brisket." He hiccups and points at the pig. "In the *diszno*, it's the Ham, Fat Back, Loin, *Szalonna*, Ribs, Plate, Boston Butt, Picnic, Jowl, and Foot." He gestures coolly to the lamb. "Now you."

The boy picks up his writing tablet. János watches him. His eyes squint. His face looks amused, but there is always the possibility for anger. The boy's throat feels tight; he can barely breathe for fear of getting it wrong.

He may as well be in a war, he thinks, and holds the pen steady. He writes *Leg*, and then *Rump, Loin, Rib, Breast, Shoulder, Shank.*

Ján checks his work. He's pleased. He even smiles a little. "That's good. That's right," he says, and kicks opens the door to the barn.

János Pfliegman sells his meat out of a small shop on Back Lick Road near the Queeconocheecook River—very near, in fact, to the field where I live now. The shop is a fragile mish-mash of boards and nails. Like a house made from a deck of cards, it is purely for display, and one month before János dies in a horrible car accident, the river will flood and drown it. The Queeconococheecook is a beautiful force, the lifepulse in this neck of Virginia, and wide masses of land will drown in the deluge. People will lose whole farms. Without Grandfather Ákos's assistance, the flimsy meat shop is Ján and Janka's only means of income, but the Queeconococheecook does not care about means of income; at the first mild pressure, the shop will collapse. The water will lift it up and deposit it in several incongruent pieces a few furlongs down the river, erasing any memory of their first and only commercial venture.

The shop is where the selling happens, but all the butchering, the beef/lamb/pork-chopping, always happens in the barn. Half of the barn is a regular, barn-like barn with splintery wooden rafters. Sheets of sunlight slide in through the cracks, and Ján keeps the pigs, cows, and sheep in this half. Today, using easy language and a gentle hand, Ján selects one of the pigs from its pen. He walks it though a narrow linking passageway which leads from the pens into a separate area. This part of the barn is floored with a peeling, floral linoleum. Iridescent track lighting hangs above in long, tragic bulbs. It *zuzzes* randomly. In the corner is a white box-shaped unit. Sensing that this barn-place is something very different than the other barn-place, the pig kicks its hooves outward and bucks up and screeches. The screeches are loud, as loud as the turkeys that roam the Virginia shrubbery in molting packs, but Ján says no one hears it. "Soundproofing," he says, and raps his knuckle against a wall of the white box. He assures the boy that the animal feels nothing. He fingers the metal knobs. "They're placed into the squeeze," he explains. "The squeeze holds them tight, forcing them to walk into the center of the white box. Cain't move that way," he says.

The boy stares at the white box. It looks like a refrigerator, turned on its side.

Is that a refrigerator? he writes.

"Carbon dioxide unit," says Ján. He turns the dial and flicks a switch and the large pig ambles into the box. From somewhere around the back, a generator kicks in. Vents start running. They only have to wait forty-five seconds.

Ján lifts the heavy lid.

Half of a pink tongue lolls at the chin, but the rest of it, the head and feet, the belly-mound, look normal. It looks like it's sleeping. On its face, a chilling, sordid grin. Ján reaches in, picks up the carcass, and holds it in his arms like firewood. "Start draining immediately," he says. "Right now the meat still has *élet*, the life, in it. Are you with me?"

The boy nods.

Ján places the carcass on the chopping block, then moves to the back corner, where a tall, three-legged structure nearly ten feet high is leaning. It looks like a gigantic tripod. The skeleton of a teepee. The legs are made of a creamy, pinking wood. Wood the color of white people. Nailed onto one of the legs is a handle and a reel. A thick strong wire runs up to the peak over which hangs a large and frightening hook.

"This," he says, "is the real secret. It's called a Coat Rack. You can't buy them in the United States. Clint Eastwood has one."

János Pfliegman beams at the prospect of sharing something with Clint Eastwood.

"You hook him to the wean, then crank the winch," he says, spinning the reel and handle. "You hang him on the Coat Rack, then you stick him. Pigs drain easier that way."

Ján removes his expensive Italian loafers. He brings out two pairs of rubber boots. The boy slides his feet in and the stale boot-air puffs out. His father goes back to the butcher block, and with both hands he carries the pig, upside-down, to the Coat Rack. The ears flop like fins over its eyes, covering the whole face except for the rubbery, can-shaped snout. The boy watches as his father cinches a rope around the feet, and hangs the pig from the hook. The little legs stick outward, straight as sticks. Upside-down, the convex belly spins.

"Crank him up," János says.

The boy grasps the winch and turns the handle. The body slowly rises. His father hands him a six-inch knife.

"Now stick him."

The boy closes his eyes and, with a lame thrust, he sticks the pig. Immediately the barn is filled with the rich odor of overripe fruit. He feels slightly nauseous and does not want to open his eyes. When he does, he sees blood spurting from the cut, ebbing in thick intervals.

"Thickening," his father says. "Another benefit of the carbon dioxide. You don't want blood going all over the place. Blood's oily. Stains. Hard to clean. This way it all lands on the dropcloth."

Ján unhooks the carcass and carries it back to the butcher block next to the white box. He gives the boy an apron and a small knife, looking at him with excitement, if not, the boy thinks, a little pride. "Hold on to that tool," he says. "Get used to the feel of it. I'll do most of the cutting today, and watch me do it. You can practice in a minute. I'll get you started on a smaller cut."

The boy watches his father cut the meat, explaining which meat-parts are which. He watches his father's fingers dance briskly around the meat and bone, making the job look easy. His hands fly over the animal quick and neat, like he was put on earth to do it. But as he works, the boy grows tired, so he glances over at the white box. The cold metal. He looks back at his father hunched over the meat, working the offal, and then with both hands, he lifts the heavy lid to find another life extinct.

One of Janka's glass jars, full of cloudy, pickled water, is tucked into the far corner. The masking tape long ago faded, but the boy leans in and reads the label: *Hal.* (Fish.) He looks closer at the jar and makes out something that looks like a fish floating heavily inside it. The body of the fish is narrow, small and blue, with a larger head. The skin, furred from the pickling, seems to hover around its own body. The boy wonders what it's doing there; why Ján keeps it in the white box. He lifts the lid all the way up and light shines in. He notices a face: thin openings of what look like mouth and nose. Two large round eyes, gray in the water. The boy knows that the hal is dead, but there is also something about it that is living. He stares at the eyes and swallows nothing down his throat. He tries to figure out how to feel. He wants to know why the fish is there, but he also knows that looking at the fish makes him sick, so instead he looks at János Pfliegman, at his father's hands flipping the meat parts—tossing the leaf fat, the cracklings—and then he turns and vomits all over the peeling, floral linoleum.

"Useless!" Ján yells. "*Szanálmas idióta!* Close that lid and get over here."
He tosses a piece of meat on the block. "You cut the meat now."

A lump grows in the boy's throat. He coughs, but the coughing does
not relieve it; it feels like his lumpy head, and then he feels horribly lumpy
everywhere. He does not know which is worse, to cry or be sick. He bites
his cheeks.

"*Cut it!*" his father shouts, and whacks him on the head with a fist.

The boy doesn't move.

So Ján jumps over and forces the knife into his hand. He squeezes,
hard.

The boy looks at the white of his father's hands, wrestling, and then
with his little teeth, teeth as sharp as lemon seeds, he bites them. He runs
out of the barn, into the horsefields. He stays away for two days, hiding in
the long grasses. He doesn't eat. He doesn't drink. Which is fine. As long
as he never has to cut another piece of meat again.

(Which, as it turns out, he doesn't have to.)

When he returns to the farmhouse early on the third morning, the
kitchen light is on. He peeks in the window, and sees both of them inside.
They are sitting hunched over the table by the stove, not moving or speaking or eating. They do not look up when he walks in.

"Where *you* been," Ján says.

The boy reaches behind his back and holds up Grandfather Ákos's
violin.

His father begins laughing. It is a wild laugh. Unleashed. He bolts
from the table and runs out to the front porch, where the laughing turns
to violent sobs—

The boy looks at his mother, her own eyes dry as bones.

"It's too late," Janka says. "He's dead."

XVI

TROUBLE IN PARADISE

Tonight, after all the meat has been sold, I settle into my Reading Center, put on the Bach cassette, and the fugues begin trickling. It's cold, with a soft, unremarkable rain outside, but the inside of the bus is snug. Mrs. Kipner hops out of his tin can and lands on my bed. His bad eye is still white and low, but the good eye is healthy as ever, black and shining. The rest of his body is healthier too: the white spots have almost completely vanished, and he's slimmed down considerably. Now he hops in and out of the tin can with no trouble at all.

I unwrap an Evermore and leisurely pick up *Your First Hamster*. The small, apricot-colored hamster looks at me in a mischievous manner.

"Oh *you*," I want to say.

It's a cozy scene, everything as it should be, until a fat drop of water splashes onto my blanket. I look up.

The diamond-shaped crack in the ceiling has gotten bigger. I'm certain of it. It looks like the entire panel needs to be patched, if not replaced. Come fall, I'm thinking of redecorating. Nothing like the busses in *This Bus Is Your Home*, with the chrome wheels, fresh paint, full-size beds, and abundant electronic devices, but I can imagine a few small but meaningful improvements: perhaps a new burner for the stove, a lamp for my Reading Center. I look at the corrugated rubber flooring and wonder if I could get away with a primal sort of carpeting—

Then two headlights appear across the field.

Cars very rarely drive on Back Lick Road at night, so I turn off the lightbulb and the tape-radio, and climb on top of one of the seats. I peer out the window. The car pulls itself slowly along the road, crunching pebbles with its enormous tires, shuddering to a stop at the edge of my field. Wide beams illuminate the grasses. Moths hurtle toward the lights as though drugged. Three men spill out, hoisting a fresh sign out of the backseat.

They produce mallets.

When they've finished pounding the sign, I think they're about to get back in and drive off like usual, but instead they turn toward the bus and start crossing the field. The headlights throw long shadows and their enormous chins swell. They're all wearing the same dark suits and carry important-looking manila folders in their hands. They curse in the distance. Their trousers are soaking wet, they complain, from all the rain.

I crouch down at the back of the bus.

"*Hsss*," rattles Mrs. Kipner.

Seconds later, they bang on the door that isn't really a door. It doesn't lock, but you've got to pull the lever from the driver's seat to make it open. The Subdivisionists don't know this.

"Mr. Pfliegman! May we speak with you?"

"Jesus, this is creepy," another whispers.

"Who *lives* like this?"

If only other Pfliegmans were here. Hair and teeth falling out, eyes squinting. They would quietly encircle these men. They would kidnap them and drag them behind the bus and, axes raised—

"Mr. Pfliegman, we have a document for you, and we think you should read it."

Something is wedged beneath the door of the bus.

I hold on to the floor, cold and wet, with my palms. Next to me are two cardboard boxes, one of which contains hundreds of crumpled up, gum-size Big M labels. The other contains the Carly Simon cassette tape. The picture on the tape is a woman with long blond hair that hangs away from her face as if freshly blown. A large, terrifying mouth. Looking at her, a sharp pain appears on one side of my abdomen. My lungs compress and my throat scratches and it's everything I can do to keep from coughing.

Helpless, I emit a suffocated sound:

"."

The Subdivisionists don't notice. I could be a squirrel, perhaps. A chipmunk. I could be a dying bird.

"It has to do with your bus, Mr. Pfliegman," one of them says. "We know you're in here. We really think you should speak with us."

"Before this becomes a matter for the *authorities*," says another.

They all murmur favorably at the word.

I hold my breath to keep from involuntarily speaking again, reach into another cardboard box and pull out one of Grandfather Ákos's coats. I bite the wooly sleeve.

The Subdivisionists, meanwhile, are negotiating whether they should throw themselves against the door of the bus—it might bend like a fan, they reason—but on better judgment decide against it on the chance that it could, in some unbelievable court, be considered Breaking and Entering. One of them bangs the door. "You'd better read that document, Mr. Pfliegman," he says. "As far as we're concerned, you're trespassing."

"I'm telling you," another says. "He's not here." He kicks the side of the bus for proof. "All right?"

"All right, let's do it."

In three deliberate ticks, the Subdivisionists turn on their flashlights. One remains at the door, shining the beam into the windows. The light reaches into the interior of the bus, illuminating the corrugated rubber flooring—

I scurry underneath my mattress.

The Subdivisionists split off and move down both sides of the bus, the beams of their flashlights dancing around the windows, and then, without warning, one of them slams his mallet into one side of the bus. It sounds like a shotgun. I start to jump up, but catch myself in time. I listen as they move to the front and smash the snout, the headlights. They even attack the grill, stomping on the bumper. It groans like a harpooned whale. They jump up to bust the windows, climbing on the tires, until one of them accidentally slips and falls.

"It's glass," he cries. "He's got glass out here!"

One of the Subdivisionists has found the Frog Pond. He tries to walk off the mirror, but it's wet and he slips again, this time twisting his ankle.

"Help me up!" he cries.

But another Subdivisionist's leg is tangled in a long piece of grass, and can't move. "What the——" he says, and tugs and curses.

From the tousle with Richie Bis, Marjorie's blade is sharp, a fresh edge. It coolly slices him across both hands.

"The fricking thing just cut me!"

I try to lift the handle to the Emergency Exit, but it's too heavy, or it's stuck, rusted to the metal, so I throw open a window and start hurling things at them. Anything I can find. I hurl the boots without laces, the stained coffee carafe, the pots and pans. I sweep my arms under a seat and discover the stale loaf of bread given to me by the well-meaning Virginian. Out it goes, soaring blindly in the dark and punching a Subdivisionist clean across one side of his large chin.

"Run!" he cries. "Back to the car!"

His partners untangle themselves and follow, tripping over each other. I grope under a seat and grab the brand-new towel rack, still in its original packaging—I tear off the plastic with my teeth and pull it like a sword from a sheath. It's silver in the light, glowing like a thing that realizes it's about to become of use. I move quickly toward the front of the bus, tripping on the tails of the coat, waving my sword, pull open the lever to the door, and burst out of the bus. But the Subdivisionists have already cleared the field and are piling into the sport utility vehicle.

I quickly limp toward them. A Pfliegman in the night—

"Drive!" they shout. "Drive!" They slam the doors, spin their huge tires, and take off down Back Lick Road, but not before turning their head-lights upon a little man in an old wool coat, kicking up his heels, holding a cold, stale loaf of bread up in the air like it's a winning trophy.

XVII
EVOLUTION OF THE PFLIEGMANS:
LOSING LILI LÁSZLÓ

During the settling of Hungary and the unsettling of every other nearby established European nation, everyone pretty much ate the same two things: meat and *ját*. Ját was a tough, fist-size ball of hard dough the color and consistency of chalk which we gnawed on. Which we tried to swallow whole and choked on. The eating of ját was an hourlong, teeth-aching endeavor, but it was all we had. Because of the unsympathetic weather, everyone always had colds, or were catching colds from stealing and gnawing on other people's ját. Sometimes, if there was not enough meat, porridge was made for the women and children, but the porridge was only ját broken into bits and boiled in water. To break a piece of ját, you had to take your axe to it, or throw it hard against a stone wall, cracking it into a dozen splintered pieces. Ját makes an obnoxious sound when hurled against a stone wall, which is how it got its name. *"These were days,"* Anonymus explains, *"when the linguistics of people in the rural regions were heavily influenced by onomatopoeia."*

Of love with fat ladies, of tidy, gruesome deaths, of bread so warm it could not be sliced, only pulled, the bread was the worst of Árpád's desires. It was the one thing he could not have. Every morning, the Grand Prince awoke to the sound of ját smacking the stones, so you might also say that aside from fleeing Pechenegs, it was for the want of thick, brown loaves of steaming bread that the kingdoms of Europe suffered Hungarian incursions for the next fifty years.

Árpád was merely a man desperate for his carbohydrates.

But now, here, on the eve of the Great Leg Wrestling Match, Lili arrived at his tent, and he beckoned her inside. He offered her a plate piled with ját.

Lili stared at the plate distastefully. She had been expecting a fair amount of pomp: exotic rugs carpeting the dirt floor, canopies of fur decorated with prized collectibles. She had seen the Grand Prince riding his great white horse around camp, and knew that he wore brilliant armor, heart-shaped across his chest. Around his helmet, the wings of the turul bird gleamed. She also knew that the leader of the Hungarian tribes ate better than anyone, so needless to say, the tent was a significant disappointment. Árpád's armor was flung messily into a corner. Two Persian rugs his men had stolen off a German merchant were rolled tight, lying like logs across the center walking area. Dogs had pissed on the rugs, filling the tent with an acrid, sour odor that seemed to linger on everything. Cracked jugs of grain alcohol lay emptied on their sides, fruit flies danced above a bowl of sweetened figs, and various flags stolen from various armies, moist from the wet country, were folded and stacked, gathering the slow, dark mold that would eventually consume them.

She picked up a clammy ball of ját and scowled. "This sucks," she said.

Árpád just grinned and lay a burlap bag down next to the rugs. He began unbuckling his outfit that once, to Lili, had looked fine and regal, and now appeared depressingly quotidian. He tossed his helmet onto a small table littered with stale shards of ját. "I don't like the crusts," he said.

Then he stripped to nothing. With his armor removed, his already small girth halved. His skin was surprisingly thin and hairless, like a sheared rabbit. His tiny body shook from the cold, and he reached for her to warm it.

Lili demurred. Although she always won the leg-wrestling contests, when it came to men she was really quite flawed. She tried many of them, like a naturalist who examines many specimens of a species to better understand the general whole. It never worked out. She sighed and removed everything but her laced boots, which frankly weren't worth the effort, and lay her fleshy body across the burlap.

Árpád jumped eagerly upon her, as though a child upon a featherbed.

In seconds, it was over. Lili barely felt a thing. It was a lesson, she decided, an important lesson about greatness and fame.

The Grand Prince rolled over onto his side and grabbed the bowl of rancid figs: "*Füge?*" he offered.

"No thanks," she said.

Árpád shrugged and popped three into his mouth. He chewed with his mouth open. A bit of moist fig flew from his tongue and stuck to his mustache. "Come again tomorrow," he said, his mouth full.

Lili shuddered. "I don't know," she said. "Maybe." She sat up and began dressing.

Árpád's forehead crumpled. "But I'm the *leader*," he said. "You *wanted* me."

Lili kept buttoning her cloak.

Árpád sat up quickly. "I'll give you anything you want," he said, and tried massaging her thick shoulders. He pecked her neck with figgy kisses. He reached over and began unbuttoning what she was buttoning. "What do you want?" he asked. "You name it. It's yours." He turned one of the buttons in his fingers.

Lili looked at him. "Anything?"

And so, over the following year, really out of nothing better than good old-fashioned pre-medieval ennui, Lili became Árpád's mistress. Árpád adored her. His own Tribal Mate for Life was a thin and delicate woman who became annoyed with him if he stroked her with a finger. He felt a kind of freedom with Lili that he had never experienced, and he greatly anticipated her visits. He would sit impatiently in his tent, lifting the flap every few seconds to see if she had arrived, and when her figure came lumbering around the corner, he quivered with want: "Love Button!" he cried.

"I'm starving," said Lili.

Árpád began ordering special food for her, and fussed over the particulars of the meals. When she came to his tent, they would engage in their lovemaking and then gorge themselves on fresh figs and deerfat. Then they would move on to a veritable buffet of spiced meats and stews, and finish with sour apples drizzled with creamy honey. Lili grew plump and cheerful. The Grand Prince wrapped his arms around her—he loved how they could not quite fit *all* the way around—and was most pleased.

"You make me very, *very* happy," he said, glowing.

"Sure, whatever. Me too," she said.

Of course, Lili was far less satisfied with Árpád. One night, again be-mused by what passed for sexual prowess, she yawned and stepped outside for a pee. A large man was lying on the ground next to the tent, curled into a huge ball, weeping.

It was the Giant. After losing the wrestling match, it proved too dif-ficult to return to work and put himself to use; he felt abandoned by Lili, by the men who had recruited him to wrestle, and was now soaked with loneliness. To want to be a part of a community that does not want you back was a savage, unsettling feeling.

Lili looked at him, and was stirred with pity. She squatted down and stroked one of his large ears. "I won the match," she whispered. "Now *you* shall win."

"If I can be of *use*," he said, miserably, and rolled onto his enormous back.

Lili climbed upon him and, bungling, was surprised at how well they fit together. His large parts fit evenly around her smaller parts. Her smaller parts fit neatly inside his large parts. Moving slowly, in a thick, strong tum-ble, Lili saw something flicker in his eyes, something similar to the flash of recognition that Szeretlek had seen when they first wrestled. It lasted only for as long as one might snap a finger or clear their nasal passages, but there it was. Lili was surprised to find herself in love with the Giant.

"*Szeretlek*," she said softly.

"That's my name," he said.

Weeks passed, and Lili's visits to Árpád became more and more infrequent. If she came, she would appear bored and uninterested. She nibbled listlessly on whatever foods he had prepared, and then laid herself down on the bur-lap and went to sleep. Once he ordered up an entire ham for her, and seven days and nights went by without a word. The ham sat, cold and rubbery, on his table until Árpád finally threw it to the dogs. They devoured it in a greedy, snarling mass. Árpád leapt from the table in his messy tent and began hurling plates and kicking the dogs with his bare feet.

"Love is a sharp-edged triangle!" he shouted. "A sharp-edged triangle is the head of a spear!"

He grabbed his sword and went looking for the slut.

In minutes, he had gathered together a search party. Árpád still rode M, though the horse was older now, and every few miles the party had to stop so M could rest. While they were stopped, Árpád wandered around camp, throwing back the flaps to every tent he could find, asking if anyone knew where to find the Woman with Enormous Thighs. Most of the Hungarians had never actually met the Grand Prince, and had only heard wildly embellished stories about the success of his incursions, east and west. The Árpád they imagined was a large and domineering man with clear, agnostic eyes, a thunderous voice, and many large and discernable pectoral muscles. When they met him face-to-face, no one believed that he was actually the Grand Prince at all. They stared at the tiny man in front of them with his dragging cloaks, his bird-helmet hanging low over his eyes, his sword looking as though it anchored his legs to the ground. They covered their mouths with their hands and begged, "You're *who*?"

At which point Árpád stiffened, shifting the sword around his belt. "I'm *Árpád. Great and noble.*"

And then they burst out laughing.

A long month went by, and eventually Árpád's own men became amused that he couldn't find the woman he was looking for. Especially such a *large* woman. "Maybe she's hiding in this," they said, laughing behind his back, holding up the horses' tails. One afternoon Árpád heard their laughing, dismounted M, and walked quickly over to the men. He grabbed the one who had been laughing the loudest by the foot, and in one clean motion, pulled him from his horse and swiftly dangled a sword above his trembling body.

"Do you desire to be cut in half?" Árpád cried.

The Hungarian shook his head vigorously.

"Do you desire to be exposed to hopeless situations?"

The man started to cry.

Árpád pointed his sword at the other men. "And what about *you*?" he shouted.

They put up their hands. They bit their lips.

Árpád replaced his sword on his belt. "Wait here," he said, and then, to give old M a rest, the Grand Prince left on foot. He walked through an orchard, collecting hard little apples and eating them as he went. Along the way, he thought a good deal about his current life-position. Despite the fact that under his leadership the Hungarians had managed to instill fear into the heart of every good and civilized member of Christian society, not all that much had changed for Árpád personally in the thirty years since he had led his people into Carpathia. His voice had not changed; the Pechenegs were still hunting Magyar for sport; the Gyepü still needing looking after. He was still gnawing ját every morning for breakfast, and now this—his fat, delicious Lili had abandoned him. He was in an exceedingly bad mood. "Muther-loving—" he grumbled, kicking pebbles as he walked. "Stupid, pooping idiots."

Suddenly the ground changed beneath his boots. The long soft green grasses became mud. Árpád took a few more steps. It began to rain. Baffled, he looked up. He was still in the region of the Hungarian camps—only seconds ago the sky had been clear. Back over the valley, through the apple trees, the sun was still shining. He twisted his mustache thoughtfully, staring at the sprawl of the sky, marveling how the dark cloud had spread over the hills. How it only seemed to cover this one particular region. Then it really started coming down.

Árpád spotted a large, poorly assembled tent, and quickly ran over.

The grass that surrounded the tent had long ago browned. For all this rain, he wondered why there were no visible gardens. There were no designated fields around the camp for animal husbandry. The only animal around for miles was a lone cow standing next to the tent, so thin you could see its scalloped ribs; so morose it didn't even look up when he approached. The Grand Prince hung back, nervously. He wondered if he had accidentally stumbled upon a crew of Pechenegs who would no doubt be pleased as punch to slaughter the leader of the Hungarians in a manner most unsavory, when a flap of the tent turned, and a dozen children scurried outside. The children saw him and halted in the rain, staring wide-eyed at his regal garments. When they understood that he would make no move against them, they splashed in the mud around his feet, and then spontaneously sprinted across the open plain.

These children were not like Normal Hungarian Children, with fat limbs, the ones who helped their parents carry water and feed the animals. Who played games in the grasses on warm days. These children were *filthy*, with black, bowl-shaped eyes. Dusty skin. Clothes hung in shreds from their arms, and many of them appeared to have some kind of notable disability or disfigurement. They limped and coughed as they ran, and their heads were atypically large, tipping side-to-side on their shoulders. They were all chasing one of the smallest children, a boy. The boy had a bad leg, and although he was clearly doing his best to escape from the others, they gained quickly and easily upon him.

As the boy hurtled himself towards the forest, it looked to Árpád as though a piece of skin had come loose from his body. It flapped over his arm, like a flag in the wind, and when the children finally caught him, he let out a helpless squeal.

"Sacrifice!" they chanted. *"Enni Hús! Enni Hús!"*

The broken boy was lifted into the air by the others and became disoriented. His eyes rolled to the back of his head and his tongue lolled out, and they carried him thus, vanishing into the forest. Árpád was familiar with gypsies. Gypsies cast spells on people and wooed them with handkerchiefs, gold chains, and other sorts of suspicious hardware. But these were not gypsies. These were—he didn't know *what* they were.

He took a deep breath, held firmly on to his sword, and entered the tent.

XVIII

TWENTY-FOUR HOURS

The following morning, I awake to find a small woman standing at the foot of my bed. She's of an indistinguishable age, wearing a brown tweed suit with both front jacket buttons neatly cinched. Her hair is tied back as far as it will go, pulling smooth the wrinkles in her skin. Her lips purse together in a dry smooch. Eyeglasses fill her face.

"Bonjour Rovar," she says archly.

She's standing in high heels pressed together at the ankle, holding the dictionary in one hand, a long stick that serves as a pointer in the other. It's Madame Chafouin.

"Get up," she says, and slaps her pointer.

I scramble out of bed.

"*Distraire*," she recites. "*To be disturbed. To amuse oneself,*" and then lowers her pointer.

Draped across the corrugated rubber flooring is a long piece of cloth or fabric—perhaps something the Indian dropped from his bag of textiles ages and ages ago? But when I look closer, I realize it's not cloth at all— It's skin. *My* skin. I take off my clothes and begin searching. Although I find the usual flakes, the smaller peels, I find nothing that resembles this pelt, this shedded towel of epidermis.

Madame Chafouin is polite. She averts her eyes. She reaches into her
blazer for a cigarette and lights it, inhaling in experienced, body-deep
breaths, then picks up *The Complete Book of Water Polo, With Pictures*. She
studies the greasy men on the cover, tracing their bare muscles with the
tips of her fingernails. "*Débauche*," she whispers. She continues smoking
and fiddles with the taperadio, but as she does, an inch of ash slips from
her cigarette. It falls lightly onto the corrugated rubber flooring and lands
directly on Mrs. Kipner, who's been lingering about her ankles. The ash
spreads all over his head, his wings and thorax. Confused, he makes a series
of unhappy clicking sounds. He starts flipping his wings like crazy, trying
to shake the ash from his body, and accidentally tosses himself upon Madame Chafouin's foot—

"*Déblatérer!*" she shrieks. She kicks the beetle from her foot and crawls
onto the mattress, cursing in words I haven't learned yet.

Mrs. Kipner soars to the front of the bus, landing backside-first on
a passengers seat. His legs jerk and scramble like fingers on a keyboard.
I capture him and wipe him off with a sleeve of the Disneyland sweatshirt,
but his antennae thrash, menacingly. I look in the meat refrigerator to
give him a tomato as a peace offering, but we're out, so instead I cull a
few droppings of congealed grease off the sink and scrape it on the edge
of the tin can.

Pleased, the large beetle sniffs the air and then expertly flutters up from
my palm, like a small hovercraft, to his perch. He forks the fat with his
mandibles and then disappears inside his can to eat.

I return to Madame Chafouin and pick the long peel of skin off the
floor.

She wrinkles her nose at it.

I take it outside to dump it, and then I get a good look at the bus. The
Subdivisionists really did a number on it. Dents pock the sides like acne,
but that's not all: the grill is bent, the bumper slants to one side, a headlight
in the snout is busted, the chalkboard has fallen face down on the grass, and
the signs, once piled neatly under the carriage, now erupt from both sides,
disturbed by whatever sleeps underneath them at night. From all this rain,
the tires are swallowed half-deep in mud, forcing the entire bus to lean
precipitously close toward the river. Everything, even the windows all look
crooked, all pointing in the direction of the Queeconococheecook—

Madame Chafouin walks to the door of the bus and squats down on the steps. She lights another cigarette. "*Décloîtrer*," she says. "*To leave the cloister. To return to the world*," and then shifts her rump. She's sitting on the letter from the Subdivisionists, wedged beneath the door last night. Balancing the cigarette between her lips, she neatly slices it open with one fingernail. She spits a fleck of ash to one side and reads aloud in clumsy English: "*Final acquisition of all land and buildings and/or Other Properties marked Property of Subdivisions LLC, will occur in twenty-four hours. Any buildings and/or Other Properties not moved in twenty-four hours will be transferred in ownership to Subdivisions LLC.*"

A funny itch suddenly tickles a spot directly between my shoulder-blades. I reach around to scratch it, and that's when I feel it— Quickly, I hoist up the Frog Pond, leaning it against one side of the meat bus. I turn around.

A long pink stripe of raw skin is running clean down the center of my back. I look mowed.

Madame Chafouin appears in the mirror behind me. "*Dépouiller*," she says, and clucks her tongue. "*To strip, to skin.*"

But when I turn around to agree with her, all that remains is the lingering smoke from her cigarette. She's gone. The smoke hangs briefly in the air and then vanishes. A cloud passing into another cloud.

I once read that most people are afraid to live alone because to live alone means to die alone. They have visions of themselves eating their breakfast, enjoying the dripping sluice of a ripe plum, and then suddenly the lights go out and they fall face-first into their pancakes. People, it seems, are less afraid of loneliness than worrying about what other people will think when they're found in some unappealing, disintegrating state, tongue out, one leg curled underneath the other, internal fluids in a puddle on the floor, etcetera. Most people are afraid that if left alone, they will not be *found*.

Being found is apparently of the utmost importance to people.

XIX
EVOLUTION OF THE PFLIEGMANS:
FINDING, AND THEN AGAIN LOSING, LILI LÁSZLÓ

Crouching, Árpád entered the tent. A dozen pairs of eyes blinked and looked up. There was barely room on the dirt floor to walk, and the ceiling was so low Árpád had to squat to move anywhere. He had never seen so many living beings occupy such a small space. The creatures that stared back at him had big, thick knees, spindly arms. Hair so matted it looked glued to their heads. The straw sleeping mats were shredded or torn; there were no tables and certainly no chairs for anyone to sit on, and as a consequence all of the creatures were lying on their backs, holding their ankles, grunting. Worst of all, Árpád noted, was the stink of the place. There were no dried-meats hanging from the dried-meat-poles, but the smell of blood hung in the air like its own, animal perfume. A little fire glowed in the hearth, over which a stew boiled, filling the place with a rancid, oppressive stench. The air flap at the top of the tent wasn't open, and so upon entry, the foul smoke seemed to grab his throat and squeeze. When the creatures saw him, they hooted, then quickly went back to chewing their feet. One of them ripped off an entire toenail with his mouth, hobbled over to the kettle and spit it in the stew.

Árpád shuddered. "Who is the leader among you?" he cried.

One of them, a sunken male, cackled. He crept over to Árpád and touched his fine cloaks, and the others quickly followed. Their hands were stained. Fingernails caked in black circles of dried blood. They stroked him with their waving fingers, pressing his cloaks against their muddy cheeks, but they did not appear dangerous. When he elbowed them off, they scattered off, whimpering. When he accidentally clocked one of them on the head, the creature fell on the floor and farted loudly.

A wave of snickering trickled through the tent.

Then Árpád noticed an old woman sitting on the hearth by the fire. She was watching him with one eye, nursing the stew with the other. It was the same woman who had handled the watery delivery of Szeretlek, the one who bit down on Aranka's nose to save the child's life. Thirty years had traveled through Kinga's body at the speed of three whole lifetimes. Most of her hair had fallen out; what remained on her scalp was just a coarse, gray halo. She had spent so much of her life squatting in the tent that her back had settled crooked; it rose up and arched behind her neck. Her skin clung desperately to her face, and her eyes were swollen from the burn of perpetual smoke. When she noticed Árpád staring at her, she unfurled her long and sinewy tongue, and pointed it right at him.

"You there!" he cried.

The old woman hissed.

The noise sent shivers through Árpád's entire body. "I can feel my own bones," he thought. "Just to look at her makes one feel dead." Were it not for his desperation to find Lili, he would have grabbed the woman, tossed her out of the tent, and, in a fury fueled by the resentment of the mere existence of these hopeless faces, smashed the entire place to pieces— Instead, he grabbed her by the shoulders and shook her.

"Who *are* you?"

Kinga giggled, her tongue hanging sloppily out of her mouth. She smiled large in Árpád's face. Her teeth were splintered and her breath smelled orange. Wormy. Árpád felt his throat tighten with nausea, and he immediately dropped her. Kinga slapped one of us on the head to make a space for him on the hearth.

The creature squealed, disappearing into the writhing mass.

Árpád sat down, closing his eyes to ease the sickness. When he opened them, the woman was looking at him with a peculiar expression. She reached one of her bony hands all the way into her mouth, to the back of her throat, and then, as though picking out a stubborn grain of food, she removed an entire, bi-pronged tooth.

She held it out to him.

The Grand Prince's mustache quivered. But he took the tooth and held it between two fingers.

Kinga gestured for him to drop it into the stew.

Not knowing what else to do, Árpád held his breath and dropped it in. This woman, he realized, was a *táltos*. A shaman. A being embodying both the real and the unreal, the body and the spirit. The dead and the undead. He watched as she pulled back a sleeve of her cloak and stuck one of her bare arms into the stew. Amazingly, it appeared to give her no pain, and after a few minutes of slow stirring, she found the tooth. With a dripping arm, she examined it. "You are a *big* and *important* person," she said, and swatted him playfully on the knee.

Árpád scowled. He did not like being touched by this woman. He was about to leave when she grabbed his cloak. "You're looking for someone," she said.

He sat back down. "I am."

"A girl."

Árpád gasped. "Do you know where she is?"

Kinga laughed so hard that she began to cough. The cough growled through her body, reaching elbow-deep as if to clean it. A marble of spit flew from her mouth, staining the front of Árpád's cloak like birdshit.

He grimaced.

"You are a good leader," she said, wiping her mouth. "For the most part, you are very good, and very kind." Light flickered across her face. "But you have forgotten some of your people."

Árpád was surprised. "Who?" he said. "Who have I forgotten?"

Kinga waved her hand around the tent. Árpád followed the hand to the hundreds of faces blinking back at him. The worst sorts of faces, with flaked skin and buttery hair—but it was the eyes which were the most difficult to look at: big and black. When they were upon you, it was impossible to tell what expression they meant to convey. Suddenly it came to him. Árpád remembered who these people were. "You're the Fekete-Szem," he said brightly. "The meat-cutters. The butchers."

When Árpád said "butchers," a rumble of disapproval grew in the tent.

"There is a *little* more to us than that," said Kinga. She removed the ladle from the soup and licked it. She held it out to Árpád, intimating that he should have a taste.

Árpád held up one hand. "No," he said. "*Please* no."

Kinga grinned a mouthful of yellow, splintered teeth. She gagged as she spoke, her tongue slipping out of her mouth. "We were there," she said, "when you led your people away from the land-mongering Pechenegs and into Carpathia; we were there when you became the leader of an entire nation, when your armies went out on the first barbaric raids. By designating us as the meat cutters, the official butchers of your new community, you have saved us from expulsion and certain death, it's true—but then you abandoned us. Despite our new trade, we still live here, on the outskirts. We spend all day butchering for your people but are only given the most marginal of all marginal payments: hoofs, tongues, intestines. The occasional collop." Kinga sucked in her tongue and continued, "Look around you. Look at the filth that surrounds you. Can you assure us that we will survive? Are you prepared to take care of us? Are you prepared to look into the mirror and see us looking back at you? Are you truly interested in creating a civilized state? A place where your people—*all* of your people—may live a comfortable life?"

"But I already made you butchers," said Árpád.

The old witch spat and pointed a bony, scolding finger at him. "Thirty years ago, the Pechenegs swam across a river to wipe their muddy hands on your grasses, kick down the posts of your tents, bust all of your precious clay pots, and to ravage the weakest among you."

Árpád blinked. "So?"

"So *we* are the weakest among you."

Then she rose from the fireplace and pointed at a mountain of burlap behind her on the dirt floor. She lifted one of the pieces, revealing an enormous arm wrapped around another arm, an enormous leg around another leg. In an altogether ribald congregation of fat and sweat and massive, leg-wrestling thighs, Lili and Szeretlek lay pressed together, sleeping.

Kinga grinned. "And the weakest force," she said, "guides the destinies of the universe."

xx

THE MOCKERS AND THE MOCKED

I decide that I have to go to Dr. Monica's today, even though it's a Friday and not a Tuesday. Even if I have to wait until the end of the day to see her.

It's freezing out. The middle of my back feels tight and small. Extremely painful. I loosen the straps of my backpack and drag my leg across the field. Along the way, a cluster of fat moths flutters up from a cold pocket in the ground. They bop around my knees. I swat at them until I see that one of the moths is different from the other moths. This moth is gray-blue, with slightly inverted, heart-shaped wings. It's not a moth at all, but a butterfly, posing as a moth.

"*The mockers and the mocked*," Darwin writes, "*always inhabit the same region—the mockers are invariably rare insects; the mocked in almost every case abound in swarms.*"

The butterflies that live in the field are orange with black spots and slender, upbeat antennae. They arrive in the warm months and then move south before winter. But here it is, barely a week into April, and this fog-colored butterfly appears. He flutters weakly, ghost-like, over the wet grasses, in and out of the heavy wings of the fat brown moths that envelop him, until he disappears in the thither. I follow the moths out of the field and into the forest to look for them, but by the time I reach the highway, the posse and their imposter are gone.

A car drives by. I wonder if the car will stop and the driver will get out and offer me a ride—this time I do believe I'd take it—but the car doesn't stop.

I can't imagine why. I'm only a filthy little Hungarian wearing a pink sweatshirt that says DISNEYLAND on it. I'm only limping along the road in boots without laces, dragging one leg behind me. I'm only holding one arm tightly to my chest—

A rumbling, abused pickup truck approaches fast. Just as it passes, the truck squeals to a stop, smoking the tires. A Virginian jumps out. His face is round and tough, burning under a leather hat. "Hey!" he shouts. "Hey you!"

The Virginian staggers towards me. He reminds me immediately of the field ticks, swollen with blood. He runs right up and stabs my chest with a thick, shit-faced finger. "What in the hell are you *doing?*" he slurs. "You're walking in the middle of the goddam road." He gives me a pause to say something.

I give it right back.

When he sees that I'm not interested in answering, he removes his little hands from his pockets. "Say something," he says, and tugs the lapels of my coat. "C'mon, say something." He flicks my beard.

I don't say something.

So he shoves me. I stumble backward, down in the ditch, onto a rock. Blood opens across my hand in an oily smear.

"You stay out of the road!" he yells. "Or I'm callin' the police!" Then he walks back up the highway mumbling *"Midgets,"* like I'm an unwanted species that's invaded his country. I hear him slam the door to the truck. The engine sputters to life. As he drives off, I try to keep the seizure at bay by thinking of Asimov: *"The Gravitational Force, by far the weakest of all,"* but the shaking has already begun.

Here, in a watery ditch off a dusty highway in Northern Virginia, a seizure feasting on my innards, the Indian stands right next to me, holding his sack of colorful textiles. He shakes his head. "You're just an image," he says, "an illusion." In the distance, a car tears around the corner, making so much noise it sounds like it's hurting the road. Trees lean back to make room. The telephone poles which line the road brace themselves for the impact. Nature holds her obsequious breath.

One particular telephone pole, leaning in the same spot that it's been leaning for twenty long Virginia years, is about to be set upright.

There's a human being at the scene: a boy, wearing pants two inches too short and a brown cowboy shirt two sizes too big that's been worn so many times it looks shredded. The back of the shirt is freshly torn. Cuts and bruises pepper his arms and legs. His eyes, the telephone pole notices, look hollow. "Go on," it wants to say. "Get out of the road!" But of course, telephone poles cannot speak. And the car is not a car after all: it's a truck. Inside, a woman with sloppy brown hair is blasting a Carly Simon pop song on her stereo. The woman loves Carly Simon. Coming around the bend, listening to her favorite song in the world, the woman feels a rush of gladness and freedom. What *isn't* there to be glad about? She's in her truck. She has a boyfriend. She likes horses. It's June 15, 1985. The sky is blue.

And it's *Virginia*, for God's sake.

She presses her foot on the gas and closes her eyes, singing, "*I haven't got time for the pain—* " and just misses the boy in the road.

At the Back Lick Bar and Grill later that evening, the woman tells her friends over a pile of nachos that it had to be a moment of premonition or something. How else could she explain why she opened her eyes just seconds before hitting the boy?

"I slammed my foot on the brakes," she says, "and held the steering wheel so hard I thought my fingers were gonna fall off. My heart was beating so fast in my chest, I thought it might pop right out."

Her friends are curious. "Then what happened?" they ask.

"I got out of the car and went over to him. He was just standing there. There was a horrible look on his face," she says.

"What did he look like?"

She thinks for a second. "Steady," she says. "Even." The woman takes a long drink of her beer and then continues. "I was so worked up, I shouted, 'What's wrong with you? I could have killed you!' But he didn't answer," she says. "He didn't even *look* at me. So I grabbed him by the shoulders. 'Do you speak, kid?' I asked him."

"What did he say?"

"He didn't say anything. So I pulled him to the side of the road and told him to go on home."

This was not *exactly* true. The woman, in a swell of fear and anger, actually slapped the boy across the face. "Speak!" she demanded.

But this particular boy does not speak. So she yelled, "Then stay in the damned road for all I care!" and returned to her truck. She started the ignition. Carly Simon started wailing. The truck tore off down the road, and just in time.

Another car was coming.

XXI

YOUR DAUGHTER IS QUITE BEAUTIFUL

Mrs. Himmel is not at all pleased to see a Pfliegman come in on an Un-Pfliegman day. She sees me stumble through the front door and groans, "This is all we need."

"We're *extremely* busy today, Mr. Pfliegman," says Adrian.

Dr. Monica is extremely busy. The Waiting Area is hot and loud. The Sick or Diseased children are tumbling all over the place.

I find a seat next to a girl in an examining gown, waiting for Dr. Monica to prepare for her X-ray. She's a handsome child with chubby cheeks and long red hair. She's sitting tightly in her chair, holding a homemade cookie and staring intensely at the Berber carpeting. She looks up at the other, fully dressed children, who are at the moment comparing shoelaces and do not have to go underneath a Big Machine. She sniffs, pitifully. Her mother has given her the cookie for a snack, but she's not eating it. She holds it limp in her hand, like a boring toy.

"You don't want it?" her mother whispers.

The girl frowns. She takes an unenthusiastic bite and keeps it in her mouth until her mother turns away. Then she spits it out behind the chair.

I reach through my coat pockets and find an Evermore. It's my last one. I offer it to her.

She looks, but does not see it: she only sees the hairy little face looking back at her. The unruly beard, the papery cheeks. The weird woolen cap and the filthy pink sweatshirt. The eyeglasses, thick as ice. She sees all of this, and, like any Good Child who can spot a Bad Adult, living proof that there's a fundamental flaw in what she believes is God's design, leaps from the chair and climbs onto her mother's lap, looking at me through squinting, terrified eyes.

I shrug and peel off the wrapper. Then I glance up—

Mrs. Himmel is staring at me with her mouth open. She shakes her head in disbelief. She picks up the phone and holds her hand over her mouth as she speaks, as though I couldn't possibly imagine what she's telling Dr. Monica: that the Creature is here on a *Friday* and not a *Tuesday*; that he's offering the children candy when they're all trained *not to take candy* from such unsavory persons as himself; and that she's *forty-five minutes* overdue for lunch already.

She slams down the phone.

Moments later, the pediatrician appears in the Waiting Area. She's not in her usual outfit today. Today, she is wearing a dress. The dress is silk. Red. Soft-looking. She shoots me a brief, exhilarating glance, and then goes to Mrs. Himmel's window. She says a few things to Mrs. Himmel that I cannot discern because her back is to me and I'm far too immersed in memorizing the heart-shaped contour of her ass to even begin to imagine, but I am marginally aware of the contents of the conversation as Mrs. Himmel's face goes purple, as her lips curl into a bitter, pusillanimous pucker—

Dr. Monica gives Mrs. Himmel a box of powdered jelly doughnuts. "I just want you to know how much I appreciate everything you do for us, Mrs. Himmel," she says, and then returns to her office.

Mrs. Himmel waits until Dr. Monica is gone, and then grabs the box and opens it. She selects one doughnut and takes a large bite. White powder sticks to the corners of her mouth. A smear of purple jelly threatens to drip out the butt-end, but Mrs. Himmel, a professional, anticipates this emission, and quickly spins the doughnut in her palm to lick the jelly from the hole.

"Can I have one?" a voice asks.

Daughter Elise is here. She's sitting in the far corner of the room next to the ficus, chewing gum and staring vacantly at *Vogue*. Her long legs are pressed into stylish jeans, and she's wearing flip-flops to dry her freshly painted toenails. Her hair is glossed with chemicals, styled into a corpulent, complex bun.

"Ha," says Mrs. Himmel. "Fat chance."

Elise turns a page and mumbles something.

"You just *watch it*, missy," Mrs. Himmel says.

Elise rolls her eyes.

"Don't you roll your eyes at me," her mother says, and wipes the sticky powder on her jeans. "You're gonna get it!"

Adrian walks in, carrying a stack of folders. Her red hair is pulled back in a thick ponytail, and she's wearing a brand new windbreaker, the kind you can unzip and roll into its own portable pouch.

"I've got the twins' folders for you, Annette," she says, and places the folders on Mrs. Himmel's desk, next to the computer monitor.

Mrs. Himmel sees Adrian and the new windbreaker and stops in midchew. She examines the jacket with narrow eyes; how it form-fits Adrian's sporty figure.

Adrian sees the doughnut balanced in Mrs. Himmel's paw and licks her top lip. She yearns for one. No doubt it's tempting: the powder sprinkled on Mrs. Himmel's blond, feminine mustache, the undeniable waft of sugar in the air. But then she considers the route the doughnut will take, down the throat, with the aid of Mrs. Himmel's meaty, elastic tongue, and all yearning disappears as quickly as it came.

She unscrews the cap of her water bottle and takes a long gug of it.

One of the Sick or Diseased children, calmly removing the pages from a *Time* magazine, also sees Mrs. Himmel's doughnuts. He asks his mother for one.

She offers him one of Dr. Monica's sugar-free lollipops.

The boy will have none of it. He throws it on the floor, breaks loose from his mother, and runs to the front of the reception desk where the doughnuts sit perched like whole cakes. He leans in close, and gently lifts his hand to touch one. It's clear that he doesn't want to eat all of it; he only wants to put his finger on the white sugar and have a taste. He's been watching Mrs. Himmel enjoy the dessert, and there was something in the ecstatic way her tongue leapt out at the jelly before it fell that has driven the boy beyond reason. "Please!" he shouts.

"No, Billy," says his mother.

"But it's so *round*," Billy wails, as though the shape is a problem that needs solving.

Mrs. Himmel smiles to herself. She enjoys having things that others want. She sips her dry tea and spins around in her swivel chair for a sugar packet. The receptionist keeps a long box of sugar packets on the shelf behind her desk and now selects three, delicately nibbling each packet open with the corner of her mouth.

I watch the sugar pour from the packets and my tongue goes fat and sticky, filling my mouth. I search the pockets of my coat for another Evermore, but it's no use—I'm out. The only place to buy them is at the G&P, and that's halfway across town. I reach around to scratch my back and fidget in my chair.

Daughter Elise sighs and looks at her watch. "It's almost three o'clock, Mother," she says. "Daniel says we have to be there at five."

"Relax," Mrs. Himmel says. "We'll get there when we get there."

"This whole dumb thing is *your* idea, not mine," Elise says.

"Just cool it!"

"You cool it," Elise mumbles. She snaps a page of her magazine.

"*Natural Selection*," writes Darwin, "*will modify the structure of the young in relation to the parent, and of the parent in relation to the young.*"

Then the front door opens. A gaggle of fifth graders stumble in.

They're all wearing child-sized suits and dresses. They quickly fill the center of the Waiting Area because there's no place to sit. A pair of twins in blue are holding hands and weeping. There was a birthday party, and one of the mothers served the children fresh cow milk from the farm to go with the birthday cake. Unfortunately, the milk was sour and has made all of the children sick. The mother, once Good, now clearly Bad, is beside herself. The other mothers smile politely but grit their teeth. They pass around knowing looks: the children won't be attending any birthday parties at *that* house again.

The birthday girl stares out the window at the darkening clouds, her yellow dress pulled tight into her fists. A look of quiet rage upon on her face.

Mrs. Himmel slides on her eyeglasses and begins handing out information sheets and organizing everyone.

The mothers all thank her, looking grateful.

"Don't be silly," she says, "I'm just doing my job." But when she's finished, she walks over to Elise and says, "Well, that's it. It looks like I'm stuck here. Go to the salon across the street to get your hair done, and then stop by the supermarket. Your father will have to take you."

Elise throws her magazine on a side table. "My hair *is* done, Mother," she says.

Mrs. Himmel stands back and examines it. "It is?"

"I did it myself."

Mrs. Himmel snorts. "This is a *professional modeling shoot*, Elise. This isn't prom."

The women gather together bundles of outfits and hair accessories and hair chemicals. Elise hoists a backpack full of makeup onto her shoulder in one hefty tug. Mrs. Himmel spits on her thumb and nabs a fleck of dust that has fallen on the daughter's cheek.

The daughter, annoyed, whacks the hand away.

"Will you just *let* me?" Mrs. Himmel says.

"Leave me alone!"

Mrs. Himmel removes her horn-rimmed glasses and breathes on them. "If I left you alone for one second, you'd gain ten pounds," she says. "You've gotten awfully chubby, Elise. You've got to be taking better care of yourself and watching that figure."

Elise throws her head back and laughs. "*I'm* not the one who's gotten chubby, Mother."

Mrs. Himmel finishes cleaning her glasses with the bottom of her sweater, and then steps forward and slaps Elise. The Waiting Area goes silent. The Sick or Diseased children stop playing and stare at Mrs. Himmel. One of them whimpers. The mothers pretend not to hear or see anything. They hide behind their magazines.

Elise says nothing; she touches her cheek and gets a funny look on her face, like she's just acquired a piece of knowledge that no one knows but her. She walks to the front door and stares outside at the picnic table.

Mrs. Himmel mutters to herself and returns to her desk.

I think about the note I wrote, and write it again on my writing tablet. I walk over to Elise and hand it to her.

She looks down at me, surprised, and then takes the note:

Your daughter is quite beautiful.

Although her skin does not possess the same radiance as Dr. Monica's, the way she holds the note, as lightly as all lovely women hold things, is stunning. What I've written on the note is true: Elise really is beautiful.

"Your-daughter-is-quite-beautiful," she reads, and then looks at me. "I don't have a daughter."

But Mrs. Himmel has seen Elise conversing with the Creature. She leaps up and runs over, standing right between us, her arms folded over her chest. Eyeglasses chained around her neck. She snatches the note out of Elise's hands and reads it, mortified.

"*Out*," she says.

Adrian returns with her folders. "Really, Mrs. Himmel, is that necessary?"

I'm sorry, I write, and hold it up.

Mrs. Himmel remains unfazed. Afternoon clouds pass across her eyes. "Out!" she shouts, and points at the door.

I gather my things and follow Mrs. Himmel's finger toward the picnic table. The sky is growing savagely dark. I look at her as if to say, "But it's going to rain."

"Get it together, Mr. Pfliegman," she says, and slams the door.

I sit on the picnic table and stare across the road at the Big M supermarket. "As if I even *could*," I want to say, as rain begins needling out of the sky. I might as well climb Mount Massive. And get *what* together? How can you *get it together* when there isn't anything there to get in the first place?

Why on earth would a person even want to recover when's there's nothing worth recovering to?

At that moment, a very tall, very lanky woman saunters around the corner of Dr. Monica's office. She's got long blond hair and a mouth so big I can make out her skeleton. She's wearing high-heeled sandals and a halter-top, and drags one finger along the brick as she walks. It's Carly Simon. Her face matches the picture on the cassette tape, exactly. She crosses the wet grass and climbs up on the picnic table next to me, swinging her sandals. She looks at me with laughing eyes as the wind whips through her feathered hair. She presses her finger on my nose and tugs at my ears. Her lips swell. "I've known you since you were a small boy," she coos, showing her big teeth. The halter-top has a wide, sloping neck that hangs off one shoulder. Her clavicle's so sharp it looks like she got a stick in the neck.

I ignore her.

"That's a nice coat you have," she says, fingering the wooly lapel. "Was it expensive?" She leans in close and looks at me. Her eyes are heavy with black stuff that falls from her lashes in little flakes.

"Are you horny, baby?" she whispers. She starts prodding me, reaching inside the lapels of the coat. I try to push her off, but she's stronger than I am. She wraps her arms around me and fiddles with my zippers.

"*Frapfth!*" I cry. "*Beschsmowg!*"

Then it really starts coming down. Carly Simon throws back her head, leaps off the picnic table and begins dances around the soaked grass in her high heels. "Whee!" she cries.

I look longingly into the window of Dr. Monica's office, and make eye contact with one of the Good Mothers. She sees me out here, getting soaked in the downpour, and although part of her knows that she should say something, she says nothing. She pretends that she never saw me at all. She goes back to filing her nails.

Adrian sees me, as does Mrs. Himmel. "He's got his coat on," she says.

Across the street, three Security Guards appear in front of the glass doors of the Big M. They're arguing, and gesticulate wildly. Shoppers linger in the parking lot to listen. Herman lumbers around the other two in his signature figure-eight until a police car pulls into the parking lot. It drives underneath the ENTER EXIT sign, right up to the entrance of the supermarket—

The siren *woot*s.

I slide down from the picnic table, grab my backpack, and hustle down the street to Mister Bis's, leaving Carly Simon dancing on Dr. Monica's front lawn, laughing in the rain, stretching out her middle parts and showing off to the entire civilized world her long and shapely legs.

XXII
EVOLUTION OF THE PFLIEGMANS:
EXILE

When he realized that it was Lili and the Giant lying together in that horrible, putrid tent, in their twisted love, my Darling, the Grand Prince completely lost it. He tore the bird-helmet from his head and started whacking us with it. He tipped over the kettle of stew, grabbed a log out the fire with his bare hands, and chucked it across the tent.

"Exile!" he cried. "You're all exiled!"

He brought the hard apples out from the pockets in his cloak and started hucking them at our kneecaps, and then, when there was nothing left to huck, he removed his gigantic sword from his belt, waved it at the burlap sacks covering his beloved in bed with a monster, cried, "*Hooy Hooy!*" and made directly for Szeretlek's heart.

Lili, awake the minute Árpád had hurled the burning log, jumped from the burlap and pulled Szeretlek out of the tent, into the rain.

"Whore!" Árpád cried, and slapped her across the face. "How could you *do* this to me?"

"You're *loony*," she said.

Then the little children, the ones Árpád had encountered earlier, poured out of the forest. They were all soaking wet, and the boy they had been carrying on their shoulders was missing. Árpád stopped them with one flat hand. "You there!" he said. "Where is your little friend? The one with the limp?"

The wet children stared at him blankly, as if they'd never heard the sound of human speech. They had clearly already forgotten about the boy, and now were only paying attention to the apples that rolled along the outskirts of the tent. They skirted around his legs and went straight for the fruit, punching each other on the heads and shoulders. One girl got her hands on a particularly fat apple, but a larger boy saw it and the girl got a fist in the eye. Árpád wondered that she did not start to cry, but instead gritted her teeth, jumped onto the boy's back, and chomped down on his ear. The boy squealed. She squeezed her eyes and bore down and managed to work off a piece of the boy's ear in her mouth. The boy burst into tears and let the apple roll from his hands. The girl comfortably spit the ear part out, blood greasy on her lips, and scampered over to collect her spoils.

Árpád scowled. He wanted very much to punish them, but they all looked so wretched and beaten that any further punishment would only seem redundant. Despite the fact that Lili had chosen this gigantic *thing*, this cataclysmic *zero*, this creature that came out of these People Who Were Barely People instead of him; despite the fact that he was nearly boiling with animus, Kinga's words remained in his ears:

"We are the weakest among you."

By designating the Fekete-Szem as the meat cutters, the official butchers of the Hungarian community, Árpád had saved us from expulsion and therefore certain death. Like it or not, we belonged to him. Watching the little girl chomp savagely into her apple, swallowing the bitter fruit in licks and gulps, Árpád realized that if he did not care for us, the lowest common denominator—no matter how filthy or backward or solipsistic—the Hungarians would become a race of monsters. He had seen what had happened to human beings exiled from their communities up North, over the Ural Mountains; he had seen how within seconds the air could freeze them into gray statues; how the wind from boundless plains of the barrens could blow the life-breath right out them.

"Nature acts on every organ," writes Darwin, *"on the whole machinery of life."*

Árpád knew that he had to somehow protect these people, even if only from themselves. So when Szeretlek crawled out of the tent and fell upon one heavy knee in front of him and begged, "Please, do not cast them out. It's not their fault—" the Grand Prince quite agreed.

"Your people may remain," he said. "But only if *you* are exiled."

The giant man bit his giant lip. His eyes watered.

Árpád raised one hand. "You will follow the river," he announced, "until the river ends. If you are ever seen here again, by anyone, you will be cut in half. Or at the very least, exposed to—"

"*Hopeless situations*," said Lili. She fake-shivered.

Árpád spun his cloaks and faced her. He lifted the lid of the bird-helmet. "And as for *you*," he seethed, "you will make a life for yourself here, among these meat-cutters. These feet-suckers. You will watch over them and take care of them until I return." He inched closer to her, lifting himself up to his tiptoes, his mustache dancing with anticipation. "And then you and I shall be reunited, Love Button," he whispered. "And we shall be very, *very* happy."

Árpád's officers waited outside as Lili and Szeretlek prepared for his departure. Inside the tent, the scene was somber. We Pfliegmans felt the heavy presence of authority and murmured quietly amongst ourselves. We watched Lili and Szeretlek pack up his things. One of us occasionally let out a weeping cough. Another sneezed. Another chewed off a hangnail too close and sniveled with self-pity. There was not much to pack: Szeretlek owned nothing beyond his cloak, his undershirt. Lili threw her head back, loudly worked a nubble of phlegm from her sinuses, and spit it professionally across the tent in one clean *thip*.

"This sucks," she said.

Szeretlek shuddered with love. "*Szeretlek*," he said.

"Me too, babe."

The enormous man gazed at her face, moving his head all the way down her torso, kissing each fold of her stomach, all the way between her rolling, dimpled thighs. "I'm not good enough for you," he said.

"Don't be stupid," said Lili. "You're awesome."

"But I've been *exiled*," he whined. "How will I possibly be of use now?"

The Giant did not know how to hunt or fish, and he certainly wasn't much of a farmer. His only unique talent seemed to involve the blunting instrument with which he had clocked innumerable cows over their innumerable heads. What use, he wondered, is a large man with a soft brain?

"I can haul rocks," he said, miserably. "I can dig holes."

"You can leg wrestle," said Lili. She threw herself on top of him, pinned him to the ground, and locked her bare legs around his. "And you *belong* here." She grabbed her crotch and grinned.

Szeretlek stared at her, and his chin trembled. "I'll be so lonely."

"You're not alone," said Lili. "You have me. You have *Ember az Égben*."

"Who?"

"The Man in the Sky."

Szeretlek thought about it for a second, then grabbed Lili's waist and buried his head in her stomach. "I don't *want* to go!" he cried.

Lili pulled her hair back and began turning it into two thick braids. "You don't have to," she said. "These men aren't going to stay here forever. Just go for a few days. Follow the river for a day or two, and then turn back. By the time you get home, they'll be gone and no one will ever know."

Szeretlek sat up. His eyes were blotchy and puffed, but he blinked with hope. "Do you think it would work?" he said.

"Why not?"

He wiped his long cheeks. Things looked considerably brighter. "I never thought of that," he said, and punched her on the arm. "You're *smart*."

"No," she said. "I'm hungry."

Lili folded up the burlap on the floor for him to wear as a coat, and she packed him a heavy bag of ját. As Szeretlek watched her, he was filled with a sweeping, unmitigated desire. He grabbed her thick waist and tossed her onto the dirt floor. Lili locked her legs in, and they both laughed as they wrestled. Their laughter echoed around the tent.

We Pfliegmans heard the laughing and hung back. We shook our wobbly heads. We knew that to laugh was a dangerous thing: laughing meant that one was enjoying oneself, and to be enjoying oneself only meant that later on, at some horrifying, unanticipated moment, one would not be enjoying oneself at all. Far better, we believed, to celebrate nothing and keep the pain constant, than to feel your body rise up, lifted high by the Man in the Sky's nimble fingertips, to only then be released, plummeting to the hard earth below. This had happened to a few of us before, this lifting and dropping. Every once in a while, one of us would rise up in the tent, hover in the air for a moment, then fall back down again, landing clumsily on some crucial appendage. So while we may not have been the most capable, the most intelligent of the early Hungarian tribes, when Isaac Asimov was nothing more than a twittering future prospect, a modern *táltos* bearing hunky white muttonchops, we Pfliegmans innately understood the laws of weakness, of gravity. We understood that what rises must inevitably fall.

Szeretlek rose from Lili's arms and strode outside to greet Árpád's officers. Standing in front of him was a large and healthy horse, as it was the custom among the proto-Hungarians that if a man was to be forever banished from the country, he should at least be given a ride.

"I don't know if he's big enough for you," one officer said. "But he's the biggest one we have."

What the men didn't know was that whether due to his size, his uncoordinated limbs, or his aching stupidity, Szeretlek had never ridden a horse. He'd never even saddled one.

Anonymus writes: *"The pagan Hungarians were among the first peoples across the entire Asian continent to ride horses with saddles, and the first among the Europeans to use the stirrup."*

But a stirrup is of little assistance to a Giant. Every time Szeretlek tried to mount the horse, the animal sensed that something it could not possibly carry was about to climb on its back, and shuffled off a few feet to the side, indignant. The officers all circled around the horse to help, but after Szeretlek had tried and failed several times, they gave up. "What can we do?" they cried. "An *animal* doesn't even want you."

"It's not a problem," Szeretlek said. "I am about as tall as horse anyway. I'll just be my own horse."

"What are you talking about?" the men asked.

"I'll walk," he said

The men shrugged. "Whatever, man," they said, and handed him a bow and a quiver packed with arrows.

"What's this for?" he asked.

Árpád's men stared at him. "Are you serious?" they asked. They looked at each other. "Is he serious?"

Szeretlek waved to Lili, to the men, to us all, and then took his first steps into the wilderness. His legs were so long that his walk was really more of an amble, a lumbering gait with his long arms swinging askew from their sockets. Szeretlek stopped before he entered the forest completely, and turned around. He had nothing but a bow, a few arrows, and a bagful of sticky ját, but he felt very fortunate. He grinned. "Lili!" he shouted. "Ember az Égben! The Man in the Sky! How he loves me!"

Árpád's men watched him go and clucked their tongues.

"That guy," one said, "is *totally* fucked."

Lili slammed a fist into his shoulder. But as she watched Szeretlek enter the woods, plodding like a large, confused bear, the familiar form of his figure slowly disappearing, slowly becoming swallowed by the tall and bending trees, she felt her waters shift uneasily inside her, as though something had deeply and permanently changed, as though the entire Danube River had suddenly sprung up between them.

There were immediate benefits to not being able to ride a horse. Without being restricted to the saddle, Szeretlek was able to shoot arrows in all directions, instead of just straight ahead, or left or right. He could shoot from behind. As he wandered through the forest over the next two days, the Giant became a rather skilled early-Hungarian foot-archer. There was only one problem: his thick fingers were not well suited for archery. So he carved for himself a longer bow from a soft, limber pine. Instead of one single curve of the bow, he made two smaller curves, cinched in the middle with several binds of leather into a tightly wound, pre-medieval EZ-Grip handle. The handle helped keep a firm hold on the tightness of the bowstring. Szeretlek placed an arrow in the center of the bow and pulled back the string until it tightened. When he loosened his fingers, releasing the pressure, the arrow soared through the trees at twice the velocity and distance of a normal bow. Grasping the first doubly curved bow in existence, Szeretlek might have been a Pfliegman, but there was no doubt that he was a self-made man in a time when there was no such thing.

He felt extremely new and modern.

Unfortunately, after only an hour or so, he became so absorbed in the game that he didn't realize he couldn't see, or even hear, the river anymore.

"Follow the river and back again," Lili had told him, but now Szeretlek had already somehow lost it.

"Crap!" he said, and kicked himself for not being smarter than he was. "How does a person *lose* a whole river?"

Whole days and nights passed as the Giant lumbered sadly through the conifers. The firs and the larches. The spruces and yews. For the trees he could not recognize, he smiled at their strange shapes as he looked for the river. He came across several streams, so there was water to drink, and he was warm enough with Lili's burlap fashioned like proper cloak, but the bag of ját was running out. Hunger set in, and his body went tight. But he was hungry for other things as well. Lili had told him he would never be alone, that he would always have Ember az Égben, and yet each day the landscape turned. The wildnerness was full of sudden, unpredictable changes. Szeretlek walked for three days in one direction until finally the trees broke at the edge of the forest, and he gasped at the white expanse in front of him. Mountains of ice and heavy snow. Wind sliced his cheeks as he stepped into the whiteness, and he gasped at how quickly his fingers and toes pigeoned, how his eyelashes curled—

He sprinted back into the warm arms of the forest. "Ember az Égben," he thought bitterly. "If He exists, this must surely be where he lives."

After the Giant had wandered in the wilderness for nearly two months, his mood changed. The hunger of loneliness was far worse than the want of food or drink as the truth of his new existence set in. He no longer marveled at the trees, the drip-drip noises. The white of the barrens. He lived to protect himself, to prevent discomfort as much as possible. He watched with a seasoned indifference how quickly his wide stomach, which in his loneliest moments he had clutched like a favorite stuffed animal, began to deflate. He did not speak to the Man in the Sky. He did not speak to anyone. He had been rationing his food, removing only the tiniest pieces of ját from his bag, but there was so little left. He would have shot and killed something, but deer tiptoed away from his loud noises and might as well have moved into another region of the world.

By the sixtieth day, Szeretlek's original size had halved. He reached into his bag and picked out the last remaining piece of ját. It was frozen. Lumpy and oblong. The color of boredom. Despite the unpleasant, bald taste that coated his tongue, he licked and gnawed the ját. He chewed harder, but the saliva that should have softened it only seemed to turn it into a mealy paste. It was utterly inedible. He sat down on a hollow log and stared at his legs. They were incredibly thin. "I will grow so thin that I will simply disappear," he thought.

A raccoon poked its nose out from under the log and sniffed Szeretlek's foot. It opened its little jaw and tried to taste his ankle. Szeretlek reached for the raccoon, but it was too fast, and he was too tired.

"I am too thin and too tired," he thought, reasonably. "I will simply be eaten by tiny forest creatures."

His ankle bled from the bite. He reached down to touch the blood, then lost all feeling in his hands and head. He leaned forward and collapsed onto the cold earth, his limbs awkwardly entwined. He could no longer move them. And although not far away was a small monastery full of men who could assist him, Szeretlek did not know about the monastery; he only knew that Lili had been quite wrong. He stared up at the enormous, empty sky. "There is no Ember az Égben," he said, and willingly slipped into unconsciousness.

XXIII

DECENT SOCIETY

Telephone poles lean, left and right, as I limp away from the Big M
Supermarket and enter the Village Square. Front Lick, Virginia, is like
most small American towns. There are subdivisions. There is community
theater. It was once quaint and beautiful, but now thanks to television,
prescription drugs, and trickle-down economics, has fallen a few notches
to "not a wholly unattractive place to live."

Across the street, three boys in spring jackets are throwing handfuls
of mud at each other. They see me shuffling into the park and stop what
they're doing. They stare at me. Their mouths are open.

"Oh my God," one shouts. "Look at the midget!"

"Nice freaking coat!"

They burst out laughing.

"The coat? Take a look at that hat!"

"Those boots!"

"Where's your shoelaces, midget?"

I move quicker down the sidewalk, bad leg dragging behind. One of
the boots slips off, and I have to stumble back for it.

The boys howl.

I may be sick. I may come from a hole in the ground. My best friend may be an insect.

But at least I don't live in decent society.

The G&P used to be a candy store called Lick's, for Lick's Candy Company, which opened a factory here in the late 1800s. The tin ceilings are original, as is the wooden floor. The planks have spread and buckled with age, but Mister Bis treats them every summer with a highly durable polyurethane gloss. "It is the *very* best you can buy," he says.

When I go inside, Mister Bis doesn't appear to be anywhere, but Missus Bis is working the register, and from across the store, Richie is trying to persuade an old man to buy an eighty-dollar prescription for back pain.

"All I want's generics!" the old man cries. "Who can afford that Rolls Royce of aspirin, goddammit?"

Missus Bis sees me from behind the register and waves me over. "Mister Pfliegman!"

She moves quickly around the counter and places her hands down on my shoulders. She air-kisses my cheeks. She is swathed in a flowing pink sari, freckled with green flowers, and leans down so that her face is as close as possible to my face. She even smells like flowers.

"I am so glad you're here," she says. "What can we do for you?"

I bring out my writing tablet.

Evermore Cough Drops, I write.

Missus Bis spins back around the counter and reaches underneath the register. She hands me three whole boxes. I slide a few bills over the counter, but she refuses them; she smiles and shakes her head. "No no no," she says, and presses the boxes over the counter. "But let me ask you: have you thought about our offer, Mister Pfliegman?"

I give her a questioning look.

Missus Bis swoops a sheet of the sari over one shoulder. "Mister Bis told me about your situation in the bus, and we would very much like you to stay with us for a while. Please. You do so much for us, and we feel it is the least that we can do for you. We would very much like to give you a place to stay."

Thank you, I write, *but no.*

"But Mister Pfliegman—"

Missus Bis continues talking, but my attention has turned to the polyurethaned floor. A few granules of sugar are shining on the wide planks.

I wander away from Missus Bis, following them around the corner to baking goods—"We'll talk about it later," she shouts—all the way up to a large, leaking bag. It's white cane sugar. I lick my finger and press it on the granules and steal one small taste. The sugar dissolves into my tongue like water on scorched earth. I press my finger into more of it, and put it in my mouth and swallow. I start using two fingers, and then more fingers, and then I rip open the bag a little. I scoop it out with my hands. The sugar starts pouring out in a white waterfall. As quick as I can catch it, I'm shoving it in, munching and gulping until the bag is empty. I stop eating, breathless and a bit bewildered. I belch a little, and then look up—

Richie Bis is staring at me.

I calmly put the empty bag back on the shelf, and turn around to my display of Pfliegman Meat.

Three men in black suits are hovering over my meat section. They're all of equal height, chatting over a pile of T-bones. They manhandle my steaks. They toss my chops, my shanks. They smell them and then toss them in a disgusted manner back onto the shelf, ruining Mister Bis's neat array. They can't seem to stop moving, and wander aimlessly around each other, twittering. They wag their large chins. Their eyes roll.

One of them has a bruise on his chin. He makes an ugly gesture with his fist and the crook of his elbow. He turns around and looks at the hairy little man wearing a coat much too big for him. He sees my thick eyeglasses, my stylish woolen cap—

"What do you want?" he says.

The Subdivisionist does not, it seems, know who I am.

I adjust my eyeglasses and show myself, rather boldly, in front of Pfliegman Meat. I begin organizing the packets of meat that have been so carelessly flung about, glaring at the Subdivisionists in the exact menacing way that Mrs. Himmel glares at me from the receptionist's window.

"What's your problem," one of them says.

If I could speak, I might retort with something intellectual. Thought-provoking. Instead I just open my mouth and go: "*Braaaaaaaaaaaaaaaagh.*"

The Subdivisionist rubs his bruised chin. "Get lost, why don't you," he says.

The others turn around. "Who is it?"

"Some homeless guy," he says. "He reeks. Check out that sweatshirt."

"Don't give him anything."

Mister Bis appears from out back and sees me in front of the Subdivisionists. He darts over to the meat section, politically inching himself between us. He looks at the businessmen. "I will be with you gentlemen in a moment," he says, and then turns to me. "Go on up to the counter, Mister Pfliegman, and Missus Bis will ring you up."

I give the owner of the G&P a stricken look. He doesn't realize what he's done. Not until he sees my face. He said the word out loud: *Pfliegman*.

The bruised Subdivisionist looks at me with fresh vitality. His eyes darken. "Hey now," he says. "Wait a second," and reaches over to grab my arm, but Mister Bis steps in front of him. He whistles at Missus Bis. His wife flies over and shuttles me quickly towards the door as Mister Bis plants himself in front of the Subdivisionists, blocking the aisle. He begins barking at them about the demise of the American business ethic with his own unique and distinguishable élan:

"Chickenshits!" he cries. "You're all a bunch of chickenshits!"

The Subdivisionists point in my direction, shouting angrily at Mister Bis. They push him a little, sending him crashing into the meat display.

In a leap, Richie clears the pharmaceuticals counter. He tackles one of them, and bites him on the shoulder, hard—

"The police!" they cry. "We're calling the police!"

Missus Bis ushers me through the door and shoos me down sidewalk. "Go on!" she says. "Go and hide!"

I hustle quickly down the rows of empty storefronts. But there really is no need for Rovar Ákos Pfliegman to hide. He's been hiding from the world even from before the day that Ján and Janka crashed into that bent telephone pole. Most people do not live out of a bus in a field. Most do not bathe in a river and shit in a bucket. Most do not keep their eyes closed so tightly in the mornings that they get dizzying, fiery headaches, but headaches they would rather have than watch the diamond-shaped crack in the ceiling. Most do not possess a general fear of exposure; instead, most people awake in the mornings and pour themselves a bowl of breakfast cereal and get in their cars and drive to work. Which is fine. He has nothing against cars. He has nothing against cereal. But it's safe to say that he's been hiding from the world ever since the day that Grandfather Ákos packed his bags in the light of the hallway and walked out the front door of the farmhouse. Ever since he climbed up the three stairs of his school bus and started the engine.

The boy ran outside and pressed a piece of paper against the door of the bus:

Take me with you.

Grandfather Ákos pulled the lever and opened it. He shook his head. "I can't, Little Ákos," he said.

The boy looked at him, at the trim goatee, the heavy coat. The white of his knuckles gripping the steering wheel.

Why not?

Grandfather Ákos stared at the boy for a moment, then reached underneath the seat and handed him a book: *The Rise and Fall and Rise of the Pagan Hungarians.* "You're a Pfliegman," he said.

What does that mean?

Grandfather Ákos scratched his chin and held the wheel a little tighter. He gave the windshield a grim, sorrowful look. "It means you're on your own," he said, and pulled the lever. The door closed shut.

The old man never returned. One day a lawyer pulled the school bus up the driveway of the farmhouse. He delivered ten Hungarian wool coats which went straight to a downstairs closet. The boy crawled into the closet and lay down underneath the coats to hide. To wait. How long should a person wait for change? What if that change never comes? And how is change even possible, when we all have a past to return to? We Pfliegmans may not have much else, but we have a past. We carry it on our backs. It presses itself against our necks. It floats in glass jars stored in white boxes, hidden away in decrepit barns, and although we can hide from many things, we cannot hide from that. Darwin writes, *"A man with all his noble qualities still bears in his bodily frame the indelible stamp of his lowly origin."*

But he writes nothing of lowly men from lowly origins.

When I return to Dr. Monica's, several of the birthday children have left, and Adrian convinces Mrs. Himmel to let me back in. "Honestly Annette," she says. "You can't just force him out into the rain. It's not humane, or something."

"Whatever," Mrs. Himmel says.

Her television program is on. She grabs the remote control and demands that everyone be quiet. She cranks the volume. We all watch as Television Elise slightly overcooks a chicken in the oven and nobody eats her dinner. She bursts into tears. At the end of the program she gets free tickets to the opera, but she's clearly still mad. "I don't even *like* opera," she says, and then they cut to commercial.

"That was a bad one," says Mrs. Himmel, having seen better rewards on other episodes. She gets up and ambles to the bathroom.

The boy with the BANG THE DRUM! T-shirt walks in with his mother. His mother has dark crescents under her eyes, and the boy isn't looking so hot either; his face is so pale it rivals my own. His cheeks and forehead are all puffed and dry. He can barely keep his eyes open.

The other Sick or Diseased children see him and instinctively shuttle to the other side of the Waiting Area.

His mother sits down in the chair next to me and reaches into her purse. She brings out a book called *If Jesus Was A Soccer Player*. There's a picture of a man wearing a cloak and a large wooden cross around his neck. He's kicking a ball into a net as the crowd behind him cheers. The mother begins reading softly, but the boy isn't listening, not even when she gets to the part about Jesus scoring the winning goal. "Go *Jesus*!" she whispers. The boy doesn't move. He's slumped over, one arm hanging listless off the side of the chair. He shifts for a moment, like he's afraid of something, and then leans forward and vomits on the Berber carpeting.

The Sick or Diseased children scream. Adrian rushes over with a roll of paper towels and the necessary powders, and the Good Mothers all hold handkerchiefs over their noses.

The BANG THE DRUM! boy barely notices any of them; he falls back into his chair as his mother quietly apologizes to everyone.

In this moment, all of the mothers, Good and Bad, are kind. "Don't worry," they tell her, looking nervously at her boy's gray face. "It's not like it's the first time," they say.

Afterward, the BANG THE DRUM! boy feels better. He gets cleaned up and is given a small cup of ginger ale. He slides off his chair to join the other children building skyscrapers out of Legos in the corner. They're uncertain about the boy—he might throw up again—so they keep to themselves, piling Legos on top of their buildings. The boy sits on his ankles in front of them, not moving. Not saying a word.

I cough a little into my fist and stare longingly at Mrs. Himmel's sugar packets behind her desk. I lick my lips. I think about the sugar at Mister Bis's and take out a box of the Evermores. I unwrap one and eat it, but it's not the same—

I spit it out into my hand.

Adrian brings me a cup of the ginger ale. "You don't look so good, either, Mr. Pfliegman," she says. The cup is warm and plastic. It smells faintly of modeling clay and peanut butter. "Go on," she says. "Drink it."

I choke it down.

"You don't *have* to stay here, you know," Adrian says. "A person has a lot of options. There are other places. My parents live in Oakland, California, for example. You could go someplace like that. Why not? Fix up that old bus and drive to California. It would be fun."

"There may be better places for someone who can do a hundred push-ups," I want to say. "There may be better places for someone who climbs mountains."

"God helps those who help themselves," Mrs. Himmel says, across the room.

Adrian nods. "That's true. It's *very* true," she says.

The BANG THE DRUM! boy waits for Adrian to leave and then walks over. "Whenever I get sick," he says, "Dad says I'm a Little Soldier." He puts his hands together into a gun and pretends to shoot me.

His mother looks up from her magazine and nods. So I shoot him back.

The boy grabs his throat and falls to the ground, rolling about on the Berber carpeting, emitting miserable, exaggerated groans. His mother goes back to the magazine, smiling from behind the pages. She's younger than I thought, wearing clean slacks and a pressed shirt, and her hair is turned up above her ears, cinched by matching barrettes. She rests her head, poised on her fingers. She appears tidy, organized. Controlling the things she can control. She puts the magazine back on the table and looks at the boy. "Sometimes I feel glued to him," she says, and laughs a little. But the laugh trails off. "Isn't that funny?"

No, I write.

Together, we watch him play.

"You're Mr. Pfliegman, is that correct? I've heard Adrian say your name. I'm Cathy," she says, and sticks out one hand.

Cathy's hand is clean and soft. Her fingernails unmarked by age or experience. I hold out my own hand, dirty and bloodied from the ditch.

She shakes it.

"It's nice to meet you, officially," she says. "You don't speak much."

I look at her.

"It's kind of nice, actually."

We watch the boy play for a while with a plastic toy, the kind where at first it's a robot and then it's a wrestler. He knows the pieces well; he turns them quickly and expertly in his hands, and the toy does not last in either form for very long. It goes from robot to wrestler and back again without a second's contemplation for what it means to be either one. Then, without taking her eyes off the boy, his mother says, "He's dying." She smiles, but her eyes don't mean it. "Do you believe in God, Mr. Pfliegman? I know it's a strange thing to ask someone nowadays. You don't have to answer if you don't want to."

I know Dr. Monica says that if you cannot be honest with others, how can you expect to be honest with yourself, but I also know that sometimes myth is preferable to truth. And here is Cathy, with her manicured hands, her coiffed hair, and her child who is not Sick, not Diseased, but Dying—

I bring out my writing tablet.

I believe, I write.

XXIV
EVOLUTION OF THE PFLIEGMANS:
THE WOMAN IN THE PIT

In the late spring of 931 AD, the early Hungarian armies launched through Bavaria and Swabia along Lake Constance to a small inlet where a gathering of monks resided with a considerable library of books, which they cherished. An anchoress named Wiborada also lived there, whom they did not cherish, but whom the monks had allowed to move into a pit in the cellar ten years earlier due to her inability to cure herself from impure thoughts and frightening visions. The visions stopped for a while, but one afternoon in the spring of that year, Wiborada was sitting calmly in the center of the floor of her pit, praying for a clear and simple mind, when the wall in front of her began to move. It moved slowly at first, and she rubbed her eyes to make sure she was seeing correctly, but when she assured herself that she was indeed watching the heavy stones of the wall creak and shift, she cried out, "The wall is moving!" The stones shifted faster, toppling over each other, until the dust cleared and a wide space unveiled itself in the dead center of the wall. There was nothing left between Wiborada and the elements. In front of her was a sprawling field with vibrant grasses. A bright and earnest sky.

Cold air rushed into the pit, making her shiver. She wiped her nose with a sleeve and backed into a far corner where the stones were safely in place.

"It's completely gone!" she screamed.

Upstairs, the monks heard Wiborada's cries, but they were enjoying a midday meal of leek and potato, which was everyone's favorite, and besides, the woman was always shouting about something. Shouting like mad was bound to happen if one immured oneself for too long, as many monks who had taken Vows of Isolation had witnessed.

They resumed sipping their meal in silence.

Downstairs, Wiborada stared at the field in front of her. The cold air disappeared to make way for the sun which now poured in, illuminating everything. "What the—" she said. From far off, thundered rumbled over the field. At least she thought it was thunder, but it couldn't be! There were no clouds. There was no dark and telling sign of rain. Wiborada stood up and walked toward the open space. She squinted, shading her eyes to block the sun, when a line appeared over the horizon. It quickly became apparent that the line was moving.

"Horses!" she whispered, as the mass rumbled over the clearing. Then she looked closer, and the anchoress realized with terror that these horses were not alone: they carried men on their backs. Men with spears, long bows and arrows, tall pointy hats covered in buttons, and bulging packs of supplies. Their flags waved. Their horses pulled long, heavy logs with which to bash open certain doors to certain unprotected monasteries.

"Holy shit!" shouted Wiborada.

At this, the monks' wooden spoons went clattering to their bowls.

"Suppose we check on the Lady Wiborada?" said one.

The monks nodded. As a unit, they rose from the wooden table and made their way to the heavy door that led to the cellar pit. Although none of the brothers would admit it, they were slightly agitated that they had not been able to finish their meal in peace. They were all thinking that by the time they returned to their tables, the soup would be cold and the bread would be hard, and this would mean the whole afternoon was shot, as there was nothing more frustrating than trying to communicate with the Heavenly Father on an unevenly digested meal.

One of the brothers jiggled the key. "Darn it all," he said.

"Patience, Brother," said another brother behind him.

"I've almost *got* it," said the first brother.

The monks all prayed silently for the first brother:

Credo in unum Deum… Visibilium et invisibilium…

The door opened, and everyone stepped downstairs, where Wiborada, dripping in sweat, lay curled into a tiny knot on the floor.

The wall, of course, was still there, in the exact place that it had always been.

Wiborada opened her eyes and stared at one of the monks. He towered over the others. He was so big he had to stoop under the doorjamb, and was now crouching down to even fit into the pit. Although she had never seen him before, Wiborada looked at him as if she'd known him for many years. She studied his face, his dark eyes, and then she gasped. A slight thread of spit hung from her lower lip.

She motioned for him to lower himself to her, and the monk did so, obediently. "If I can be of *use*," he said.

But Wiborada could not understand his gawky, foreign tongue. "What is his name?" she asked.

"We call him Brother Lignarius," the monks said.

Some years back, the monks had found the Giant lying in the woods half-starved, looking as if all of the air had been sucked out of him. A skeleton with skin. They unanimously agreed that God had delivered the man for a purpose, and decided to watch over him until he recovered. At first, the arrangement worked quite well. As soon as the Giant regained his size and strength, they were delighted by the breadth of his utility: he could haul six full barrels of potatoes at once. Fix a leaky roof without a ladder. The man could enter, bare-armed, into the forest, and emerge minutes later carrying an entire cord of winter wood. On top of this, his personality suited the monastery: all of these tasks he performed without complaint. "If I can be of *use*," Lignarius always said.

The monks knew that Brother Lignarius was not intelligent; his face rarely changed expression; his eyes did not possess even a flicker of the curiosity that speaks to an enlightened mind. But eventually they were able to teach him a few simple prayers, which he mimicked lightly on his large lips: "God is love," they said, and he repeated the words even if he did not understand them. "The age of the myth is over," they explained, distinguishing God from the stories of the Greeks and their shape-shifters. These were false gods, they said, the ones that became bulls and swans and oxen. Gods that assumed earth-forms to deceive. Manipulate. They had heard rumors of a pagan deity, some "Man in the Sky" capable of bringing sunshine and rain at his own inestimable whim, and they made sure to explain to Lignarius in simple terms that there could never be a Man in the Sky, because, reasonably, men require ground to stand on. Could he disagree with that?

He could not.

"*Credo in unum Patrem?*" they asked.

Szeretlek shrugged his shoulders. "Credo," he said.

And then they would give him his breakfast.

But as time passed, the monks spoke less and less to Lignarius, and Lignarius rarely spoke to them. He developed a lingering cough which no one could cure; he suffered from nosebleeds, crippling headaches. Mysterious pains grabbed random places on his body, and his skin dried in flakes and itched him terribly. He was always lifting his arms up around his back to reach one particularly tortuous itch which brewed in the exact place where neither hand can reach.

But his change in behavior disturbed them the most. The monks watched as Lignarius started wandering the woods, snapping trees he was not supposed to snap. He would not cut them or pile them neatly as before; instead he dragged the logs back to the monastery and abandoned them, strewn haphazardly all over their nice front lawn. The giant monk walked for hours in the vegetable gardens, coughing until his chest rattled and making funny gestures with his arms and body, as though pretending to shoot imaginary targets with imaginary arrows. The honey pot was always empty, and there was Lignarius, ducking out of the kitchen, furtively licking his fingers. He began mumbling to himself in a tongue so unrecognizable it did not sound like human speech at all. If scolded, no look of contrition crossed his face. Lignarius would only say "Credo" and then walk away.

The monks tried offering him gifts: a fresh piece of cloth, occasional shoe leather. But Lignarius just looked blankly at the objects. He displayed no gratitude. No emotion at all. One afternoon, the matter grew quite serious when Lignarius was served his supper and right away he began slurping his tomatoes. Without prayer. If he realized the brothers were staring at him, he did not show it; he sucked down the meal quickly, without regard for anyone else at the table. When he finished, he looked up, skin flaking from his cheeks.

"What of grace, Brother Lignarius," they said.

He looked at the monks and their soupbowls. "Credo," he said coldly, then stood up from his place at the table and left.

That day, in the darkness of the pit, Wiborada grabbed the monk's gigantic head between her hands and stared at him with wonder. A thread of spit dangled from her lower lip. "God cannot save you," she said.

The monks gasped. "God saves us *all*, Little Sister," one protested.

Wiborada eyed him coolly. "An invading horde of men approaches from the east. You must move the monks and the treasury, but most importantly the library. All of this will be destroyed if you do not."

"And how does the lady know this?"

"I've seen it," she said, and pointed to the wall. "God moved the wall and showed me. It's a blessing."

The monk looked at the stones, at the moss which had grown undisturbed for decades, and were amused. If God would choose anyone to proffer a vision to, it would likely be himself, he thought, certainly not anyone else at the monastery, and *certainly* not a female. He laughed all the way up the stairs, across the gardens, and well into the night. Under his bedsheets, he tickled himself with the idea that he lived in the same place as a woman who thought she saw invaders coming through the walls of a monastery. No barbarians would ever invade God's house. They wouldn't, he snickered, have the gall. He took his nighttime tea and slept in peace. Only a week later, when the early Hungarians came as Wiborada said they would, burning houses, stealing gold and jewels, destroying the entire neighborhood of Lake Constance and moving, positively *brimming* with gall, to the front door of the monastery—only then, in fear and astonishment, did he believe her. A long log swung and the front door burst open.

All of the monks ran out the back entrance, crying like frightened children: "*De sagittis Hungarorum libera nos, Domine!*"

"*That day*," writes Anonymus, "*the monastery at St. Gallen was abandoned to the invaders except for a large and friendly, but not terribly bright monk, who plunked down in the middle of the courtyard and refused to leave because he had not yet been given his monthly allowance of shoe leather, and the anchoress Wiborada, who remained in her pit, listening as the invaders approached.*"

The Hungarians thundered into the pit. They were expecting to find barrels of wine, and were more than surprised to find a woman there, hunched in a corner amongst towering piles of books. The leader of the invaders, a short man with a mustache which broomed over his lips, stepped forward. "Who are you?" he demanded.

Of course Wiborada could not understand him. "Please," she begged. "Kill me if you want to, but leave the library intact."

Árpád sighed. "Can anyone understand this woman?"

Wiborada glowered at Árpád. "*Paganismo transnatauerunt*," she said, her chin quivering. "Transient pagans." She grabbed a book and held it tightly to her chest.

Árpád looked around. "Can anyone tell me if her life is worth a hundred books?"

"I'd say fifty," the men said. "Fifty-five."

"Forty!"

"A dozen!"

"*Nulla!*"

Then it was everyone chanting, "No books! No books! No books!"

The Hungarians banged their swords and axes on the floor.

Árpád sighed. He was never happy when the men got carried away. "Leave the books," he said. "Get the wine."

"*Bor!*" they shouted happily.

Árpád followed them upstairs to check on the bread supply in the pantry of the monastery's kitchen. In the courtyard, he came upon the large, sickly-looking monk, sitting with his legs folded on the flat stones. The monk was moving his large arms randomly about, appearing to shoot at imaginary targets with imaginary arrows. Other Hungarians quickly gathered around him, holding their swords high above his head. "Why do you not flee?" they cried.

The Giant turned his invisible bow upon them, held it, and then released his fingers. "I can be of use," he said.

The Hungarians looked at each other. They demanded to know how this monk, way out here in the remote regions of Swabia, knew how to speak their language. So as they sat around the long wooden table that afternoon, Szeretlek, in a spattering of consonants, confessed that he was not actually from the monastery; that he came from a small camp of tribes somewhere further east.

Árpád was amused. The man clearly had come from Carpathia. "What else?" he asked, pouring himself some wine.

Szeretlek shrugged. "I'm in love," he said.

"With whom?"

"A woman," said Szeretlek.

The men roared.

Árpád held up his hands. "What sort of woman?"

Szeretlek looked patiently around the table. "She has very large thighs," he said.

The men lost it. But Árpád's ears perked up. "Large *thighs*?" he said.

"Like loaves of fresh bread."

Árpád paused. "Tell me about your tribe," he said. "Who are your people?"

The large man lifted his large face. He looked the Grand Prince in the eyes. The look, Árpád felt, was unsettling.

"I am a member of the *Fekete-Szem Hentes*," he said.

Then Árpád recognized the man's face, his body. The Giant looked different: his body was thinner, more brittle, and something horrid had happened to his face and skin. Suddenly Árpád very clearly remembered how the same gigantic arms and legs had entwined themselves around the legs of his beloved Lili under the burlap. It had been nearly five years since he had spoken about the Fekete-Szem, but the image of the creatures packed into the tent still flooded his brain. Each time he closed his eyes they were there, staring at him, licking their teeth, shaking nits from their hair, blinking their enormous, frightening eyes. And that woman! The táltos! Despite the fact that he had given them Lili, a proper Hungarian, to stay and watch over them, Árpád felt that he still had not satisfied the old witch. He felt that she had somehow cursed him. Ever since the day he stumbled into that tent, Árpád had awoken in the middle of the hot night, gasping for breath, thousands of those black eyes blinking back at him in the darkness, her words *"We are the weakest among you"* running full speed through his brain. How the image of these creatures persisted, like a second, insatiable conscience! He was stunned he had not recognized the Giant earlier, but it hardly seemed possible that Szeretlek could have survived Exile. And yet here he was, displaying one of his enormous leg-wrestling thighs to other members of the cavalry, who were *ooh*-ing and *ahh*-ing admiringly.

"Can we bring him with us?" the men begged. "Please?"

"We have enough oxen," said Árpád.

"But he'll be of use," the men said. "Get a load of these legs!"

They slapped Szeretlek's thighs and beamed.

Árpád threw his helmet across the table. "Fine," he snapped.

Fueled by the prospect of a homecoming with Lili, Szeretlek ran off to collect his belongings. Árpád reached over the table and grabbed bowls of food from his men. But they were empty. The Hungarians had eaten everything. There was no soup, no fruit. No fresh bread. He grabbed a large gray piece of ját, the size of a small skull. "Is this all that's left?" he said. The men looked at each other.

"That's it!" he shouted. "Everyone up! We're leaving! Get your horses."

In a flurry, the men began assembling their belongings and leaping upon their horses. When Árpád realized that Szeretlek had no horse to ride, he threw a fist in the air with fresh enthusiasm, jumped on top of the table, and cried out, "Hooy Hooy!"

"Hooy Hooy!" the Hungarians howled.

In the mere seconds they were famous for, the Magyars signaled everyone together with bugles and fire beacons. They quickly gathered their plunder, threw themselves over their saddles, and began galloping east across the Swiss plains, leaving one person, the one who would save them from their deaths, behind.

XXV

ANGEL, DANCING ON THE FINGERTIPS OF GOD

Adrian enters the Waiting Area with her clipboard. "Pfliegman," she says. "There's been a cancellation. You're up."

The Sick or Diseased children stop banging blocks as I limp past Mrs. Himmel's desk and into the narrow corridor that leads to Dr. Monica's office. I am going where they're going. Perhaps they're curious to see why I'm going. Perhaps they're curious to see if I'll return.

They quickly go back to the banging.

Adrian sits me down on the examining table, hands me my gown, and wordlessly closes the door, leaving me to the intense privacy of Dr. Monica's office sans Dr. Monica. Some improvements have been made: white curtains now hang down each side of the window like an open robe, a brand new humidifier purrs next to the door, two small chairs with painted daisies are in one corner, the examining table is in another, Dr. Monica's swivel chair is in the third, and in the fourth all of the stuffed animals have been piled into one big amalgam of fun.

I admit that part of me does not want to have impure thoughts about Dr. Monica. But I cannot help myself. It's like Pfliegmans were born to suffer such urges. Lovely Lily, I think. Exquisite Flower! I could take you. I could take you right here, our bodies splayed across the children's examining table.

It could happen—My Darling, I would beg, won't you let me sniff your soft chin? May I, if for only just a moment, squeeze the fat of your calves? Is not lust, after all, the fertile and exacting seed of love?

Adrian pokes her head in. "Everything okay?" she says.

"Get out!" I want to scream. "You're ruining the moment!"

"Undress, Rovar," she says, and closes the door.

I undress. I go to the closet and hang up my coat. My trousers fall to the floor in a pile, heavy from the caked-on dirt and the weight of my belt buckle. At home in the bus, I often let the clothes stay where they are, in the accordion shape into which they fall from my body, but not here— Here, I fold the trousers and sweatshirt neatly, and place them on the floor next to a small white chair. The boots remain on my small feet, the tongues hanging out the front as though panting. I hold the paper gown over my head.

It floats on.

Dr. Monica knocks briefly and enters the room, my manila folder embraced tightly to her bosom. Pieces of blond hair are everywhere. They decorate her face. Her cheeks, pink and round, perfectly complement the red dress, which hangs over her in U-shaped drapes. Her body is an altar. The dress, *la nappe d'autel*.

New curtains? I write.

Dr. Monica beams, admiring her windows. "It makes a difference, I think," she says.

I look down. Usually Dr. Monica wears puffy white sneakers, but not today; today she flaunts these red, open-toed heels. There is no rational reason why the extra space is afforded the toes; it doesn't appear to have anything to do with comfort. The red shoes are a tease; a deliberate act of vanity. And suddenly my Darling is removing her tiny white hat and letting all that hair go. She's unbuttoning her white doctor's coat and pulling low the neckline of this unbelievable dress. She climbs on top of me, straddling the examining table, and her thighs emerge from underneath the dress like two pale hams. She flips her hair over one shoulder and presses herself into me, biting the outer orbit of my ear, and me, all the while, grabbing her by the buttocks, quietly kneading—

It looks nice, I write.

"Thank you," she says, opening my folder. She brushes a leaf of hair from her face.

Where are you going tonight?

Dr. Monica looks at her watch. "Mr. Pfliegman," she says. "You're not being completely forthcoming with me."

Aren't I?

"What are you doing here? You don't have a temperature, and you look fine to me."

Do I?

Dr. Monica sighs, and tosses my folder on the counter by the sink. "I'm sorry, Mr. Pfliegman, but I can't stay for this. It's been a difficult day, and I really do have somewhere to be."

I slide down from the examining table, turn around, and part the examining gown for her. I show her my back.

"That's not good," she says.

I climb back up on the table. *NO*, I write.

"Let's have a look."

Dr. Monica stands up and snaps on the rubber gloves. She begins prodding. She places her hands flat on my back and examines the skin at the shoulders, rubbing all the way down each of my arms. The full breadth of my torso. She whistles. "So this has never happened before?" she says. "Nothing happened to instigate it?"

I shake my head.

She sits down in front of me, my folder poised on her lap. "Mr. Pfliegman," she says, "Why do you have to stay in that bus? Can't you at least move back into your old house? The farmhouse? Isn't that an option?"

No, I write. *That is not an option.*

"Why not?" she says.

The animals are there, I write.

"What animals? The animals you butcher?"

No.

"Then what animals?"

It's better not to discuss things like this.

"I completely disagree," she says. Her eyes flutter. "I think things like this are *exactly* what we should be discussing. Your parents, for example. Where did they—"

Give me something, I write.

"What do you want?" she says. "A drug? No drugs."

I shake my head. *Sugar.*

"Definitely no sugar," she says. "Water."

Dr. Monica goes over to the sink and runs tap water into a paper cone. She hands it to me. I reach for it, and a sharp pain suddenly enters the left side of my body. It tears its way right across my abdomen, and exits on the right. It feels like I've been sliced in half. My tongue sticks to the roof of my mouth and I start coughing in dry, fiery bursts. Dr. Monica's got me firmly by the shoulders. This time it's not a ploy—the pain holds constant.

"Mr. Pfliegman? Are you all right?" But I can't shake the coughing— Dr. Monica takes my hands in her hands. "Write it down," she says gently.

Shaking, I pick up my pen.

"I want you to try and visualize each pain specifically," she says.

I give her a quizzical look.

"It's what I ask the children," she explains. "It helps to try and visualize what's hurting you. Like it's an enemy that can be conquered. If your pain were a person, for example, what would the person look like?"

If I could speak, I know what I should say. He would have a small, pointed face. Dark hair and eyes the same color as mine. The same thin, lame muscles. He would be wearing those creamy slacks, the shirt with a long collar and an anachronous paisley print, those shiny Italian shoes— But it isn't him. The person I imagine has no discernable face. Instead the person I see behind my eyes is a young man with bright blond hair. He wears a short-sleeved blue dress shirt. Fancy black trousers with even cuffs. A black belt neatly cinched around his middle. He keeps one hand in one pocket of his pants, and the other hangs casually to his side, showing off a glittering silver wristwatch. It's nice out. The wristwatch shines in the sun—I swear that I've never met this man before in my life, but when Dr. Monica asks me this question, there he is, standing before me, as still and brutal as my own reflection. How can this be? How can I imagine the worst about someone I've never met?

Dr. Monica looks at me. "Mr. Pfliegman, I want to try something."

I thought you had somewhere to _be_.   —

She's quiet. It is a dangerous line, the line between the Creature and his Pediatrician. There are many, many unspoken rules. Certainly the Creature knows that if he confessed everything to her, if he confessed that his sicknesses are not always as terrible as he makes them out to be; if he confessed that he has spent whole hours gazing at the lines of her rump as though they were sculpted from fine marble; if he confessed that because of this rump, he has in the past helplessly suffered Thoroughly Benevolent But Nonetheless Highly Unsavory Erections in the company of Sick or Diseased children; if she knew that the car accident which killed Ján and Janka Pfliegman was not an accident at all, but something else entirely, there is no question that she would banish him from her office. If she knew what her hairy little convalescent was recovering into, she would stare at him, open-mouthed, and back away in cold fear. She would refuse to see him at all.

But the line has not been crossed this afternoon. Dr. Monica, thick-skinned, cracks a smile. "I suppose I do have somewhere to be," she says. "But it's not a big deal. We're just seeing a movie. To be honest, I don't even like movies. Isn't that funny?" She sighs, fingering and twisting the cross around her neck. "I'm just not any good at this dating business. Never was."

Ange, valsant sur les bouts du doigt de Dieu.

She slowly pulls on her rubber gloves. "Just relax, Mr. Pfliegman," she says. "We're in no rush. There's no rush at all." She walks over to the sink and runs the faucet, wetting a sponge, then opens a cabinet and removes a small blue bottle. It's some kind of lotion. She squeezes an inch of it onto the sponge and says, "This is just a clinical dermatological cream. It might feel a little like clay as it dries, but it's good for you. It pulls toxins from the body, and will clear away all that dry skin." She starts moving the sponge over my body. The lotion is light blue, the exact color of the bottle, and odorless. She coats my arms, chest, back, and even my face with it. "This should help loosen things up," she says. She spreads it all over my cheeks and beard, under my eyeglasses. It feels oily, and it burns.

"It can burn at first," Dr. Monica says. "But the burning goes away after a minute." She deposits the old sponge and produces a fresh one, along with a small stack of fresh handtowels. "When we wash it off, it will pull some of this dead skin away, okay? This stuff can be a little messy sometimes, so we've got to use these," she says, and pats the towels.

I look up at Dr. Monica, startled. She's never used "we" before. I stare at the dry sponge, nervously.

"Okay, let's see what's going on here," she says, and begins wiping.

As soon as she touches me, globs of lotion and skin begin to slide off my arms, my shoulders. Dr. Monica tries scooping it up with the sponge, but there's so much of it. She throws the sponge in the sink and scoots the HUMAN WASTE bucket to the examining table with her feet. She flicks the wet pieces from her hands into the bucket, but misses— They splatter to the floor. "Oh my God," she says, and quickly cups her hands around my chest as she tries to catch another jellied peel. It gets all over her gloves, her arms. The astonishing dress. She darts around the examining table and somehow maneuvers a wide, gelatinous piece off my back. She carries it slowly, like a ticking bomb, to the bucket— It collapses apart in her hands. Dr. Monica looks at my skin, pink and shining, and wipes her eyes with her wrists. "That's it," she gasps. "I think that's it. It's over," but then she remembers my face.

Trembling, she lifts a finger and touches my beard.

In one piece, it slips from my chin and falls onto my lap, quivering like a hirsute jellyfish.

As usual, Dr. Monica is entirely correct. I am not being completely forthcoming with her. But how could I possibly? How could I explain to her that the reason for my illnesses both is and is not biological? That my body is chained to a legacy of a thousand other crippled bodies that lived and died over the last millennium? That perhaps the Pfliegmans, the foul, ineffective few, were not as ineffective as we had always thought? After all, wasn't it for the protection of us—the weakest among them—that the Hungarians fled the wrath of the Pechenegs? Weren't we, therefore, the ones who drove them into the Carpathian Basin in the first place? Weren't the Pfliegmans, in that sense, actually *necessary* for their success? Isn't it for the protection of the weakest members of our race that all good change happens in the world? Isn't it true that if we do not care for the least among us—no matter how filthy or backward or solipsistic—we will become a race of monsters? What some historians and other official-sounding officials try to call "progress," all the while asking themselves whether history should be written this way or that, we Pfliegmans have never asked, knowing full well, deep within our rotted cores, the sacrifice that we must make for the survival of the greater good. "*Throughout nature*," Darwin writes, "*one species incessantly takes advantage of, and profits by, the structures of others*"—

"We have to get you to a hospital," Dr. Monica says. "I'm going to call the hospital."

No hospitals, I write.

"Why?" she asks.

You're my doctor.

"But I'm just a pediatrician, Mr. Pfliegman. I know colds and flu and ADD—I'm not a dermatologist."

But it has to be you, I write.

Dr. Monica wipes her eyes again and looks at me. "Why me? You aren't even honest with me, Mr. Pfliegman."

What do you mean?

"Your parents?" she says. "Your health records?"

I don't answer.

Dr. Monica looks up and down at the hairless little Creature occupying her examining table. Her face softens. "Okay, then, but you'll have to wait. I have to get this all cleaned up and see a few other people." She goes to the cabinets and removes several square boxes of gauze and unfurls the bandages. "You'll need to cover up first," she says, and starts wrapping the bandages around my body. She winds them around my neck, my shoulders. My chest and back.

As she's working, I notice my folder lying open by the sink, and lean forward to read it:

"Pseudomaniacal tendencies," it says. *"Invents various illnesses for personal attention."* And at the very bottom, printed out in painstakingly deliberate letters: *"PHYSICALLY, THERE IS NOTHING WRONG WITH HIM."*

Dr. Monica finishes quickly, snapping her scissors and applying thumb-sized pieces of medical tape. "How does that feel?" she asks. "Is it too tight?"

I don't answer.

She tidies up my face in silence, snipping underneath my nose, my eyeglasses, barely leaving room to see or breathe.

XXVI

THE INVISIBLE MAN

"Look at him, Adrian," laughs Mrs. Himmel. "He looks like the Invisible Man!" She has to hold her sides. Apparently to keep from rolling off her office chair. "The Invisible *Midget*," she howls.

Adrian covers her mouth with both hands. Her eyes water.

It's brutally hot in the Waiting Area. The Sick or Diseased children are sluggish, lying flat on their backs all over the room. They seem to be barely breathing, barely feeling well enough to do anything at all. They look drugged. When they see me enter, their eyes widen at the bandages, but that's all they can muster. The BANG THE DRUM! boy looks at me and slides off his chair.

"What happened to you?" he asks.

I saved a child from a burning building.

"You did not," he says. "You were in the back the whole time."

Spiders, I write. *They were living in my beard. Pesky.*

"No," he says, and laughs.

All of my skin fell off, I write.

The BANG THE DRUM! boy shouts across the Waiting Area to his mother: "All of his skin fell off!"

At this, the children perk up. They give another curious glimpse at my wrapped face, my eyeglasses hovering over the wrapping, and then lie back down again. The BANG THE DRUM! boy spies my writing tablet, and remembers the cowboy picture.

"Draw me a soldier," he says.

I pick up my pen and draw him a picture of a soldier with tall boots, a feathered hat. A military sash.

"That's just a man," he says. "Give him a gun."

I give the soldier a large, handsome rifle.

The boy touches the page with light fingers. "It's good," he says. "But now give him some bullet wounds."

I start attacking the soldier. The bullet wounds look more like the soldier's wearing polka dots, but the boy gets excited. "Get him!" he cries. With tiny circles, we shoot the hell out of that soldier. We shoot until there isn't any space left and the soldier is completely blacked out. The boy looks at me and grins. He sways in front of me, as though to imaginary music. "I'm going to have a baby sister," he says.

Really? I write.

"It's very good for Mother."

Why is that?

He looks at me like I'm an idiot. "Because that baby will be healthy, of course," he says, and runs back to his mother. She puts the magazine down on the side table and draws him in, holding his face with both hands.

"This is a Human Kiss," she says, and pecks him on the mouth. Then she rubs her nose against his nose. "This is an Eskimo Kiss," she says. "And *this* is a Butterfly Kiss." She places her face right next to his face. She flutters her eyelashes. He giggles warmly.

"Oliver?" says Adrian.

The BANG THE DRUM! boy and his mother stand up and follow her out of the Waiting Area. On his way out, he waves to a friend lying flat on the carpet. "Bye Brian," he says, but Brian doesn't wave back. He's too hot. He's wearing corduroy pants and a long-sleeve shirt, and his hair is sticking wet to his forehead. He looks like a washed-up starfish. He watches Oliver leave, then rolls up from the floor and stands in front of his mother. "I'm hot," he whines.

"Go get yourself a drink," she says.

He darts over to the water fountain and slurps the water. He plays with the knob for second, then returns to his mother. "It didn't work," he says. "I'm still too hot."

She ignores him.

Brian draws in a deep breath and holds it until his face goes purple. Then he bursts, spitting into her face.

"Please don't do that, dear," she says

The boy starts whacking his mother on the knees with little fists. "I want to play the drums," he says.

His mother turns a page of her magazine. "Mm-hmm."

He stares at her, furious that he received no reaction, and then begins stomping around the room, naming all of the musical instruments he wants to play. "I want to play the guitar!" he says. "I want to play the trumpet and the clarinet and the saxophone! I want to play the *trombone!*"

Wearily, she tells him to shush.

Suddenly a girl sitting across the room, perhaps motivated by the boldness of the boy, climbs up onto her chair, grabs one of Mrs. Himmel's unframed barnyard paintings off the wall, and bonks her own mother on the head with it. "Bonk!" she shrieks, and flies off her chair to bonk some other people. The mother, clearly Bad, does nothing. In fact, she looks relieved the girl's attention is elsewhere for a while. The girl bonks three other kids lying flat on their backs. The heat has them beat. Listless, they let her bonk them.

One of the mothers finally stands up. "Excuse me, Mrs. Himmel," she says. "Would you mind turning the heat down just a smidge? It's awfully warm in here."

Mrs. Himmel nods. "Of course," she says, and waddles over to the thermostat. Behind her desk, the sugar packets from the shelf beckon. The itch on my back digs in sharp, and underneath all these bandages my skin feels raw. Suffocated. Sweat slides down the center of my back aggravating the itch. I reach around to try and scratch it, and Mrs. Himmel catches me fidgeting. She smiles a little at my discomfort, and then, consciously or not, cranks it up a notch. Another cloud of heat puffs out of the radiators. The Sick or Diseased Children moan and roll onto their sides.

I unwrap three Evermores and close my eyes, and start chewing ferociously. When I open them, the little bonking girl is standing right in front of me.

"Why are you wearing that coat?" she says. "Aren't you hot?"

"Cynthia," her mother says, and gives her a scolding look.

But Cynthia is unfazed. She remains standing in front of me, clutching her painting. She wants to bonk me with it. "What's that picture?" she asks.

I show her the picture of the soldier.

"That's stupid," she says. "Draw me something, now."

I draw her a quick picture.

"What is it?"

It's a trombone.

"That's a penis," says the girl.

Her mother looks up. All the mothers look up. They lower their women's magazines and sit up in their chairs. They are transformed from Good Mothers and Bad Mothers into a pack of Mother Bears. Claws extended, nostrils flared. The girl hesitates for a moment, holding the picture of an idyllic farmhouse above my head.

"Cynthia, no!" cries her mother.

Cynthia bonks me. "Bonk!" she says.

In one spontaneous, exaggerated movement, her mother drops the magazine, darts from her chair, and grabs her child. They back away slowly.

Confused, Cynthia bursts into tears.

Mrs. Himmel rises from behind her desk like the sun over a battlefield. She hurries over to me, her eyes shiny as bullets. She grabs a corner of my writing tablet. *"Give it to me, you little creep,"* she seethes.

The mothers stand grouped behind her. I surprise myself and growl a little—Mrs. Himmel steps back, but does not let go of the tablet.

"It's a *penis*," says Cynthia, sobbing.

Mrs. Himmel finally yanks it from me and looks at the picture. "Lord in Heaven," she says, and runs into the back room to show Adrian.

A moment later, Adrian appears, filling the doorjamb. She pushes her sleeves to her elbows. I've never seen her look at me this way before; her eyes have shrunk into half-moons. Her back seems to arch up all on its own. "Mr. Pfliegman," she says.

The Sick or Diseased children all sit up and look at me with excited faces. I'm a scoundrel, and I've been discovered. *"Fleeg-man,"* they say. They whisper it like it's a swear word. *Fleeg-man.*

"Get out!" yells Mrs. Himmel. "Now!"

I want to leave—I know that I should leave—but I can't; I need my writing tablet. I gesture for it, waving my bandages as if to say, "Please, just give it to me. If I get the tablet then I'll leave."

But Mrs. Himmel holds it tight. "You're not getting *this* back, Mister," she says, and steps behind Adrian. "This is evidence!"

Helpless, I look around for a pen and paper, but there's nothing. Children's building logs. The withering ficus plant. *Highlights.* I try to show them what I drew—it's not a penis, see, it's a trombone—I hold my hands to my throat and rub quickly—I try to get the words out but they just won't go. I look frantically for Oliver, he might come to my defense, but he's still in the back, so I stand up and pretend to play the trombone to show them what I mean. I stand up and start moving my hands and blowing.

"Good God," Cynthia's mother says.

"That's enough of that," says Adrian, and she moves in a big red flash. She pins me to the floor of the Waiting Area and twists my body beneath her weight. "I don't care if you're sick or wrapped in bandages or not, Mr. Pfliegman. I don't know or care *what* you are." She puts one foot on my spine and then lifts me up. "Out you go," she says.

Mrs. Himmel holds the door open. I'm deposited, coat and all, out on the lawn. Rain hits at once. Cars driving in and out of the Big M parking lot slow down to watch as from the dripping grass, the Invisible Man reaches one arm toward the picnic table.

Adrian slams the door and locks it. Mrs. Himmel watches from a window. "Get away from that picnic table!" she shouts. "This time you're not coming back!" She folds her arms. I stare up at her with pleading eyes, but she's not buying it. "You're-not-coming-back," she mouths, and casts a look upon her face that only belongs to a person who has satisfied a prejudice.

The Sick or Diseased children all run to the window and start shouting. Oliver has returned from Dr. Monica's office and presses his palms against the glass. I look at him, and he looks back at me. He blinks. His mother rushes up and tries to pull him away from the window. He cries out in protest.

"The police!" shouts Mrs. Himmel. She stabs her thumb and pinky finger at me. "We've called the police!"

I look over at the supermarket in the rain. The enormous M glows red over the wet parking lot. No Security Guards are guarding the entrance, so I jump up and sprint across the street, the tails of the Kabát Tolvajok dragging behind me. I skirt around puddles, all the way up to the front entrance of the supermarket where the wide glass doors swing open.

I duck behind a chubby Virginian in a tracksuit, and follow him past the rows of vegetables, through condiments, and abandon him at the frozen dinner entrees. There is a back entrance to the Big M behind the bakery, where the bakers unload their trucks at night, and right next to the meat section. I make a run for it, but a familiar figure is in the way, blocking the exit. It's Daughter Elise. She's leaning over the bakery counter, piling powdered jelly doughnuts into a waxy white bag. She looks over her shoulder, then shoves one of the doughnuts in her mouth.

I glance back to the wide glass doors, but the Security Guards are now gathered there, circling—

"What are you doing?"

Herman Himmel comes up right behind me. Underneath the high ceiling of the supermarket, the bright, fluorescent bulbs, he looks even bigger. He bends forward like a curious bear. "What's with the bandages?" he asks, and adjusts his baseball cap.

I lightly touch the bandages, but avoid eye contact. Instead I look over at the refrigerated display units, at the long pink rows. A football field of meat.

"Buddy," he says. "Why aren't you at the bus?"

But just as he asks it, Herman realizes it is a question he already knows the answer to. "Buddy," he says again. "I can't save you." Slowly, he points a finger towards the ceiling. Three cameras, each with one red eye, are all pointed right at me. Herman gives me a sad, defeated look and grips the sleeve of my coat. He picks up his walkie-talkie. "I've got him," he says.

The other Security Guards throw their walkie-talkies into their holsters and dart from the glass doors. Their billy clubs swing in unison.

"You got him!" they shout.

"The man in the coat!"

"Take him to Management!"

Herman holds up a large flat palm. "Wait," he says. "Just wait." He looks at his clipboard, and gestures to the other men, who then also look at their clipboards. "Stay right here," he says to me, and moves the Security Guards a few paces away. They talk with each other, glancing occasionally at me. It's possible to dart around them; we're close to the sliding glass doors, and through them is the ENTER EXIT sign, the cars that fill the parking lot. But then I see the Indian running underneath the sign. He's tearing across the parking lot in the heavy rain, waving his arms. His hair is plastered to his head, but he doesn't wipe it away. He looks frightened. Behind him, a black sport utility vehicle rolls beneath the sign and into the red glow of the parking lot, wipers thrashing across the windshield. It finds an empty space and parks. Three men in black suits step out. They slam the doors and, protecting themselves with manila folders above their heads, walk quickly toward the entrance of the supermarket. The Indian darts around the men as they approach the glass doors, he tries to punch them—it's no use. Herman picks up his walkie-talkie from his holster and barks, "We've got Disneyland, repeat, we've got Disneyland," but I keep my eyes on the doors. The Indian swings and swings, but keeps missing them. One of the Subdivisionists is holding something familiar in his hand, something square and white which they stole from my bus when they went there today, after leaving Mister Bis's, after they kicked in the door of the bus. It's a business card. They found it perched on the windowsill next to an abandoned tin can smelling faintly of tomatoes. The card says DR. MONICA BOTTOM, PEDIATRICIAN, and there's a picture of a blue butterfly above the name. Below the name is her street address and telephone number.

Mrs. Himmel was only too glad to tell them where I'd gone.

In a final, wild effort, the Indian moves behind the Subdivisionists and throws himself on top of them, but his body simply moves through them, as if they were air, as if they were never there at all. They walk up to the glass doors of the Big M, pointing their large chins in all directions. The doors swing open. They spot what they're searching for and run over, and suddenly Rovar Ákos Pfliegman, the last of all Pfliegmans, finds himself surrounded by enemies, both east and west.

IMAGO

1. The final and perfect stage or form of an insect after it has undergone all its metamorphoses; the "perfect insect."

2. A subjective image of someone (especially a parent) which a person has subconsciously formed and which continues to influence his attitude and behavior.

—*The Oxford English Dictionary*

XXVII
EVOLUTION OF THE PFLIEGMANS:
THE BATTLE OF THE RED VALLEY

Dust shimmered in a line along the horizon. Szeretlek the Giant stood on the steps of the monastery watching morosely as his fellow Hungarians rode off without him. He watched until they were out of sight. It felt as though someone was holding him by the throat, tight around his esophagus, even though he hadn't a clue about esophagi. A large tear slipped down his large face. He closed his eyes and tried to feel Lili's soft hair against his palm, the mould of her fat back, the smooth wide roll of those spectacular thighs, but he could not. To be abandoned by one's people was one thing; it was quite another to be abandoned by one's own mind.

"Stupid!" he cried, knocking his head with the hoof of his palm. "Stupid stupid!"

It was all because he had wanted to be of use. But what use was he now to Lili? To himself? To anyone? Kinga had once told him that a useful man is never lonely, but here, now, after thirty-five years of quiet obeisance, the Giant was more alone than ever.

Szeretlek stared up at the clouds curling above. He shook his fists. "You Miserable Punishing Man in the Sky," he shouted. "I am of use to no one!" And then, as though resigning himself to some stronger, more authoritative philosophy, cried out: "I have no useful purpose!"

At that moment, something jabbed him from behind. Szeretlek spun around to find himself nose-to-nose with the biggest horse he'd ever seen. The horse was enormous, big and white. Magnificent-looking. Truly it was the most magnificent horse he had ever seen. It was M. Earlier that day, as the Hungarians were preparing to leave, the horse had gotten into a barrel of wine, become swimmingly drunk, and passed out, hooves to belly, in a nearby barn.

Árpád had tried to rouse him, but the horse just lay there, sleeping. The Grand Prince did not realize the horse was asleep; he'd assumed that one of the monks, sometime during in the hours of the Hungarians' indelicate arrival at the monastery, had poisoned him out of revenge. So he'd left M lying on the floor of the barn and instead mounted a speckled and far less impressive horse named Paprika, who suffered from backaches and perpetual foot rot. "Death to the man who stole my horse from me!" he'd cried.

Of course Szeretlek hadn't heard him; at the time, he had been clear on the other side of the monastery, assembling his things. He packed the doubly curved bow that he made in the wilderness. He packed shoes, his cloaks. He'd spent a few extra minutes wandering the fields and gardens, gathering gifts for Lili: an unusually long blade of grass which wound around his finger like a wedding ring; from an assortment of insects creeping in the grass, he selected a large shiny beetle; he found a small, funny-looking caterpillar, bearded in fur. When he'd returned to the courtyard, he was astonished to find the monastery empty. He'd been abandoned. He had no horse to carry him home.

And now he had a horse. There was just one niggling, inescapable concern: Szeretlek the Giant had to somehow get on top of the thing.

He tossed a saddle over M and tried to mount him in the manner which he had seen the other Hungarians mounting their horses. He promptly fell off. His feet were like paddles. They slipped from the stirrups, and he couldn't get a good enough grip to swing his legs over the back of the animal. As he tried, he grew so frustrated that a peculiar itch developed between his shoulderblades. He reached behind his neck to scratch it, but couldn't reach. He continued trying to mount M, but the more the Giant tried and failed, the more intense the itch became. It got to the point where he couldn't even get a running start to throw his foot into the stirrup without stopping to claw his back. "Ack!" he gasped, and threw himself on the ground, rubbing himself against the stones. It didn't work. Szeretlek stood up again and removed his shirt. Twisting his body, he reached both hands around to try to figure out what was happening, and then, suddenly, his body lifted. Like a puppy grabbed at the neck, Szeretlek the Giant rose up. He jerked and struggled to stay put, but whatever was carrying him would not let go. It was a ridiculous feeling; he wasn't high up, he only hung a few feet above where he was previously standing, but there he was: a Giant, dangling in the air! He tried to crane his neck around to get a glimpse of the carrier, but his neck seemed stuck in an awkward, forwardly bent position, and he couldn't see. He struggled only for a moment more and then gave up. Almost involuntarily, his long arms and legs went loose. It was as though they had suddenly lost their utility. He felt his body tugged upward a few more inches and then, just as quickly, without logic or reason, the Giant was lifted above the horse and dropped onto the wide white back of M.

The horse groaned, stunned by the massive weight. He trotted back and forth unhappily.

"I am *awesome!*" Szeretlek cried.

He was so pleased that he had finally mounted a horse and would now finally be able to return home to Lili, that it did not occur to the Giant that there was anything all that different or unusual in the manner of the mounting, or even that he had landed backward on the animal and was facing entirely in the wrong direction. To him, it was obvious what had happened: after five long years, Lili was right. He was not alone. It was Ember az Égben. The Pfliegmans often chattered about such a thing happening, and now it had happened to him. He had been lifted up by the nimble fingertips of the Man in the Sky and dropped. It was exceedingly fortunate, he felt, that when he was dropped, he landed directly on top of the animal. Belief, new and raw, coursed through his body, and Szeretlek did not question it again. He did not, in fact, give it another thought. He did not even dare to think of turning around to ride the horse properly; his only thought as he sat backward on M, as he leaned forward and slapped the horse's hind end, was to return to the Carpathian Basin, throw back the flaps of the tent of the Fekete-Szem, and run as fast as he could between Lili László's large, imposing thighs.

"The Giant rode backward for two days in the direction of the rest of the Hungarians

and did not stop," Anonymus writes. *"Not until he arrived over the crest of a dense and bristling forest. Before him was a grassy field at the bottom of an open valley where Árpád's armies had pitched their tents. It was evening. The sun burned the horizon, cloaking the valley red. The mud, the grass, the river, the uneven ground, all the way over the hills to the distant, luminous mountains. Everything glowed."*

Szeretlek rode a winding path into the valley, and despite the fact that these very same men had abandoned him at the monastery, the Giant felt the presence of someone watching over him, and he had never felt more love or generosity. "My brothers," he thought. He wept openly. And had he not lost himself in the Carpathian wilderness five years earlier; had he not spilled the beans about Lili at the breakfast table; had Árpád's white horse not taken so much of a liking to warm, Swabian wine; had Szeretlek the Giant indeed not been born a Pfliegman, he would never have been in a position to see the fires of the enemy light up the hillside that evening. He rode quickly down the mountain, shouting, "Pechenegs! On the eastern hills!"

From the belly of the red valley, the Hungarians watched, open-mouthed, as a large, shirtless man rode Árpád's great white horse backwards down the mountainside. He was shouting his head off. They saw him and howled with laughter. They slapped each other on the back. They held their middles. But as one of them wiped a joyful tear from his eye and looked gleefully over the eastern hills, an arrow appeared through a red cloud above, hurtled speedily toward him, and before the Hungarian could speak or breathe, or even blink, it sank deep into his heart.

The Hungarians stared at the fallen soldier, astonished.

The backward rider came closer. They still couldn't see his face, but now his voice echoed over the valley, and the Hungarians discerned what he was shouting:

"Pechenegs! Pechenegs!"

They mounted their horses just as the foreign army rolled over the hills. They were outnumbered. Six to one. A soldier rushed into Árpád's tent just as the Great and Noble Grand Prince was about to settle in for some boiled ját and masturbation: "Pechenegs!" he cried. "On the eastern hills!"

Árpád jumped to his feet. His entire army had mounted their horses and were shooting arrows as fast as they could without dying. He soberly evaluated the situation. Pechenegs wore black armor and bared their teeth and carried long, floppy spears with points at the end, and on top of the points were the heads of their victims. But these men wore metal helmets, expensive green cloaks, and their swords were strong and firm. Their beards were combed, and their green banners waved arrogantly. The perfume that clung to the air smelled too clean to be Pechenegs. Then Árpád noticed the crosses on their banners.

"Those aren't Pechenegs," he said. "They're Germans."

"Kyrie Eleison!" the Germans cried, and charged down the mountain.

"Hooy Hooy!" shouted the Hungarians.

Árpád pulled on his bird-helmet, leapt upon Paprika, and galloped down the mountain, skirting trees and rocks, into the heart of the valley. He had always felt safe while riding high atop the wide back of M, and now, for the first time in his life, the leader of the early Magyars became uncertain. He quickly realized that Paprika, well-meaning as the horse might be, simply was not fast enough.

Almost at once, a German arrow stabbed him in the leg.

Árpád raised up his hands. "Is this the moment of my death?" he cried. Then he noticed a hawk circling the valley. It flew into the fight, as if to show him something, and in the crowd of men zipping arrows from their horses, shiny German metal clashing against Hungarian cloaks and pelts and buttons, Árpád saw a flash of white. He rubbed his eyes. It could not be—but it was! How on earth had M made it all the way here from where he'd left him, dead at the monastery? And the enormous man riding him! He was shirtless, and turned the wrong way around, but it was very decidedly him. It was the Giant. The woman-thief.

"Well, I'll be damned," said Árpád.

Now, Szeretlek was no warrior. After crying out his warning, the Giant had, in a manner classic to Pfliegman behavior, made his way through the chaos, swerving in and out of danger's way, hiding behind the swords of other, braver soldiers, and then had turned tail, fully prepared to find the first clear route away from what appeared to be Certain Death, and back into the arms of his pragmatic, rotund Lili. But flight from the red valley was not so easy; certainly not when one was riding backward upon an animal accustomed to riding *into* battle, and not away from it. Before he knew it, Szeretlek found himself riding into, and facing away from, the Germans.

"Lili!" he cried, as if she might appear from the bushes and start throwing punches.

A German soldier rode up behind Szeretlek. He held up his weaponry, fully prepared to shoot, when he realized that he was looking not at the back of a man's head, but at his face. Confused, he lowered his arrow. He saw the ass of the horse but the face of a man, when the *backs* of men were supposed to be the same as the *backs* of horses. He deduced that the rumors about these horrible people were true: this enormous, brutal Hungarian was indeed Two-Faced. Very clearly, he had faces on both sides of his head! Choking with fear, the German stammered, "But it's the wrong—"

At that moment, Szeretlek did what Nature had intended him to do ever since she scrawled the messy plans for his invention. Ever since Kinga bit down Aranka's nose and he burst forth into this wet, unhappy world. He did something that would change the course of the battle, and, henceforth, the course of the Hungarian Incursions for the next thirty years, all the way up to 955 AD, when the Germans, fired by the fury of this great loss, would gather all of the European armies together at the Battle of Augsburg and slaughter every Hungarian soldier but seven—Szeretlek dug his heels into the horse's gut, reached into his quiver, removed his doubly curved bow, and shot the German.

The victim looked stunned for a moment, but then, with no stirrups to hold him in, tumbled easily from his horse.

Árpád had never seen anything like it. "Look!" he cried. "He's shooting *backward!*"

Collectively, in one dignified movement, the Hungarians looked at each other, then spun around in their saddles and began shooting backward at the enemy in what would eventually become a signature Hungarian method of attack. All of them, every last greasy-haired pagan Hungarian, picked arrows from their quivers, placed them over their bows, and pulled back tight. Then they turned in their saddles and sent the arrows singing through the air.

The slaughter was massive. For every Hungarian soldier killed in the battle, six Germans fell. No one was spared. And the Hungarians, barbaric reputations now firmly sealed, watched how the panorama of the valley changed: how the grass and trees and even the mountains beyond the eastern hills, all of it, which once glowed red from the terrific, dying sun, was now red for other reasons. German blood soaked into the earth, creating small pools in which the early Hungarians frolicked. They would give them their schadenfreude, but years later, when King Stephen's corrupt nephew

Peter takes the throne, demanding that the entire country enter into German bondage, that only Germans hold the Hungarian thrones, attributing ownership of all castles and private estates to the Germans and slaughtering any pagan slave who disobeyed his Christian master—then the Germans would give it right back. *"Eventually,"* Anonymus writes, *"the Christians win a bigger battle, the battle for Hungary itself."*

But now, this evening, the Hungarians were celebrating the victory. They encircled Szeretlek, begging him to show them his doubly curved bow.

"If I can be of use," he said.

The Hungarians watched as the bow sprung arrows twice the distance of a normal bow. "It shoots marvelously well," they said, patting his legs.

Then the soldier who had first spotted Szeretlek riding backwards down the mountain got off his horse and helped him to turn around. He helped him to face the proper direction that a man is supposed to face when he is riding a horse. When he is civilized. He took the bow and held it high in the air so all of the other Hungarians could see it, and Szeretlek, regarded for the first time in his life not as a Giant, a Pfliegman, a Fekete-Szem, but simply a man among other men, felt the burden of his great body no longer. He spread out his arms, lifted his chin and unleashed a deafening scream:

XXVIII

WE'RE ALL CHILDREN

"Don't move," a voice says. "Just relax."

I open my eyes. Blond hair falls away from her face in tired pieces.

"Mr. Pfliegman, can you hear me?" she asks.

It's morning. I'm lying on top of Dr. Monica's examining table, wrapped in a pale blue hospital blanket. Outside the window to her office, sunlight beams on the arms of the oak tree. I motion for my writing tablet.

"You spent the night here," she says. "You had a bad fever."

What happened?

Dr. Monica stands up to wash her hands. She turns on the faucet, runs her hands under the water, and then dries them. She takes her time. When she faces me, her arms are folded tight across her chest. The red dress is gone, replaced with clean slacks, her turtleneck sweater, and her white pediatrician's jacket. The gold cross shines arrogantly between the lapels. It looks like it's flipping me off.

"Mrs. Himmel told me what happened," she says. "Her husband, Herman, is a security guard at the supermarket, and he says that you've been stealing meat from the Big M. Selling the meat out of your bus. He says that you've been doing it for some time now."

I gaze over at the far corner of her office, where my Disneyland sweatshirt is dry, folded on top of one of the daisy chairs. My trousers hang from a hook, with the stylish woolen cap perched over them. The Kabát Tolvajok is folded thickly in half on her counter, telling me that things have been taken care of. Things have been done.

And you believe them? I write.

Dr. Monica sighs and looks at me. "Elise was there, Mr. Pfliegman. She said you started a fight. She said you were throwing packages of meat at people. It took three people to hold you down. It was the fever, I think— You were delirious, so they carried you across the street and brought you in here. You bit a Security Guard on the leg." She gives me a stern look. "Why did you do that?"

I don't know.

Dr. Monica reaches over, pulls one of her paper cones from the dispenser, and fills it with water. I accept it, but do not drink. She presses her hands around my face and neck, tightening the bandages. "There are some people outside who want to see you," she says.

I move to get up from the examining table, but she pushes me back. Her eyes soften, and she relaxes a bit. "Wait," she says, and presses down on my forehead. "They can wait. At least until the fever breaks. It was nasty out there last night. There've been reports of flooding all morning. It's affected three counties, they say. I don't remember ever seeing rain like that before. Not in twenty years at least."

Dr. Monica walks back over to the sink and picks up a familiar piece of paper next to the throat swabs. It's a yellow page torn from my writing tablet with a drawing on it which is clearly a musical instrument and not an instrument of any other kind.

"Mr. Pfliegman," she says. "What's this?"

I squint at the picture.

It's a trombone, I write. *The kid asked me to draw it. I swear.*

Dr. Monica's eyes flutter. "Well, I don't know if it's a trombone or not," she says. "But it certainly doesn't look like—the other thing." She smiles and circles around the examining table. "Look, Mr. Pfliegman. There's something I need to tell you. I don't care about the meat, I really don't— But Mister Bis is coming over this afternoon when you're feeling better. He was worried about you with all this rain, so he went out to the field to check on you yesterday."

I sit up and adjust my eyeglasses. I look at her.

"But when he got there," she says, "the bus was gone."

Gone?

"The whole field is gone, and not just your field. The river flooded. People have lost whole farms. I can't tell you how relieved I am you weren't out there when it happened. It's all over the news— Anyway, I don't want you to worry about that now. Everything's arranged. Mister Bis has agreed to take you in. He has an extra room. It's just a cot in his basement, but it's safe and dry. I think it's a good place to stay until we can help you make other accommodations."

I'm sorry. But I can't.

Dr. Monica frowns. "You may not have a choice. The Big M is pressing charges— But look, I don't want you to worry about that now," she says, and walks over to me. She places her hands on my kneecaps. "Things have been taken care of, Mr. Pfliegman. I just want you to lie back so I can have a look at you."

Why?

"Why what?"

Why do you want to help me?

She looks at me, surprised. "It's my job."

It's your job to care for children, I write.

Dr. Monica sighs and looks at her watch. "We're all children, Mr. Pfliegman," she says. "Just lie back. Relax."

I lie down. Dr. Monica prods her fingers along the bandages covering my clavicle to my sternum, all the way down to my pelvis. At this point in an examination with Dr. Monica, I might suffer urges, or even just a floating immodest thought, but now that Things Have Been Taken Care Of, now that there are Other Accommodations, now that Everything's Arranged— Dr. Monica presses down on a small place on the left side of my abdomen.

I cough, violently.

"Do that again," she says, keeping her fingers in place.

I cough again. It feels like one of my lungs is leaning against the other. Dr. Monica presses a little harder, then walks around the table. She takes a few minutes and unwraps the bandages, then she presses the other side. "Does this hurt?" she asks.

I shake my head.

"Weird," she says, and crumples her brow. "Mr. Pfliegman, there's something wrong with your stomach."

I look down at my stomach. It's one round bulge, swelling out between my ribs and hips. It looks like my gut's full of air. I trace it with a finger.

"Let's get rid of the rest of the gauze," she says. "I want to do an X-ray. You can keep the examining gown on."

Wait, I write. *There's something I have to tell you, too.*

Dr. Monica looks up from my writing tablet. "Yes?" she says. "What is it?"

XXIX

EVOLUTION OF THE PFLIEGMANS:
EXEGESIS

Lili László normally wore the kinds of clothes that the men wore, a cape-like shirt secured with a rope for a belt. During her pregnancy with Botond, she loosened the rope a few notches, but that was all. The nurse in charge of the delivery was an old, crooked-looking woman with furry yellow teeth and hair that grew in places where hair has no business growing. Kinga's cheeks had long drained of color, her eyes squinted at light and at darkness, and she slowly accepted the fact that she was going to be blind and there was nothing to be done about it. She did not mind the loss of sight. She had spent too many years observing how the stronger Pfliegmans tried and failed, often fatally, to participate in any activity in society that went beyond butchering; she had seen how the meeker Pfliegmans, the ones who kept to the tents and did not mingle with society, the ones who spent days waving the flies out of their eyes, coughing their lungs out, managed to *keep hanging on*; she saw our bleak and unforgiving future and the old witch retreated into herself. She was, in ways both physical and spiritual, shrinking from the world, which might explain why, upon helping Lili give birth to Botond, the tiny, slippery baby boy, she felt no gentle tug of conscience, no whisper of remorse, when she told her the small secret she had carried, like a pin on her shawl, for the last thirty years.

Lili was sitting up, nursing the child, as we Pfliegmans hung back. After the birth of Szeretlek, we'd become highly suspicious of the whole experience, so when it appeared that Lili was entering labor, we'd scattered to the flaps of the tent, watching fearfully. Waiting for the water to begin. But it had been an easy birth. Kinga removed the one bowl of body-water from the tent to dump it outside.

"He's small," said Lili. "Should he *be* this small?"

"Small's good," Kinga said. "You were big. Too big." She rubbed her sagging cheeks, then squatted down to the fire. She poked it with a stick. A burning log fell over and rolled out onto the hearth. She jammed it back in again.

"You were there?" said Lili, adjusting herself.

The baby whimpered.

Kinga sucked her lower lip, which slid easily in and out her mouth. Over the years she had lost her teeth into various meats and stews, and the lip now flapped against her gums with each breath. "Your mother died when you were still in the womb," she said. "She couldn't deliver you. So after your brother was born, I reached in and pulled you out."

Lili laughed. "You're crazy," she said. "I don't even have a brother."

Kinga grabbed her leg and squinted fiercely. "We are *all* brothers," she hissed, sucking her lip.

We must go back, for a moment, to the day Szeretlek was born. To Aranka lying sprawled across the hearth. To the water and fish, the long arms of algae, pouring from her body. The other Hungarian women have swum out of the tent to save their own skins. But Kinga stays back to check the lifepulse. To be absolutely certain of the death. She is chilled, chest-deep in the water, and quickly runs her hands over the body. The little Pfliegman woman is dead. But when Kinga reaches the belly, something quivers beneath it. The belly is still large with fat, which Kinga knows is common, but she also knows that it should not be moving like that. The belly wobbles and jerks, like a baby bird trapped in its own egg. She presses one hand into it.

The belly kicks back.

Kinga pushes up her sleeves and reaches inside the dead woman. She feels a pair of feet. The baby is turned around. Kinga gets one foot, wrapping her thumb around the ankle and grabbing it, and then she gently pulls the baby out. It's a girl, and she screams louder than any baby Kinga has ever heard before. The scream is disconcerting, and Kinga has to concentrate to keep her grip. Once she affirms her hold on the child, she severs the umbilical cord and paddles toward the open flaps of the unsteady tent, holding the baby high above the quickening current.

The child cannot see Kinga, but feels for her. She stretches her legs out as far as they will go, down Kinga's left arm. "Steady!" Kinga cries. But when she reaches the elbow, the babe wrestles both of her legs around the arm, squeezes tightly, and then turns it with surprising strength— Kinga's grip loosens, and the child drops, splashing into the river. Frantically, Kinga tries to swim to catch her, but she is not fast or strong enough. She watches the baby float away, perched on a fat bed of algae and cradled by the current, disappearing around the bend.

It is one thing to learn that you're in love with your brother—your *twin* brother. It is quite another to learn you are a Pfliegman. After Kinga's story, Lili picked up Botond, wrapped him in cloth, and fled the fetid Pfliegman tent. She fled from all of us. She made her way across camp to the outskirts of the outskirts, where the trees had not been logged, where there were no barnyard animals milling cozily about, where the congregated populace thinned from ten paces per tent to one hundred paces to an even thousand. Lili spun around and stared back at her home, the home of the butchers, a lazy patchwork of animal hide pieced onto the frames, hastily sewn in uneven stitches. These people were her people. She looked down at little Botond and was frightened: the boy now seemed foreign to her, a wriggling, unfamiliar creature that opened and closed its mouth like a begging bird. She began to notice failings in the child: the eyes were off balance, the ears stuck out much too far to be normal. The stomach ballooned with air. The small arms and legs that had once seemed endearing and delicate now looked displaced next to the head.

It was spring. The gray, wet sky roiled above as Lili walked to the edge of Aranka's river and stood in the mud of the embankment. "It would be so easy," she thought. "All I have to do is let him fall from my arms in the exact manner that I would drop a load of firewood. A stack of burlap." She moved closer to the edge, to the place where weeds fall into water. She put her toe in. It was freezing.

Botond screamed in her arms.

Lili thought of Szeretlek as she looked down at his face, at his watery gray eyes, eyes that would one day turn black with no discernable pupils, and could not do it. He felt glued to her. Lili had seen so many of the Fekete-Szem walk out to this spot to send a *hal* back where it came from, but although Botond was small and weak, he had not been born *hal*— She could not send this little fish back. She held him tight and ran away from the river, back to the tent.

After some pushing and shoving, she commandeered a corner for herself and Botond near the hearth, and then Lili László, the unflagging Leg-Wrestling Champion of Tenth-Century Hungary, herself grew lethargic. Kinga ran errands for her, stealing rinds of fat peeled from deermeat from the proper Hungarians. Armloads of ját. She would return to the tent and dump everything on the food mat on the floor, but still Lili's appetite waned. She never left the tent. Never. She would gnaw indolently on a piece of ját and then toss it on the floor in the manner of every other Pfliegman. She grew disinterested in meat, and only ate the droppings of tomatoes Kinga gathered from the ground below other people's stews, until one day she lost interest in the tomatoes. Often she ate nothing at all.

She spent each day growing thinner in her corner of the tent, nursing and then eventually feeding the wee, misshapen Botond only when she had to, speaking only when it became urgently necessary to do so, and eventually, after five years had passed, after it became clear that Szeretlek was not returning, that he most likely had been consumed, somehow, by the barrens, Lili stopped speaking at all.

Of course, Szeretlek was not dead. Far from it. As a reward for saving the Hungarian armies, Árpád had given him M, and Szeretlek rode the great white horse back to the Carpathian Basin. For weeks he scanned the populace, searching for the one specific tent, the tent that leaned both east and west, but Lili had moved us, and Szeretlek could not find it. He lumbered along the riverbanks of the Danube, his giant arms swinging, inquiring of strangers if they had ever heard of Lili László. The Hungarian population had expanded considerably over the last five years: many people eager to get on board with a prospering nation were new to the community, and had never heard of her. Others had only vague, imprecise recollections. Some of the older Hungarians remembered when Árpád had searched for her, and cried out, "She's lost again?" If they remembered anything, they remembered a compact woman with impressive thighs, but most had not seen or heard anything about her since the Great Leg-Wrestling Match, and that was—well, it was a long time ago. Most didn't even remember the match.

"Time," thought Szeretlek. "How you float so effortlessly by."

Always, he asked who among them had cut their meat, and their answers always varied: "The creepy butcher-folk," they said. "Those sickly little meat people." Or sometimes, in a slightly deferred murmur: *"Enni hús, enni hús."*

A new pain appeared at his ankle, from the very place where the raccoon had nipped him on the heel. It grew upward to the knee, then the stomach, the shoulders, like a rising flood. Once again, he began to feel the weight of his body. No matter how strong or able, his thick arms were useless. A burden. His back drooped as he rode M along the river, and his head hung low. Without Lili to return to, there would be no reason ever to look skyward.

As he rode past them, the Hungarians whispered amongst themselves: "How sick he looks!"

"And how sad!"

"Is there anything sadder than a sad giant?"

One desultory afternoon, while slumping around yet another embankment, Szeretlek found himself barely able to sit upright. He felt stabbed, and yet, when he lifted his shirt, there was no cut. The pain traversed from the left side of his body to the right in a clean half-orbit across his belly, and he could endure it no longer. He slid off the great white horse and into a lick of the river. He paddled along in a strange and foreign daze until he saw it. The tent was bigger than he remembered, but there was no denying the clumsy handiwork, the sour smell of the boiling stew, the clouds leaking into the sky overhead. The Giant crept from the water and crawled up on his knees. Exhausted, he fell on his side.

The ground shuddered.

We Pfliegmans felt this disturbance, and it frightened us into a flutter of discontent. We stopped whatever foul thing we were doing and squealed, "The earth is shaking! It will swallow us whole!"

We nominated a wispy young Pfliegman named Elod to investigate the sound.

Fearfully, Elod poked his head out of the tent where Szeretlek's enormous body lay in front of him, unconscious. Elod whimpered and ducked back inside. "It's a giant," he whispered. "A dead giant!"

Of course, we Pfliegmans had no understanding of the gray areas of human existence—a body either moved or didn't move, that was all—so after poking him with a few sticks to be certain, four of us emerged from the tent and grabbed his hands and feet. We dragged the body to the back of the tent, behind the Moving Rock Pile. We did not recognize him. We had forgotten him in exactly the way that we forgot everything else. What part of a Pfliegman life, after all, is worth remembering? Memory is for the strong, the well-nourished, and we Pfliegmans could only endure each brutal second as it presented itself— Besides, the Giant certainly didn't *look* like one of us. We huddled around the fire that evening, swatting the flies, yelling and batting each other over the head, all in a manner common to the Pfliegman urbane.

Here was the issue: in order to be a sacrifice, the sacrifice had to be alive at first, and then killed. But others argued that when the Giant came to the tent he was alive, if only for a short time. We Pfliegmans very much enjoyed a good sacrifice.

"What shall we do?" we cried.

"Sacrifice!"

"But we could use his clothes and body parts!"

"Sacrifice!"

"Let the body rot, and we'll keep out the villains!"

"Save the bones for lumber!"

"Enni hús! Enni hús!"

Szeretlek gagged and coughed, and then awoke.

People, so many people, wiggled and squirmed around him. It was impossible to move. Embers burned low in the hearth next to him, smoke circling and rolling in the tent, heavy as a moving fog. His eyes! How they stung! The flap in the ceiling was not wide enough for proper ventilation. Szeretlek tried to look for Lili, but his eyes burned and he couldn't see. Too many arms and legs cluttered his view. Too many black eyes peering down at him, trying to evaluate whether he was alive or dead. They picked at his hair. They tasted his feet. He tried to move his arms and legs but found them to be bound.

"Help me," he choked.

A young boy scampered between the legs and knelt down next to him. Szeretlek grabbed his arm. There was something in the boy's face that spoke of Lili, something in the way his dark little eyes blinked back at him, something about the crooked way he held his small body. But it could not be. As the boy twisted his arm unhappily, Szeretlek held on. He knew what was about to happen; he knew that however glorious his victory with the Hungarians in the Battle of the Red Valley, the Fekete-Szem did not belong to the Magyars; we belonged to the Man in the Sky.

"*Credo*," he whispered.

The boy blinked back at him with curiosity.

"It will save you," he said, and turned onto his back.

The boy waited for the Giant to say something else, but the enormous man just closed his eyes. His limbs went limp. The boy jumped up and ran over to two nearby Pfliegmans and told them what happened. In a flash, they were upon Szeretlek, hopping and bouncing around his mammoth torso. They jabbed him with pointy sticks. "He's alive!" they cried.

"Now there can be a sacrifice!"

Across the tent, Lili heard the commotion and stirred. Enough time had now passed that the truth did not repulse her. Her brain felt soft. Uncooperative. Which was fine. Slowly her own memories faded, until there was just one left: she thought back to the day of the wrestling match, how strange it was that both of their bodies just seemed to fit so well together. She now understood that they fit for a reason: that they had been linked once before, tumbling about in Aranka's extraordinary womb.

Lili coughed and picked up the clay pot where she kept her grain alcohol. It was empty.

She smashed it on the stones.

No one paid any attention. Everyone was gathered at the far end of the tent, hooting and dancing around the hearth. Lili stood up and stretched, her hairy legs tingling from the blood moving for the first time in days. She looked for Kinga, but the old witch was nowhere. Lili bent her knees and straightened them. She placed her hands on her legs and thought how they were shadows of their former selves, so scrawny they hardly felt like legs at all. She ran her tongue over her wooly teeth. A few nits nibbled her scalp. She picked them from her hair and ambled over to an old man crouched before the fire, fluids dripping from the holes in his face, teeth poking out from his lips in tiny shards.

"What's going on?" she said.

"Thabbs-thiffice," he spit.

"What?" she said.

"Thabbs—"

"Nevermind," Lili said, and pushed her way into the center of the circle, where she found Szeretlek lying uncomfortably on a pile of logs that were being ineptly tended by a dozen scurrying Pfliegmans.

"Get back!" she cried. "Get away from him!"

She tried shoving us back, but there were so many of us, and Szeretlek could not assist her. His arms and legs were bound. A rotten gag was wrapped around his head. We were trying to light the fire using anything we could get our hands on. We tossed on old bits of food, broken clay pots, animal hides and straw mats, but nothing caught. So Lili fanned the smoking coals, and it became difficult to breathe. We screeched at her, but her plan worked: we coughed and fled outside. As soon she had the tent to herself, Lili held her breath and quickly began to untie him. If it had been another millennia ahead from what it was, she would have rolled up her sleeves and performed CPR, but alas, she did not know CPR; she only knew that Szeretlek's chest was not moving, and therefore he was not breathing, and she quickly reasoned that if she could breathe and he could not, there was no reason why she could not *give* her breath to him. She placed her lips on his lips and began to blow into his body, thinking nothing of the past, nothing of how they were related or unrelated, nothing of Botond. Lili breathed into Szeretlek until Szeretlek breathed into Lili. The Giant began to realize who was trying to give him life. With relief, with weak and stupid love, he began to pull her in with him. His mouth grabbed at hers as though he was drowning, and she gave her breath to him until the smoke took over, the ground spun, and she collapsed on top of him.

Kinga, meanwhile, had been watching from behind the flap in the tent. Covering her mouth and nose, the old witch stepped inside. She saw Lili and Szeretlek lying next to the hearth and stood over them, for a moment, in the fog of smoke. Then she reached down and quickly snapped a twig from a log. She stuck the twig into the embers until it caught, then she watched as the two bodies slowly became one body, and then no body at all. "What goes up must come down," she thought. "But sometimes it will rise again."

Sixty years later, in 1000 AD, the creaking turn of the new millennium, we Pfliegmans are standing among the pagan tribes vying for inclusion in the brand-spanking-new Christian Hungary. Those who believe in God will be saved; those who do not will be killed or made into *uhegs*—slaves to the Christians. We Pfliegmans line up in front of the first Christian king, Istvan. King Stephen. He is by far the cleanest human being we have ever seen: the long cheeks, the golden crown. The luminescent, blowing hair. We stare, gaping, at the whiteness of his cloaks. Standing next to him is a man named Kristoff Dorff, one of his German counselors.

"This is the eleventh tribe," says Dorff.

Stephen frowns. "There are only ten tribes."

"They're butchers. They can be of use."

But the king sees our flaking, hairy skin, our curved backs. Our toes curled into tiny toe-fists. He sees our lumpy heads, our eyes, black and whole, and cannot see anything else.

"They may be of use," he says, "but they will not believe."

Dorff looks at us with genuine pity.

But then one of us shuffles forward from the pack. Who knows why—perhaps he possessed some flimsy scrap of bravery, or maybe he was moved by a bubble of gas trapped in his greasy lower intestine—whatever the reason, Old Botond steps forward. He hobbles over to Dorff, clears his throat, and then whispers something into the ear of the German administrator.

Dorff turns his head, amused. "Credo?" he says.

The German knows that there is no possible way that we believe in God because, let's face it, we just don't look the part. But then the sky shifts, and the sun appears. Although a full century has passed since the sacrifice of Enni Hús, the Fekete-Szem still crave sunlight. It's the heat on our faces baking us, reducing all of us to a common denominator: human, with human needs, which is why when the sun comes out this day, my Darling, we all raise our arms to better feel its warmth.

Dorff watches as the pack of fetid little people begin reaching for the sun: we are so short, the top of our heads just barely reach Dorff's large chest; we are so thin, Dorff can strangle us with one hand only; our eyes so deep and round, so eerily black, they look glued to our faces. And cast out from each one of us is a thin, oblong shadow. With our arms raised, our shadows resemble a flock of skinny, out-winged birds. Dorff looks over one shoulder, ensuring that King Stephen has moved on to another tent, and then he gives us a name:

"I will call you Fliegendenmann," he says. "A nice German name to make you stronger."

We will not be killed or made into uhegs; our name, although about as far linguistically from our own people as we would like it to be, allows us to survive. And although from this point on, we must say that we believe in order to survive—to be regarded as *worth* saving—in truth, it is not what we Pfliegmans really believe: we believe in hiding. We believe in sacrifice. We believe that the stars are holes in the sky.

We believe in the power of the swerve.

And from here, where we are, we begin to watch and wait for some other leader, a leader like Árpád, to find us and care for us. We wait as King Stephen marries Gisela, daughter of Henry the Quarrelsome, duke not of any Hungarian camp, but of Bavaria; as he turns our entire barbarian nation into a Roman Catholic state; as he orders the slaughter of his very own cousin. We are there, and we say nothing. We are waiting in 1038, as the country is brutally invaded by Pechenegs and in 1058, as Andrew the First declares independence from the Holy Roman Empire. We are there, watching, waiting, all the way up to 1241, as Béla the Fourth is defeated by Mongols and half of Hungary's population is slaughtered. We Pfliegmans are there in 1485, when Hungary is once again the strongest power in Europe, and in 1514, when there are peasant uprisings: for the first time, Hungary argues over its own ethnogenesis, and even then, knowing what we know, we say nothing; we only wait in our moist tents, bored, licking our feet, as Hungarian society splits between the nobles who acknowledge Stephen as the first true ruler of the country, and the peasants who acknowledge Árpád. We shake bugs from our hair. We pluck our own teeth from our mouths. And we are still waiting in 1541, after Hungary has lost five campaigns and the Turks take over, forcibly incorporating Hungary into the Ottoman Empire.

With cloudy eyes and knobby fingers, working hard balls of ját down our gagging throats, we watch and wait as the peace treaty in Westphalia is eventually signed; as Vienna invalidates the Hungarian constitution and appoints an imperial governor; as imperial forces are driven out of Hungary. We are there in 1684 when the Reconquest begins. Buda is liberated, Transylvania is reunited with Hungary, and we are lying on the floor of our nimble misshapen tents, waiting all the way up to 1844, when Hungarian is declared the official language and a national consciousness emerges. It emerges, somehow, without us—but we Pfliegmans are still there in 1848, witnessing the revolutions which are exploding all over the place. We are watching in 1867 as the Austro-Hungarian Compromise is swiftly signed; in 1873, as the Stock Exchange crashes and the League of Three Emperors is created: Austria-Hungary, Russia, and the German Reich; as Austria-Hungary occupies and then annexes Bosnia-Herzegovina; as tensions with Russia continue through the Balkan Wars, as the Serbs gain territory, and on June 28, 1914, on this day in history, Eldridge Cooner, you miserable, insular *délinquant*, we Pfliegmans are standing on the side of the cobblestone road, hands deep in our pockets, squinting with our black eyes, as the Archduke Franz Ferdinand, heir to the Habsburg throne, is assassinated in Sarajevo. His body tumbles from the carriage.

We lick our hairy chins. We hide and wait.

Rumors of Transylvanian vampires spread across Europe, but there are no killers in the shadows of the Carpathian Mountains, there are only the Pfliegmans pinched into the darkness, our woolen coats heavy on our shoulders, blinking at the rich, the full, the cared for. There we are in 1918 (fewer of us, for sure, squirming in our boots) as Austria-Hungary joins the German quest for ceasefire, as the Hungarian Soviet Republic is led by Béla Kun and Admiral Horthy's brutal White Army enters the scene; we are there in 1920, as the Peace Treaty of Trianon reduces Hungary to a third of the lands occupied by King Stephen, and despite the fact that no one is noticing, there we are waiting in the unemployment lines, stomachs rumbling, feet burning, hats pulled low over our heads when in 1929, an economic crisis yields massive unemployment in Europe, the Americas, and the whole world over. We Pfliegmans watch the outbreak of a second war, as Hungary opens its borders to a hundred thousand Polish refugees, and we are there, coldly watching, only one year later, as Hungary joins forces with Germany, Italy, and Japan. Our backs press against the wall as the Germans invade Yugoslavia; as our prime minister commits suicide; as Hungary occupies previous Magyar regions in Yugoslavia and declares war on the Soviet Union; as Britain declares war on Hungary; as Hungary declares war on the United States; as secret negotiations with the Western Allies about changing course fail; as German troops occupy Hungary. We Pfliegmans are there in 1944 as 437,000 Hungarian Jews are shoved onto trains to Auschwitz.

Many of us are among them.

By 1945, only a scattered few of us remain as the Soviets occupy Budapest. We wait, patiently, lying on the floorboards of our shacks, as Hungary becomes a Peoples' Republic. We are part of Rákosi's new "collective farms"; we are the *kulaks*, the peasants. Our stomachs burn with hunger. We are told to deliver impossible amounts of food, we have none left for ourselves, and it would seem that someone, then, kicking over the empty pots and tin cans of our various farmhouses, would find us, but no one does, and by 1956, only nine or ten of us are there, wringing out our dirty bedsheets as a student protest ignites a revolution, as Prime Minister Nagy declares withdrawal from the Warsaw Pact, as the Red Army crushes counter-revolution, as the Soviet troops stationed in Hungary wickedly demand the extreme opposite of what all of Western Europe has been pressing us to believe, that *no one* believe—

And *now* look at us. There is only one of us left. When he is gone, what happens? If the Pfliegmans are not around to suffer the worst the world has to offer, who, may I ask, will take our place?

XXX

THE GATHERING

Holding my writing tablet with one hand and the back of my examining gown with the other, so as not to expose any parts of Rovar Ákos Pfliegman that the world does not need or want to see, I leave Dr. Monica's office and make my way way down the long corridor behind Mrs. Himmel's reception desk to the X-ray room. A Good Mother is standing with her Sick or Diseased child in the hallway next to a tall metal scale. The child weighs forty-two pounds, but the mother, sweater tied in a V around her neck, is not looking at the scale; she's staring at down at my tiny feet, so flat, so thin, they hardly look like human feet at all; then it's my ankles, like sharp little rocks; then my calves, two sticks of bone and skin and only a scrap of meat between them; my wrists pared into two rusted hinges, barely hanging on; and finally the skin underneath the gown: pink. Shining. Demanding everyone's complete and total attention.

The Good Mother grips her child by the shoulders. "Stay close to me, Stevie," she says, as I hobble closer toward them.

Stevie steps off the scale and looks at me.

"Stevie!" his mother whispers, and hustles him down the hallway.

"*Pthbbb*," I say, behind her.

She gives me a frightened look.

I limp along in quick, uneven movements, passing the doorway to the Waiting Area. The Sick or Diseased children see me and their faces blanch. "Mommy," they whimper, clinging to their mothers' kneecaps. "Mommy, what *is* that?"

"*God only knows,*" they whisper back.

I place my stylish woolen cap over my head. I cackle a little, then continue down the hallway.

Mrs. Himmel meets me at the door, holding my folder tightly over her chest. "I don't want to be doing this," she says. "I just thought you should know that you've inconvenienced a lot of people, Mr. Pfliegman. You're not going to get away with it."

I produce my writing tablet. *You're a fucking star*, I write, and hold it up.

Mrs. Himmel smiles at me. The smile is thin. Threatening. She looks like she's ready to hit me, but she doesn't; instead, she lifts one fat arm and grabs a plastic cup from the shelf behind her. "Drink this," she says.

What is it?

"Barium. You have to drink it so we can see what's going on."

I take the cup.

"Go inside now," she says, and shoves me into the room. "Get up on the table. Lie down on your back."

The X-ray room is a small, narrow space, with a high ceiling that reaches all the way up to the roof. There's just enough room for one person to lie on the table and cover himself with the appropriate protective materials. I climb up on the table, clutching my gown. It's freezing in here. The X-ray machine is an old one, cream-colored with a fat red stripe along one side. An enormous moveable arm hangs over the table, and nailed into it is a small plaque that reads THE INDUSTRIAL. Mrs. Himmel watches me shiver. She smirks a little, and then walks over. There's barely space enough for her to fit.

"Give me your hat and your eyeglasses," she says.

I shake my head at her. I growl a little.

"This is an X-ray, Mr. Pfliegman," she says. "You can't wear your eyeglasses. You just can't. It's not allowed."

She tries to snatch them, but when her arm crosses over my face, I grab it first.

"Jesus H.!" she shouts. "You bit me!" Mrs. Himmel flies out of the room and slams the door. From an outside switch, she turns off the lights, leaving me in darkness. I listen to her arguing with Dr. Monica out in the hallway:

"I'm going to need the darn rabies shots now!" she shouts.

"Take it easy, Annette."

"You take it easy! I'm not taking it easy. Not anymore. If you make me do this, Monica, I swear I'm quitting. I mean it! I'm not putting up with this crap!"

"Don't quit," says Dr. Monica. "Please. Just relax. There are people waiting outside to take him away, and he won't be back again. Let's just take the X-rays, and that's it. That's all."

Mrs. Himmel flubs her lips. "Not until you admit it," she says.

"Admit what?"

"It was a mistake."

"Now, Mrs. Himmel, I don't say things like—"

"Admit that it was a mistake to take him on. Admit that he's a Lying, Dangerous, Psychopathic Lunatic Midget who was never sick to begin with, and who now has conjured up some kind of weirdo skin disorder. I've read his folder! I know what's going on! Admit that he has the hots for you, and stares at you like a darn fool whenever you come into the Waiting Area! Admit that it was a mistake to allow him to wait all day around children, who are now all practically traumatized! Admit that there are some people who don't want help, who don't deserve it! If you admit that, then I'll stay."

Dr. Monica is quiet for a moment. "Please, Annette," she says.

Mrs. Himmel laughs out loud. "Do you admit it?"

"Fine," says Dr. Monica. "You were right, I was wrong. Now let's go."

Mrs. Himmel opens the door to the stairwell and stomps upstairs. Moments later, two lights appear. The first is the square X-ray light from the Industrial, and the second shines from a plastic window about five feet up, where Mrs. Himmel now stands. There's a panel in front of her, and she fiddles with the knobs as the Industrial groans to life. The metal arm shifts in one controlled movement over my body, spinning on a pivot, locking in place over my abdomen—

My bad leg begins shaking.

Mrs. Himmel reaches over and presses a button. There's a click and then a scratchy version of her voice emerges into the darkness: *"This is just a test,"* she says, and clicks again. *"Hold still until I tell you to move."*

She sighs and shakes her head.

I try to hold my leg down with one hand. I hold my breath and close my eyes. The arm wails and groans. It moves sluggishly over my body.

Mrs. Himmel clicks in. *"Turn over,"* she says.

I turn.

"Other way, Mr. Pfliegman."

Lying here on my back, my arms and legs flat on the table, the Industrial hovering over my chest, the barium sinks to a lower part of my stomach. As it moves slowly through me, I think of Oliver in the Waiting Area, expertly moving the toy from robot to wrestler and then back again. I close my eyes and breathe, *Enter, Exit, Enter*— What goes up must come down. "If your pain were a person," Dr. Monica once said.

I open my eyes. A strange man is standing at my feet, just inches beyond the light of the Industrial. He's wearing a black T-shirt with a glow-in-the-dark galaxy on it, and the swirls of the galaxy are vibrantly green, shaped like a hurricane. I inch up the table, away from him, and try to get Mrs. Himmel's attention, but she's working the knobs and doesn't see him. The man steps right up to the table, into the light, and grins. He's wearing square black eyeglasses, and is sporting the fluffiest, whitest sideburns I've ever seen. It's Isaac Asimov. Mr. Asimov smiles at me, and the smile is genuine. He clears his throat. "The Gravitational Force," he says, "by far the weakest of all," but before he's even finished speaking, the others all begin to gather. The Captain struts up to the table, into the light. He's still in his Speedo. The yellow ball is tucked under one bare armpit, and the silver whistle hangs over his chest like a glittering jewel. He has dark circles under his eyes, like he hasn't slept all night. "Hiya sport," he says, and grins. He gives me a thumbs-up. The Indian steps up to the table, and there's some shaking of hands. "We're all images," he says. "Illusions." Then he reaches into his bag, produces a warm bottle, and pops it open. Beer runs down the side of the bottle, and he quickly sucks the foam to avoid spilling any on Dr. Monica's clean floor. He offers one to the others, but only Asimov accepts.

"Cheers," the Indian says.

"Cheers!" says Isaac Asimov.

Carly Simon crawls up from underneath the table and immediately spies the Captain and his shiny muscles. She giggles, chomping her gum in his ear. Her lips are coated in greasy, bright red lipstick that smears onto her big white teeth. Her smile glows, Cheshire-like, in the light of the Industrial. She hangs a thin arm over the Captain. "You're *foxy*," she whispers.

Suddenly it's getting crowded in here. I shift my body a little to make more room and Mrs. Himmel crackles in: "*Lie still, Mr. Pfliegman.*"

Pointed, high-heeled shoes tap the floor behind me. Everyone acknowledges Madame Chafouin. She puts her cold French hand on my cheek. "*Démence*," she says affectionately. "*Madness.*"

"Not madness," the Indian says. "Company."

"Whatever," says Madame Chafouin. She reaches for a cigarette.

"You can't smoke in here," says the Captain.

Madame Chafouin gives him an icy stare.

"What's *happening?*" whines Carly Simon. "Why is this taking so long?"

"Quiet! All of you!" shouts Mr. Asimov.

Around the table, everyone quiets down as the last figure steps into the light. He is older than the rest, with a low, probing brow. It's a kind face, with a particular beard. He possesses small hands with thick fingers, a sunburned nose, and he's wearing a baseball cap with a beagle on it. "Sorry I'm late," he says.

Mr. Asimov sees him and claps his hands with delight.

The bearded man fidgets, standing here among the others, but when he realizes that the hairy little Hungarian is staring at him, that we're all staring, he knows he has to say something. He steps forward. Everyone listens as he speaks. His voice is soft and high. Unexpected. A voice that betrays a gentle spirit, too gentle for a man who spent his life squatting on alien beaches, digging in primordial pits and holes; a man with a spirit too gentle for his own aggressive species.

"*At some period of its life,*" Charles Darwin says, "*during some season of the year, every organic being has to struggle for life and suffer great destruction.*"

"What does that mean?" the Captain says.

Darwin shrugs. "Sometimes waters rise."

What he's saying is that under the laws of heavy rain, of wind, of the groaning earth, last night, the Queeconococheecook, for all her effort and restraint, could not contain herself. He's saying that the broken school bus was picked up and carried on the current, gliding along underwater until it creaked and groaned, collapsing into several disparate pieces, exactly in the manner of a certain flimsy butcher shop twenty-two years ago. He's saying that neither I nor the Subdivisionists own the field that I live in, that ultimately life cannot own life, and when the waters finally subside, along the soaked banks the Virginians will find a busted tape-radio, a drowned lightbulb, old wet cuts of meat from the Big M supermarket, remains of a splintered bookcase, and an empty tin can of Mrs. Kipner's Hungarian Goulash. They'll find a waterlogged copy of a pamphlet on raising hamsters, a book about outer space, one about Hungary, one about water polo, a heavy French dictionary, and the remains of a paperback copy of *The Origin of Species*, so cheap that at the first kiss of water the pages curled, broke away from their spine, floated for a mile or so downriver, and then disintegrated into the mouth of the Queeconococheecook.

Suddenly the door opens and Dr. Monica enters the room. She walks right up to the X-ray table and everyone fidgets, stepping on each other's toes to duck out of the light. They quietly groan, pressing up against each other to make room. They hold their collective breath.

Dr. Monica comes right up to the table and places a hand on my forehead. "How are you feeling, Mr. Pfliegman? It looks like you kicked that fever. We're going to get started now. Oh, but you can't wear these, though," she says, and removes my eyeglasses.

Which is fine. I no longer need them. I open my eyes, and, for the first time, look right at her. She sees my eyes and gasps. Instinctively, perhaps protectively, she covers her mouth and slowly backs away from the table.

Darwin tries to explain. "Insects cannot easily escape by flight from the larger animals that prey on them," he says. "Therefore, speaking metaphorically, they are reduced, like most weak creatures, to trickery and dissimulation."

But Dr. Monica's already fled the room.

Mrs. Himmel clicks in. *"We're starting,"* she says, and flicks a switch. The Industrial hums to life. My limbs ache like an adolescent's, the bad leg pounding at the knee. My lungs feel like they're caked with mud. I breathe in.

And then it begins.

XXXI

JUNE 15

It's the day of the earthquake, the nebula, the agoraphobe. On this day in history, on June 15, 1985, Ján and Janka Pfliegman are speeding down Back Lick Road in their shitty, dilapidated Rambler. The car flies past farmhouses filled with Virginian families behaving themselves, following the rules, up and down; it flies past the grassy fields that line the road; past the muddy embankment of the Queeconococheecook; past interminable clouds that linger over this county like jobless men in front of convenience stores. It flies past schools, churches, public buildings. It flies past a hundred telephone poles. But a few miles ahead, there is one telephone pole that is not standing upright like the others. It leans forward, as though looking for the speeding car that's about to come roaring around the bend and drive headlong into its spine. The pressure from the accident will not, the experts marvel, break the pole, or even splinter it; instead, the car will set the pole upright. The likelihood that the car would hit this particular pole in this particular way and the pole would not break or splinter or uproot completely is a billion to one.

It is the day of the telephone pole.

It begins in a coat closet. The boy is lying on the wooden floor underneath a dozen wool coats, smelling the sweet, rotting wood, pawing the tails with one hand. The coats are gray with gold buttons. Heavy on the hangers. Outside, Ján and Janka shout his name, looking for him, but the boy lies still. He doesn't move or even blink. The coats above stop swinging, holding themselves close together as if to cover and protect him, but then the closet door creaks open, the light pours in, and there's nothing the coats, however big, however heavy, can do.

"Found him!" cries Janka.

They're drunker than he's ever seen them. Ján, especially, has a new, wild look. He's holding the violin in one hand, a bottle in another. He chases the boy from the closet, out of the house that leans both east and west, out into the front yard, yelling *here pig, here pig* until he catches him.

Janka squeals and claps her hands. *"Now* what?" she shrieks.

Ján holds the boy by the shoulders and leads him over the horsefield, into the barn, and beyond the regular part to the linoleum part where they keep the white box. "Get in," he says, and hiccups.

The boy obeys. He tugs his leg a little.

"You can fit," his father says.

His mother closes the lid, and it seals above him, tight. He hears her laugh above him. It's a game. The boy starts sweating. He doesn't know whether it's toxic amounts of carbon dioxide or just the heat of his own body, but the air around him becomes smaller. The walls close in. *Turn the dial*, a voice says. *Flick the switch!* He tries desperately not to think about the fish in the jar behind him, but he can feel it watching him. As if it knows something that the boy does not know. The boy closes his eyes and presses his hands against the inner wall. He produces a sound, a small wail, but they don't hear him. They don't respond. They do not know that he is capable of making sound. He has not spoken before, so they wouldn't know what he sounded like even if he did speak, which he does now:

Janka covers her ears. "Let him out!" she laughs. "I can't listen to that!"

Ján opens the lid. Inside, the boy is holding on to the walls with his palms. He looks at their faces and doesn't know which is a worse place to be: inside or out of the box. They take him out. "Hook him to the winch!" they cry, and lift his body up. The hook catches the back of his shirt and they turn the handle. Up he goes on the winch of the Coat Rack. They watch the boy dangle from the hook, sputtering, until they tire of him. They decide to take the Rambler out for a spin through the back roads of Virginia. They drive at a very fast clip: eighty, then ninety miles an hour— There are, it turns out, many ways a Pfliegman can fly. They drive so fast a molting pack of turkeys darts through the forest and doesn't even see them. There's just a roar, a flash of brown, the dirt and dust of the road kicked up and spinning in the air, but that is all. The turkeys chatter fanatically. But only a few miles past the turkeys, smoke begins to pour out from underneath the snout, and Ján is forced to pull over. He parks the car at the side of the road.

"What'd you do now," says Janka.

"Shut up," says Ján.

Janka swings open the heavy door and climbs out. Ján follows her. He lifts the hot hood with his bare hands.

"Transmission," he says.

"Great," says Janka, and she hiccups. "You done it now."

At first, Ján says nothing. He walks away from the car, his hands deep in his pockets. But he only gets ten feet from it before he changes his mind. He rushes back at her and gets her clean in the stomach. Janka bends over and howls. She stumbles back a few steps as Ján stands over her, amused. She stays down longer than she needs to, then lifts her legs and swipes him viciously in the groin. Ján falls to the ground, holding himself. He grits his teeth. "God help me!" he cries, but God is nowhere in the vicinity. They are children. At play. And when the parents are children, the child becomes a butterfly.

"Get back now," the Captain says. "Everyone make room."

In the dark, on a table, in a room no bigger than a closet, in a town no bigger than a sneeze, my legs begin to grow. They grow long and lean, thin as needles. An unfamiliar pain enters the left side of my body, digging in sharp. It travels across my body, exiting on the right, and in its place, two appendages, one on each side of my torso, unfurl themselves across the table. As they grow, the ache they carry dissipates. My arms shrink up, elbow-first toward my chin, into small, reduced forelegs. The legs lie still at first, flopped over the edges of the table, but as my body feels the presence of new passages, blood moves quickly into them and they wave awkwardly in the air. The one bad leg has not miraculously healed itself—it will always droop off to one side—but now there are other legs to compensate. I now have six. Six legs, with several knees separating the coxa, femur, and tibia—

Carly Simon screams.

Janka, half-bent, crawls away from the car. She gets about ten feet away and turns to look at Ján. He's still lying on the ground, curled in a ball, so she stands up and starts walking. She can't go home because the boy is home, hanging from the winch, and she doesn't feel like dealing with him. She walks down the road on those brutal clogs until her ankles pinch, and then she takes them off to go barefoot. After a few minutes she comes to a building with a large glass window in the front. Painted on the glass is a circle, and inside the circle is a picture of a galaxy. But Janka doesn't know that it's a galaxy. She doesn't know about outer space. She does not, in fact, notice the logo at all. All she notices are the shiny new cars displayed behind the glass. She throws her feet into the clogs, opens the door, and walks into the place like she owns it. She walks up to the counter like she owns it. "I want a red one," she tells the clerk. "Like one of the ones in the window."

The clerk is blond and tan. Conventionally handsome. He's wearing a short-sleeved, blue-collared shirt. Black trousers with an even cuff. A black belt is neatly cinched around his middle, and he wears an expensive, silver wristwatch. "That's a Porsche," the clerk says. "Not a rental."

Janka scratches her legs. "So?"

The clerk takes a long and steady look at Janka. She's terrifically short, and about forty pounds overweight. She's wearing cut-off jeans with strings that hang down her hairy legs like broken cobwebs. A boxy T-shirt. She looks top-heavy, with legs too thin to fit her body right. Her teeth have not been brushed for months, and she's defensive. She is not, he decides, the kind of customer they want at Galaxy Car Rentals.

"So you can't rent it."

Janka reaches into her purse and holds up a credit card. She curls her lip. "Listen," she snarls. "I can rent anything I want. Or I'm calling the manager."

The clerk smiles at the little woman. She can barely see above the counter. "About what?" he asks.

"About how you discriminate."

"Against who?"

"Midgets."

The clerk sighs and looks at his watch. He works on commission, and it's been a slow day. It's already three o'clock. So he takes her out behind the building to a small outdoor lot of less new, less expensive cars. He offers her a worn-out Escort.

"I want a red one," she hisses. "Brand new."

Another customer walks in. The clerk looks over his shoulder and winces. "Look, here's a red one. It has some miles on it, but it's still pretty new."

"How much?" she says.

"Twenty dollars for the day."

"How much for two days?" she says.

"Forty."

"Three days?"

The clerk looks impatiently at Janka. "It's the same price *every day*, ma'am."

Janka opens and closes the doors several times. She honks the horn. She's taking her time because she has a bad credit card, and she knows that once she drives the car off the lot she won't bring it back. Maybe they'll leave town with it. Or she could give a fake address and they could keep the car in the barn. Either way, it's a winner. "What kind is it," she sniffs.

"It's a Mustang."

Janka follows the clerk to the counter and smiles sweetly at him as she signs all the paperwork. He gives her the keys. Slipping on her clogs, she practically runs back outside to the car, and starts the ignition.

It howls to life.

Dr. Monica is correct: there is indeed something wrong with my stomach. Inside, it coarcts and bifurcates into two stomachs, the fore-gut and the hind-gut, bulging into a long, impressive abdomen that grows fatly down the table, shredding the adult-sized examining gown, moving away lengthwise from my body in ten even and distinct segments. I am growing in all directions now. The fingering, obstinate pain is gone. Chest down, my body glows, big and round. *Healthy.* A glistening sheen covers my skin, coated with a brush of soft, dark hair. My neck broadens into a thick thorax and suddenly tightens, making it impossible to turn my head.

Mrs. Himmel clicks in. *"Remain still, Mr. Pfliegman."*

Two quick, club-ended antennae sprout from the strange lumps on my head, tossing my stylish woolen cap onto the floor, which the Indian quickly grabs and throws into his bag of textiles.

"Damn fine antennae," says Isaac Asimov, chugging his beer. *"Damn fine."*

Then Dr. Monica comes back into the room. She walks briskly over to the table to make adjustments. There is a blank look on her face. Not unkind; professional. She is doing the job that she has to do.

Mrs. Himmel presses the button and crackles in. *"You should leave, Monica,"* she says. *"It's not safe."*

Dr. Monica looks up at the window and protects me from Himmel's view. "You're wrong. I'm staying," she says, and begins placing longer pads over my gigantic abdomen. Her gold cross shines.

Behind her, my forehead grows upward into two pointed and furry labial palps, the pink and raw skin hardening into scales. My mouth and nose spiral out into two long straws. It is a strong and perfectly formed proboscis. Coiled like a watch-spring.

"Beautiful," breathes Darwin.

Even the Captain's rooting for me. "Attaboy, Pfliegman!" he says. "Woo hoo!"

But suddenly it's become very uncomfortable to be lying down this way. I shift my entire body in one gigantic motion.

Mrs. Himmel crackles in. *"Don't move, dammit!"* she commands, as the wet roots appear, heart-shaped, across my back.

"Make more room!" cries the Indian.

When Janka reaches Ján, he's recovered somewhat, sitting on the side of the road cross-legged, holding his ankles, not unlike the way Szeretlek awaited the Hungarians in the inner courtyard of St. Gallen. But of course, this is no monastery courtyard. This is a millennium later, in a ditch on the side of the road in Front Lick, Virginia, and the man is most certainly not a giant in heart or mind. Mosquitoes loiter around his head, taking pot shots. He sees the red car drive up and rises excitedly. "Where'd you get that?" he says.

"It's a Mustang," she says. "Get in."

They switch places. Ján drives. "This is a *helluva* nice car," he says, and whistles.

"Did I do good?" says Janka.

He kisses her sloppily on the mouth. "You did good," he says.

They turn the car around and take off down the road. They're stopping by the farmhouse to get a few things before they leave. A few shirts. Some kitchenware. The boy. But after packing their things, they go out to the barn and discover that he's gone. He's not where they left him. They go back into the farmhouse and look in his room. They look inside the coat closet. It's empty.

"He's probably just out in the horsefields again," says Janka.

"I'm sick to death of looking for anything in those horsefields," says Ján.

They stand there, for a moment, in silence, then agree they'll come back for him later. As soon as they can set up their butchering shop somewhere else. As soon as they get settled.

They return to the Mustang.

Wet and heavy, the wings take over, flipping me over to give them the space they need to stretch out from my body. My abdomen presses against the edge of the table, and then the swelling starts to go down. Fluid pushes into the veins of the wings. Mrs. Himmel leans on the intercom: *"If you don't stop moving, I'll come down there,"* but Dr. Monica shakes her head. "Ignore her," she says. "Just concentrate," so I concentrate on the wings. They rise up from the table like four large flags. The larger, more triangular forewings appear first, dripping a sticky fluid all over the X-ray table— Then it's the hindwings. They reach out, wet from my body, assembling like tectonic plates, millions of scales shimmering against the light of the Industrial. They are so tall, I can feel the tips brush the ceiling— All orange, with veins of running black that delta into spots of white— How beautiful they are, everyone marvels. How they shatter the light! Even Madame Chafouin nods in approval. The wings crack open slightly, like the binding of a book, and then, quite involuntarily, flap down.

"Duck!" cries the Indian.

It's 3:30 p.m. János Pfliegman is driving around the dusty, curved back roads of Northern Virginia in a shiny red Ford Mustang. He's looking to move from one place to another place successfully, in a manner not dissimilar to the exodus of the early Hungarians over a thousand years ago, but he would not know that. He has no sense of his heritage or his people. He has no real interest in history, just like he has no real interest in the present. He swats a mosquito on his neck; it leaves behind a bloody smear.

Janka, however, feels a small tug of remorse as they leave. She cranes her neck around and watches the farmhouse disappear around the bend. Her ankles ache. But as they turn the corner onto Back Lick Road, Ján and Janka look at each other, and each of them knows, as they often do, what the other is thinking: the Creature is not coming with them.

I notice, first, the absence of the cough. I'm breathing freely for the first time through new spiracles alongside my abdomen. I take several deep, satisfying breaths. I hold them and release without coughing or obstruction. My antennae swoop in circles as a wet wing smacks the metal arm of the Industrial, sending it spinning. My feet tingle, maneuvering into a hundred smaller joints, ending in a pair of claws that scrape the table, clutching the edge for support. They cannot hold. My thorax turns, and I accidentally slip off the table, the base of my long abdomen bumping the floor. I stand up, and for the first time there's no nausea— The fore-gut and hind-gut are working as they should be working. I'm glad they cannot see my bug-face in the dark. My strange pointed head, my eyes huge and unblinking. Eyes like black pearls— Then there's the lust. The absolute, matter-of-fact, irrevocable, insect lust. I scan the dark room for her and spot the fuzzy outline of her white pediatrician's coat pressed against the table, and how she, along with all of them, cannot tear her eyes away from my spectacular wings— They are so beautiful, it's difficult for anyone to speak. They shimmer in the pockets of light around the room. Moments of brilliant orange. Flashes of fire. They flip together and apart at their own will. I cannot seem to control their urges. It is their job. Body parts doing exactly what they are supposed to do.

"*That's it,*" yells Mrs. Himmel. "*I'm coming down there!*"

It's true. The boy is not in the barn, hanging where they left him. As soon as they drove away, he wiggled off the winch from the Coat Rack. The shirt tore, and he fell. He ran over to the white box, picked up the glass jar, and then fled the barn, the farmhouse, making it a few miles down Back Lick Road before coming to the top of a hill, right next to a line of telephone poles, which is where he is now.

The boy clutches the jar tightly to his chest.

A river gurgles nearby. So he crosses the road and walks over a sprawling, weedy field. He follows a narrow path all the way down to the Queeconococheecook. The embankment was once grassy, but the recent flooding ruined it. In his bare feet, the boy steps into the mud. It squishes between his toes. With some difficulty, he unscrews the lid of the glass jar. Then he holds his breath, dumps the watery contents into the river, and watches as the little fish, the *hal*, gets picked up in the whirling current, spinning in the froth and foam. Then it's gone. Sent back to wherever it came from. The boy turns and walks away from the embankment, back over the field and up onto the road. But at 3:40 p.m., just as Ján and Janka are driving away from the farmhouse for the last time, the boy stops walking. He looks up at the telephone poles and admires the smaller, bent one. The one that leans forward. He likes bent things. Things wrecked, broken, rusted. Things that have no useful purpose. "Eldridge Cooner never writes about the small things," said Grandfather Ákos, so the boy usually tries to appreciate any detail of the world around him: the spinning clouds, the wet, everlasting grass, the caterpillar embracing the leaf— But not today. Today he cannot seem to forget being stuffed inside the white box for fun; he cannot forget hanging by his shirt on the winch; he cannot forget the sound of the *hal* spilling into the cold running waters of the Queeconococheecook.

The boy moves quietly into the center of the road. He looks at the telephone pole and holds out his arms.

He lifts his chin.

A truck nearly hits him. A woman gets out and starts yelling, but the boy does not respond. She becomes angry and slaps him. He barely feels it. In the background, the radio goes on and on: "*You're so vain, you probly think this song is about you...*"

The woman returns to her truck and speeds off. Seconds later, the boy spies a shiny red Mustang flying around the corner. He smiles inwardly, thinking how close he is to feeling better, or at least to feeling something, and steps into its path.

But something unexpected happens.

On June 15, 1985, at 3:42 p.m., just as the car is about to hit the boy, Janka sees him standing in the middle of the road and grabs the steering wheel. The car swerves left. The edge of the front bumper knocks him on the leg, turning the boy around to watch as if in slow motion: he watches the red car swerve again, this time to the right, and crash headlong into the telephone pole; he sees how the telephone pole, once bent, now stands up straight, pulling down a neighboring telephone pole six inches. Wires snap. Birds pitch and flutter around them. The hood of the car elbows into two distinct sections. Smoke rises up as though from a campfire.

It is a sacrifice.

The boy holds his sore knee. The leg will heal, but grossly, leaving him with a debilitating limp for the rest of his life. He hobbles over to the car and sees the driver lying against the left side window. His father's hand is split neatly from the middle finger to the wrist. His eyes and mouth are open. His nose is twisted like someone turned it with a crank. Blood covers the rest, clothes and body. It glistens on the steering wheel. Pieces of shiny glass decorate his face like someone sprinkled it with sugar. The boy's first thought is that his father is alive because his eyes are still open. He looks alert, like he's going to growl to life at any second and reach for the boy's neck. But his father doesn't move.

The boy walks around the car to the passenger's side. He looks at his mother.

Her face is hidden underneath a mass of tangled hair. Her right arm has been sliced at the elbow, and the boy can make out gruesome strings of bone and tendon. He stares at the wound; how similar it looks to the thousand wounds that he's seen before. The meat separates in the same way from the bone. The Hind, Rump, Loin, Short Loin, Flank, Rib, Plate, Brisket,

Chuck, and Shank. The body is different from the spirit. Her shirt is all blood. Her feet are turned at the ankles on the floor of the car, still firm in those unbearable clogs. The boy dares himself to move the pieces of hair and look at her face. Her eyes are also open, and her mouth is open, and she also looks as though she might blink several times and snap out of it. The boy snaps his fingers in front of her eyes, but there's no response. He leans forward, closer to his mother than he has ever been before, and breathes in. For the first time, he smells her skin. Her greasy head, her hairy neck. He watches her mouth for movement, for the chance that she might recognize her son and whisper *all of this terrible life is your fault*. Then he looks back at Ján and recalls what Grandfather Ákos said:

"It's in the eyes, they say."

The appearance of the Pfliegmans has not changed much over the course of this last, brief millennium. Their skin is the same, weathered and flaked. They have the same greasy hair, brittle bones, toes that reach up and out like tiny fingers. They have a terrible time finding shoes. Wide, uneven eyes, eyes so dark they look black. They are sick a lot, but ignore their sicknesses. They do not know that their sickness is a legacy; that if given love, their decrepit bodies are capable of extraordinary beauty. It is the single missing ingredient. If Ján and Janka had been a little bit wiser, a bit more curious about their people, they might have understood why they, as teenagers, left home and came to Front Lick to start their own butchering business; why the Queeconococheecook, in her unpredictable wrath, flooded; why Nature would not select all of their best attributes (Ján had good kidneys, Janka had nice earlobes) for their accidental off-spring, but their worst; why the boy would stare at them every day with those same slippery, terrifying eyes as if to say: "How could you *do* such a thing?"

Another car comes speedily around the bend. When the driver sees the accident, he stops and steps out. He is tan and blond, wearing a blue col-lared shirt. One hand he keeps in the pocket of his black trousers, the other hangs to one side, displaying an expensive silver wristwatch. It is the clerk from Galaxy Car Rentals.

"Gosh," he says. "Golly. You okay, kid?"

The boy nods. "I'm fine," he says.

The man walks over to the smoking car. "Holy Mother of God," he says, and skims his hands over his beautiful blond hair. "The card bounced," he says. "I was chasing them because the card bounced. That's all."

The Captain stares at the power of my hind legs. So thin, yet they hold so much weight and heavy movement. The wings flap down and my mouth turns sticky. I need sugar. But there is a second need, from some deeper, sadder part of my abdomen. I wave my antennae and feel the scales on my wings, pigmented in thick, velvety patches, spreading my scent, searching for her, and she, who once smelled like tuna-fish sandwiches, now radiates a thousand smells: it's her sweat, the cloudy, angelic pheromone, her pale skin, her vegetable hair, the meat of her own dark places. I smell it all and shuttle my numerous legs toward her. She freezes, watching me with careful eyes as I reach down and take her in my creeping arms. She allows me to fall onto her body, allows the orange wings to rise up into a full four-spread, allows me, as my blood pressure surges and the proboscis slowly uncurls, to lightly swipe her lips with mine. Which is wonderful.

"*Szeretlek,*" I whisper.

Time feels different now. Slower. Seconds churn by like big, interminable hours. Every movement, every pulse, is important. Small and important. I think only about movement, about the present, and leave her in the X-ray room, wide-eyed and stammering, turn my gigantic segmented body, squeeze through the door, and make my way in a very peculiar hopping fashion down the hallway, wings crashing into the walls, knocking down images of bucolic farmyards as I go.

"*Hey!*" cries Mrs. Himmel, but I ignore her. I throw all my weight on one foot—tarsus—and then I throw it all on the other. The wings expand into fans that scrape and bend on the ceiling. They wave and waft behind me as I tug them down the hallway, past the Good Mother and Stevie, who throw themselves against a wall. I turn every facet of my compound eyes to look at them, thousands of lenses linked to the optic nerve—

They scream.

I scuttle to Mrs. Himmel's desk where she keeps her rows and rows of sugar packets. There are other sugar items as well—cookies and broken pieces of cake and a berth of individually wrapped chocolate bars, but they hold no appeal. I swipe the sugar packets to the floor and crush them with my forelegs until they open, white granules spilling out over the Berber carpeting. I bend down and try to drink the sugar, but it's too dry. The granules stick to the tip of my straws—the sugar, it seems, must be fluid— I look up. The entire office is staring at me.

Spotted, orange wings fill the Waiting Area.

Mrs. Himmel comes hurtling down the hallway, and I quickly move back behind the reception desk. She picks up a broom from the closet and holds it in her meaty hands like a rifle. She threatens, *Caw, caw, caw!* I back away from her in large, uneven steps. My wings involuntarily beat down, crashing across her desk, snapping the telephone wire, shoving her computer monitor to the floor. She chases me back into center of the room where the wings have the space to explode from my body, beating in swoops, elevating me a few inches off the floor. There are flowers on the wall and I try to suck them, but they're not real— A confusing, wincing noise chatters behind me, and I spin around to blue flashes of light flickering from a box hanging from the ceiling. I jab at it with a leg but it doesn't stop. Something pushes against my backside, and I turn back around and stare at a thousand fractured images of a fat woman with a broom, jabbing at me. *Shoo, shoo* she cries, but I'm hungry. Libidinous. The need to eat and procreate is so overwhelming, I break the hinges to the door and press myself outside where everyone, the Police and the Security Guards and the Subdivisionists and the Mothers, are all standing in a semicircle, clutching each other.

One mother screams and runs across the street, her babe in her arms, but the others can't move or even look away as I flutter up to the picnic table and stay there, out in the open air, beating my wings to stir the smells, the first of the summer sun.

ACKNOWLEDGMENTS

A great deal of thanks goes to my parents, Thomas and Susan Anthony, for their unbending encouragement and support; Jim Rutman, for his extraordinary diligence and camaraderie; Eli Horowitz, who worked so tirelessly to help me better see what this book could become; also Dave Eggers, Anthony Schneider, and everyone at McSweeney's, for the great honor of selecting me for the Amanda Davis Highwire Fiction Award; Jacob Magraw-Mickelson, for creating such an accurate, jawdropping cover; Alan Cheuse, Susan Shreve, Stephen Goodwin and Richard Bausch, for giving me the first year of this book at George Mason University; Elena Vizvary, for taking me to Budapest; Michael Jones and Katalin Vescey at Bates College, for their wisdom of all matters Medieval and Hungarian, respectively; and a special thanks to the following people who all assisted in ways large and larger: Robin, Tom Hop, MacGregor, Maya, Tiné, Spitzy & Dave, Struve, Chicken, Amy, Ben, Tracy, Courtney, and my sisters, Kate and Julie. Finally, this book would not have been possible without the time and sustenance afforded to me by the MacDowell Colony, the Millay Colony, the Virginia Center for the Creative Arts and the Ucross Foundation.

INFLUENCING LITERATURE & RESEARCH

The Origin of Species: Charles Darwin, Modern Library paperback edition, 1993; *National Audubon Society Field Guide to North American Butterflies*: Robert Michael Pyle, consulting lepidopterist, Chanticleer Press, Borzoi, Knopf, New York, 1981; *Your First Hamster*: Peter Smith, T.F.H. Publications Inc., The Spinney, Parklands, Denmead, Portsmouth, England, 1996; *Home Butchering and Meat Preservation*: Geeta Dardick, TAB Books Inc., Blue Ridge Summit, PA, 1986; *The Complete Book of Water Polo*: Ralph W. Hale, editor, Simon & Schuster, New York, 1986; *The Collapsing Universe*: Isaac Asimov, Walker and Company, New York, 1977; *Cassell's French Dictionary, Concise Edition*: J.H. Douglas, Denis Girard, W. Thompson, editors, Macmillan Publishing Company, New York, 1968; *The Hungarians: A Thousand Years of Victory in Defeat*: Paul Lendvai, Ann Major, translator Princeton University Press, Princeton, NJ, 2003; *Magyars in the Ninth Century*: C.A. MacCartney, Cambridge University Press, 1930, reprinted 1968; *Gesta Hungarorum (The Deeds of the Hungarians)*: Simon of Kéza, ca 1280 AD, László Veszprémy and Frank Schaer, editors and translators, Central European University Press, 1999; *A History of Hungary*: Péter F. Sugar, Péter Hanák, and Tibor Frank, Indiana University Press, Bloomington and Indianapolis, 1994; *The Story of Hungary*: Arminius Vámbéry, New York & London, Knickerbocker Press, G.P. Putnam's Sons, 1886; *History.com*, "The History Channel: 'On This Day in History.'"